SHERLOCK HOL[

-

TANGLED SKEINS

Stories from the Notebooks of
Dr. John H. Watson

by
DAVID MARCUM

Paperback ISBN 9781780927527
ePub ISBN 978-1-78092-753-4
PDF ISBN 978-1-78092-754-1

Published in the UK by MX Publishing
335 Princess Park Manor, Royal Drive,
London, N11 3GX

www.mxpublishing.co.uk
Cover design by www.staunch.com

CONTENTS

Introduction:
In Praise of the Deerstalker, *and*
A Truly <u>Great</u> Hiatus, *and*
How This Book Came To Be

Part I: In Praise of the Deerstalker

As I've related elsewhere, I started reading about Holmes and Watson when I was ten years old. Not long after, my parents gave me a copy of William S. Baring-Gould's *Sherlock Holmes of Baker Street*, and it greatly influenced my future enjoyment of the World of Holmes, so much so that I have been collecting and reading stories about him ever since. I was amazed at all of the sources that Baring-Gould referred to in the back of the book, and I wanted to *be* one of those people who actually *knew* about Holmes, rather than just a casual visitor to Baker Street.

One cannot think about Holmes without seeing the iconic, universally recognized, and archetypal figure of *The Man in the Deerstalker*. It can be argued that Holmes never actually wore such a hat in the original Canon (although his "ear-flapped traveling-cap" was mentioned in "Silver Blaze") and that the use of that type of hat was simply a touch added by that incredible illustrator, Sidney Paget.

But when one becomes acquainted with Holmes at an early age, and when he is wearing a deerstalker during that initial introduction, as he was on the cover of the first Holmes book that I acquired, one comes to associate it with him, whether it is strictly accurate or not. And from an early age, I wanted a deerstalker of my own.

I can still see it clearly, the very first deerstalker that I constructed from a plain blue cap of my father's. It had no logos, insignias, or advertisements. It was simply blue. I didn't permanently damage it, although I *did* destroy a different cap with a red bill, in order to sew the red bill onto the back side of the blue cap. Thus, one deerstalker, rather odd looking, and without ear flaps. I don't know why I thought that the red attachment on the back was acceptable, but I did. And I wore it proudly in connection with the detective agency that I opened in the basement of our house. (We actually made a little money, performing chores for a neighbor that took pity on us, but those cases are *not* resting in a tin dispatch box somewhere, and they will never be written or read about.)

At some point I lost track of that first deerstalker, and my father snipped the threads holding it together, removing and discarding the red bill and reclaiming his blue cap. But even as I grew up, I wanted a *real* deerstalker.

When I was nineteen and a sophomore in college, I went home on my birthday, where my parents proudly presented me with the real thing, a true and authentic deerstalker. It was a houndstooth pattern, heavy tweed, and the earflaps were tied up with thin leather thongs. It had actually been made in England, and my parents had ordered it from somewhere quite expensive in New York. I was thrilled and amazed.

So I was back at college the next day with my deerstalker, and it was time to make a decision. Did I keep this thing as a treasured souvenir to sit in dust on a shelf, or did I wear my Sherlockian Pride on my head, proclaiming my beliefs and walking the walk? I decided to live up to my convictions and *put on the hat!* And then I walked to the dining hall for lunch. No looking back.

The hat caused some initial comment around campus and amongst my friends, but amazingly not as much as I'd feared. It became *my* hat and look for the remainder of my time there until graduation. I wore it to and from class, and for walks in the college woods, and to the mall or out to eat or to the movies, and wherever else that I went. I wore it in yearbook photos. I'm sure it attracted some stares, since one did not and does not see that type of hat where I live. I've had a few comments from passers-by over the years, but they are rare. One person pronounced that

I must be a Robert Downey, Jr. fan. (No.) One wag cleverly called me Inspector Clouseau. Even when I've worn my hat during trips to New York or Washington, D.C. and walked the streets, no one has really said anything. And in the last thirty years, since I received and started wearing that very first hat, I've never yet encountered anyone else who was simply wearing a deerstalker in his or her everyday life as an everyday hat.

A few years ago, some of my family got together and bought for me the ultimate Christmas gift, a real Inverness and matching Deerstalker, custom made for me in Scotland. While I'm used to wearing a deerstalker everywhere, I must admit that it is more difficult to find excuses to go out in full Inverness and Fore-and-Aft, but I have occasionally done so, and even then I did not attract the excessive attention that one would expect. Possibly I carry it off with such swagger that it elicits no curiosity. Or perhaps I look eccentric or even dangerous, and people are giving me a wide berth. In deference to my wife, and the point when I would definitely cross her mortification line, I don't go out often in full regalia, but I still wear a deerstalker on a daily basis for most of the year.

So I've always worn a deerstalker as my only hat, from the time that the weather cools off in the fall until it becomes too warm to wear it in the spring. And it goes without saying that I wore a deerstalker when I was finally able to make my trip-of-a-lifetime Holmes Pilgrimage to England.

Part II: A Truly *Great* Hiatus *or* The Holmes Pilgrimage

I had wanted to go to England for most of my life. It called to me. I couldn't watch any movie or television program about the place without wanting to put my feet there. In most directions back, my family tree is English or Scottish. (My mother was a Rathbone, and my great-grandmother was a Watson.) And most of all, I wanted to visit all of those places that I had only imagined when reading the Holmes Canon. Finally, after making exhaustive lists, giving my employer plenty of notice, and consulting my collection of over a dozen Holmes travel books, I was ready. This trip was just me and the places that I wanted to go. And my sole companion on the journey was my deerstalker.

I wore that hat everywhere while I was over there. For a few weeks in September 2013, a man in a deerstalker roamed Baker Street once again. Of course, I went to the Sherlock Holmes Museum in Baker Street multiple times, and tried to visit the sites of all the other possible theorized locations for 221b up and down Baker Street as well. I stayed in the Sherlock Holmes Hotel on Baker Street on every night that I was in London, and it was there that MX Publishing held a book-signing for me. (To be honest, I didn't actually *wear* the deerstalker during that event, but I had it with me, and it sat on my lap while I did a reading from a previous book.)

I went to as many Holmes-related sites as I could while I was there. If it wasn't connected to The Master one way or another, I pretty much didn't do it. I didn't go up on the London Eye, for example, because it wasn't something that was there in the good old days. (The few exceptions to my Holmes-only rule included visits to Poirot's lodgings, James Bond's house in Chelsea, and most of all, 7B Praed Street, the residence of Solar Pons and Dr. Parker. It certainly doesn't look the same now as it did in the old pictures – what a loss!)

My deerstalker and I ate well at Simpson's. I went to the Sherlock Holmes Pub with it – and through the courtesy of a kind Sherlockian friend, was actually able to go *into* the exhibit room/museum and touch many of the Sacred Objects, and then this same noted Sherlockian gave me a personal "Empty House" walking tour through various streets and mews to the back of Camden House. I went to Montague Street and visited the exact building that Michael Harrison identified (in *The London of Sherlock Holmes* – 1973) as the one where Holmes lived in the 1870's, when he first came up to London. I roamed Pall Mall, identifying The Diogenes Club and Mycroft Holmes's residence across the street to my own satisfaction. I went to both of the old Scotland Yards. I went to the front door of each of Watson's identified residences – Paddington, Kensington, Queen Anne Street – based on information culled from the Holmes travel books in my collection. I journeyed up to Hampstead to visit Milverton's house. I explored up and down the river and around "Upper Swandam Lane," The Tower (the location of many pastiches), and sites in the City. I went to Paddington and King's Cross and Charing Cross and Victoria.

Since Holmes has been in so many pastiche encounters with Jack the Ripper, and I have over two dozen in my collection so far, I went through Whitechapel twice – the first time on a drizzly night with *the* Ripper expert Donald Rumbelow, who added some extra Holmesian content to his tour because I was wearing my deerstalker. The second time was by myself on a quiet Sunday morning, when the deerstalker and I went to each murder site in order, as well as other related locations, such as the Juwes doorway, and the Ten Bells pub, where I had lunch. Possibly the man in the deerstalker making his way up and down those streets caught someone's attention.

The deerstalker and I made our way into the lab at Barts, where I pulled out my Complete Sherlock Holmes and re-read about the first meeting there between Our Heroes. I went west by train to Dartmoor, where I explored the Moor and read "The Man on the Tor" and the "Second Report of Dr. Watson" from *The Hound* while sitting atop Hound Tor. I went to Edinburgh, because I wanted to go to Scotland while I was there, and where better than to visit the Holmes statue and the Conan Doyle pub? (Some excellent pastiches are set in Edinburgh, too.) Back in London, I took a river tour, trying to imagine chasing Jonathan Small and Tonga after departing from the very same dock that Holmes and Watson and Athelney Jones used, below Scotland Yard.

I also spent a couple of days in and around East Dean, Birling Gap, and Beachy Head in Sussex, because Holmes actually lived the majority of his lifetime in his retirement cottage there on the South Downs. (If you believe Baring-Gould – and I do – Holmes resided there from the fall of 1903 until his death in 1957, having lived to the ripe old age of 103 years, thanks to Royal Jelly!)

In East Dean, I stayed at the Tiger Inn, a smuggler's inn from hundreds of years back, where I encountered a ghost – one of the few events of the trip that wasn't strictly Sherlockian. The inn is across the village green from a building that has a historical plaque, supposedly identifying it as Holmes's retirement villa. I don't agree with that location, as my research led me to decide that my personal choice for Holmes's retirement villa is nearby Hodcombe Farm. I went all around there as well.

While in that area, I found a seat on the ground at the top of the cliffs of Beachy Head, directly across from Hodcombe Farm, and re-read "The Lion's Mane," while looking down at the farm and "Fulworth" (Birling Gap) and Maud Bellamy's house, The Haven, in the distance. (It's actually there, just as described in the story! You can see it if you go to Birling Gap. It's the house at the top of the hill and the end of the lane, "the one with the corner tower and slate roof," as Holmes describes it in "The Lion's Mane"). While there, I also re-read the final chapter of Baring-Gould's *Sherlock Holmes of Baker Street* describing Holmes's death there on that spot on January 6th, 1957. Very moving, I assure you.

Throughout my travels, I kept my eyes open for fitting souvenirs. I wasn't buying the usual tourist items. I purchased some Holmes trinkets, and a bust of Our Hero, and Holmes-related books that I couldn't find in the U.S. But mostly I bought some more deerstalkers. A lifetime supply of them. Eighteen more of them, as a matter of fact – added to the six that I already owned – from various spots in London (the Sherlock Holmes Museum, the Sherlock Holmes Pub, a shop on Baker Street, a shop in Whitehall, a shop across from the British Museum around the corner from Montague Street) and even a really nice one in Edinburgh. Some were obviously souvenir quality, but others are definitely the real thing, solid and heavy. In each case, the vendors where I shopped looked oddly at me, a man already wearing a deerstalker, as I would take mine off in order to try on one of theirs. What could I possibly need with *another deerstalker*? (I'm sure that my wife has asked herself that question many times over by this point.)

On my Great Hiatus, I crammed in more Holmes-related sites than I can possibly list here. But one of the places on my list – which was actually four places – directly led to the existence of this book.

Part III: How This Book Came To Be

In "The Problem of Thor Bridge", Watson states:

> Somewhere in the vaults of the bank of Cox and Co., at Charing Cross, there is a travel-worn and battered tin dispatch box with my name, John H. Watson, M. D., Late Indian Army, painted upon the lid.

I had specifically wanted to visit the site of Cox & Co. of Charing Cross. My research in the various Holmes travel books revealed that there were at least four past Cox & Company locations, so I visited all four. There was one on the Strand that is now a Lloyd's bank. I went inside and used my card to get some money while I was there. Another was in Craig's Court, off Whitehall. (That location is also the site of the office of Cyrus Barker, Holmes's "hated rival upon the Surrey shore," mentioned in "The Retired Colourman," and as chronicled in an excellent series of books presented by Will Thomas.) A third former location of the bank is at Whitehall Place, where there is currently a business occupying the old site, its stylized sign covering the still-visible "Cox & Co." carved in the stone over the door.

The final location of one of the old Cox & Co.'s is at 16 Charing Cross Road. This narrow shop, still involved one way or another in the matter of money, was one of the places that I visited on September 25th, 2013. Little did I realize that my deerstalker and I were being watched.

As I mentioned in the introductions to *Sherlock Holmes in Montague Street, Volumes I, II,* and *III,* I had been at that particular Cox & Co., taking pictures, before making my way down Charing Cross Road for a nearby appointment with Catherine Cooke, keeper of the Sherlock Holmes Collection at the Westminster Reference Library. As expected, visiting the collection was incredible, and I'm very thankful for the chance to see it.

When I departed the library, it was still mid-afternoon, and I was trying to decide where to go next. I had returned back to London from Dartmoor the day before, and I was due to journey home in just a few days. I had been successfully crossing Sherlockian locations off my list, but there were still so many places to find and visit. I turned down the hill, zigzagging my way toward Trafalgar Square. I had only gone a few steps before I sensed that I was not alone.

That is a strange statement to make in one of the world's busiest cities, but a traveler hopefully develops and cultivates some survival skills along the way, and sensing that I was being followed was one of them.

As I stopped and looked around me, a small man approached. He had probably always been short, and now that he was quite elderly, the years had only robbed him of whatever height he'd once had, as he inevitably collapsed in upon himself. There was nothing unusual about his clothing. It was his manner that was odd, as he approached slowly, almost fearfully, holding a package and darting glances between the ground and my hat, without meeting my eyes.

His story was hard to follow, especially due to my awkwardness in deciphering his rather thick accent. Essentially, he had seen me earlier in my deerstalker, taking photographs while standing outside of the old Cox & Co. in Charing Cross Road. He was one of a series of people who had been told, many years ago, to deliver the package that he was pressing into my hands to a man in a deerstalker. (At least that was what I understood. Some parts were not clear, and it was possible that he said that the original delivery instructions had been given to *his father*. This made sense after I read what was in the package. If he himself had been the man who had first received the package, he was a *very* old man indeed.)

While I was still trying to puzzle out what he was telling me, and looking at the package in my hands, he finished what he was saying, gave a great sigh of relief at a job finally finished, and turned away. In a few steps, he had vanished into the crowds.

I made my way to a small shop selling juice and snacks on the south side of Leicester Square. Purchasing something to drink, I sat down and carefully opened the package. And then I quickly rewrapped it, terrified that someone was going to come and take it away from me.

I considered, just for a moment, returning to the Westminster Reference Library, just to show what I had found. But selfishness overtook me. I wanted to keep this for myself, at least until it could be prepared to share with the world.

As I've mentioned elsewhere, part of the package consisted of the documents that were later edited and published as the three volumes of *Sherlock Holmes in Montague Street*. But there were other documents, including a collection of additional adventures already prepared by Watson for publication. As he explains in his "Foreword," he chose to leave them with someone, intending to pick them up later. There is no explanation given for this decision, or why he never came back to get them. Based on the date of Watson's comments, it is apparent that events overtook Our Heroes.

I have prepared this volume for publication by correcting – when necessary – the places where the manuscript has faded or blurred. In addition, I have also Americanized the spellings in the manuscript. Any dissatisfaction about the spelling choices, as well as any identified errors or discrepancies, are completely *my* fault, and should not be laid at Watson's feet.

As in previous volumes, I wish to dedicate my efforts involved in preparing this manuscript for publication to both my wife Rebecca and my son Dan. They continually put up with my ever-increasing interest in Holmes and Watson, and the exponentially rising number of Holmes-related volumes that keep finding their way to our house. They helped me prepare for my trip to England in September 2013, realizing that it was an almost religious experience for me. And they are still willing to go places in public with me while I continue to wear a deerstalker. My wife knew what she was getting into when we became a couple and later married, now over a quarter-of-a-century ago, but my son had no choice in the matter, having been born into this Holmesian Household. I am exceedingly blessed to have both of them!

David Marcum
January 6, 2015
The 161st Anniversary of the Birth of Mr. Sherlock Holmes

The Editor and his Deerstalker
in
Baker Street
September 17th, 2013

Foreword
by Dr. John H. Watson

If I have given the impression, while recording certain examples of the adventures of my friend Sherlock Holmes, that he suffered from long spells of inactivity between cases, then I must apologize, and explain that, except for those early years when he was first establishing his practice as what was then the world's only consulting detective, my friend's plate was usually very full indeed, and the cases frequently overlapped one into another. It was during the times in the mid- to late-eighties, when I first attempted to arrange some of my notes into published narratives, initially with *A Study in Scarlet*, and subsequently with *The Sign of the Four*, that I realized I must be carefully selective regarding which threads I chose to weave into my tapestry, or else I would find the resulting tangled skein simply overwhelming, and unpleasant to look upon as well. And if I were to feel that way about it, I can only imagine how distasteful the finished mess would appear to the casual reader.

Often, one case did not have a clear and definite finish before bleeding into the next. For example, this became most obvious to me when trying to recreate the events of the Sholto murder, and the subsequent pursuit of the Great Agra Treasure, which I recounted in the aforementioned *Sign of the Four*. That particular investigation, only the second that I had prepared for publication, took place in September 1888, which was no doubt part of the busiest and most complex period of time that I can ever recall facing Holmes, and only to a slightly lesser degree, myself.

That fall was crowded with events, and my notes for the months of September through November alone fill five thick volumes. Our involvement with the steeply escalating problem of the Whitechapel Murders, as well as taking care of the many other calls upon Holmes's attention – including one notable and lengthy trip to Dartmoor – are narratives that I have either already presented for publication, or that I may record elsewhere at another time. Suffice it to say that when it came time to write up *The Sign of the Four* two years later, at the request of an American publisher in 1890, I was faced with the considerable dilemma of deciding how to record *only* the events of the Sholto murder, while leaving out any references to the other matters which were occurring concurrently.

I believe that I accomplished my mission, and that the final published narrative appears to be self-contained, with no indication in the least that between and woven throughout the events surrounding our pursuit of Jonathan Small, we also visited Whitechapel on a number of occasions, including one grim trip to view the murder site of one of the Ripper's victims, on that very same early morning following our ill-fated trip to the Thames with that amazing dog, Toby, detouring by way of a creosote barrel.

Later, in the spring of 1891 when I believed that Holmes had died at the Reichenbach Falls while locked in mortal combat with Professor Moriarty (of evil memory), I again set out to record some of Holmes's cases, both to preserve his reputation for posterity, as well as to protect it from the malicious aspersions of the Professor's brother, the Colonel. Reaching an agreement with a periodical that had only recently gone into business a few months earlier, an arrangement that I believe has been beneficial to both of us over the years, I began to write about my friend Holmes. And I was faced with an overwhelming amount of material from which to choose.

I have always tended to favor those cases which showed various aspects of my friend's gifts, rather than selecting the most exciting tales simply for the sake of titillating the reading audience. Thus, in 1891 I was again forced to narrate specific and isolated pieces of each day involved, stitching them together to make single self-contained tales while carefully leaving out references to many other cases that were occurring simultaneously.

As Holmes's practice developed over the years, so did his abilities, and he was able to juggle successfully a number of cases at the same time. Careful reading of my narratives might reveal that a breakfast conversation, for instance, is the only recorded action that occurs on an identified day that is related to that specific case, without alluding to what else happened with some other completely unconnected investigation occurring at the same time. Hopefully I may be forgiven for writing in such a way as to imply that this was the sole occurrence that actually took place on that day, and that Holmes then spent the rest of those hours on just that one solitary matter. I also plead for mercy for giving the impression that Holmes spent a great deal of his time simply waiting around the sitting room at 221b without purpose, ill-tempered or worse, as he wished for cases and clients to appear. This device, making each case into an isolated island on its own, was used – against my better judgment, perhaps – to increase interest at the dramatic start of a published narrative, and was suggested to me by my literary agent. It was not a device that I always favored, but it had its uses.

In fact, Holmes's cases overlapped one another considerably, often with the next beginning while the current was still in motion. Some moved linearly from start to finish without interruption, while others stretched, a piece here and a piece there, across weeks, months, or even years and decades. There are cases from the past that resonated into the present, or times when Holmes's path was detoured from the middle of one case into a completely different matter without warning. A few never reached any conclusion at all. Sometimes, as in the matter of the stolen Dickens letter which I propose to include in this collection, Holmes would find himself surrounded by the returning ripples of a matter that he had believed to be concluded years earlier, with the guilty miscreant supposedly far behind him. I have chosen the other cases in this portfolio to reflect these same aspects.

I trust that this collection will meet with approval, as have others in the past. I am gratified with the continuing interest in narratives related to Holmes's methods, and I plan to continue providing them to the public for as long as I am able. In the days which lie ahead of us, I believe that reminders of my friend's skill, as well as his unflagging patriotism and chivalry, will be of value to us all.

I go now to join Holmes in another investigation, this time on the Continent. I shall depart as soon as I complete this introductory material, only stopping on the way to drop off the manuscript with my friend Lomax for his review and amusement, where it will be held until such time as either Holmes or myself can retrieve it and take it on to the publisher. I trust that, barring any unforeseen circumstances, it will soon be in your hands, dear reader, and that you find as much joy in the reading of Holmes's adventures as I have had recalling them.

John H. Watson
2 July, 1929*

* Editor's Note: Sadly, Watson passed away on July 24th, 1929. Obviously, he never retrieved these notes from his friend, Lomax, who, along with Lomax's heirs, waited a long time for someone in a deerstalker to show up and take possession of them. I don't know why Holmes never retrieved them, but I'm glad that I was able to receive them.

The Mystery at Kerrett's Rood

Mr. Sherlock Holmes finished lighting his pipe, and concluded by stating, ". . . and I cannot say that it is likely to weigh very heavily upon my conscience." With that, he flipped his spent match out the window and into the warm April air of the English countryside.

Holmes was referring to his own recent actions, which had resulted just hours before in the death of a particularly evil man, and I could not disagree with him at all. We had only met the dead man once during his lifetime, but that was all that had been needed to size up the black-hearted villain. We had just spent a horrifying night, hiding in silence while waiting for a diabolical murder attempt to take place. The murderer's scheme had been turned back on him, and he had fallen in the same agony and terror that he had caused for his first victim, and had attempted to impose on his second. The killer, one of the most grim and immoral men that Holmes and I had ever faced, was now dead himself, no doubt because of Holmes's frantic and successful efforts to repel the lethal creature that had been sent to kill the dead man's poor stepdaughter.

I had been grateful the previous night for the warm and dry spring weather, as we made our way in darkness from the local inn at Stoke Moran, and through the dense undergrowth of the neglected estate to the manor house. Now, however, the balmy air, along with the relaxation that inevitably arrives at the end of a tense adventure, threatened to put me to sleep.

We were returning from Harrow, where we had taken the unfortunate surviving stepdaughter to stay with her aunt, following the previous night's events. The train was unusually crowded that morning with travelers going up to London. As we pulled into some small station in the vicinity of Sudbury Hill, I could see the press of humanity stepping toward the great resting beast, anxious to board before it renewed its relentless journey to

17

the capital. I sighed and shifted. Holmes and I had been unable to get a private carriage, and I knew that we were about to have fellow sojourners joining us.

I was soon proved correct. The door opened to reveal a small middle-aged woman, who began to carefully step up into the compartment. Behind her was a large man with a case, wearing a slightly-too-small billy-cock which accentuated his red meaty face and great untrimmed moustache. He was quite impatient for the woman to get out of his way so that he could entrain as well.

I was amused to see that the woman paused for the smallest of instants, glancing back and forth from myself to Holmes. Her eyes narrowed when she observed his pipe. This helped to make her decision, as she turned to her left and sat down beside me. The large man took the opposite seat, settling in by Holmes, who glanced at me in wry amusement. The man put his oversized case on the floor behind his feet, and began to pat around his coat before pulling out the makings of a cigarette.

Beside me, the woman gave a small disapproving cough, as only the ladies can do, spurring the large man to glance up. She glared at the tobacco pouch in his hands with fierce yet concentrated subtlety, causing him to deflate somewhat and return it to whence it came. I knew that there was no prohibition on smoking in this compartment, and I wondered what Holmes would do when the lady inevitably turned her gaze upon him, and his recently-lit pipe.

As I expected, he ruefully smiled, nodded to her, and reached over to the window, knocking out the ashes and still-unburned tobacco onto the ground below. I hoped that gallantly surrendering to the woman's wishes would not cause a track fire. As the door slammed shut and the guards' whistles signaled our departure, Holmes returned the offending implement to its resting place underneath his Inverness.

Our strong-willed feminine companion did not feel the need to gloat over her victories. She simply turned and looked out the door to her right as the train resumed its movement towards London.

The large man, deprived of his stimulant, chose a different path and settled into an immediate doze, his face appearing to collapse around the fixed constant of its wild moustache. I envied him.

We rode in silence for some moments, and my feelings of drowsiness, due to the warm weather and the complete lack of sleep the night before, began to overtake me. Only the fear of appearing to be like the softly snoring bear across from me kept me awake at all, although I have no doubt that my struggles were visible to my other companions. Finally, as though taking pity on me, Holmes began a conversation that was certain to revive me.

"Do you believe in Providence, madam?" he asked the woman to my right.

She looked up sharply from whatever inner thoughts she had been pursuing, and frowned as might be expected, possibly fearing that she had stumbled into a nest of proselytizing zealots.

Holmes smiled, as if to dispense with her concern. Finally, as if deciding that he was harmless, or if not, that she was worthy to stand against him, she replied in a slight Scottish accent, "I do, but I also believe that the Good Lord expects us to help ourselves along the path of life when we are able."

"Then," replied Holmes, "you will be happy to learn that your efforts to assist the Divine Plan come to fruition have been successful, and you have been delivered to what, or rather whom, you seek. I am Sherlock Holmes."

This odd statement made no sense to me at all, and the woman seemed as surprised as well for just a moment, before a look of comprehension led to a smile on her face. I would have been surprised that such a grim visage as she had first presented could warm so quickly and pleasantly. "I see that what I have been told about you is true, Mr. Holmes."

"By your sister, no doubt."

"Why, yes. How did you know? I have not been to visit her in a good five years."

"But obviously you must regularly communicate with her, to have some knowledge of me," replied Holmes.

"Certainly," said the woman. "We are constant correspondents, and tales of your activities make up a substantial portion of her letters."

"Yet you did not tell her that you were coming up today?"

"No, for I believed that she might discourage me. Again, how did you know?"

"Because Dr. Watson and I have obviously been away, and if you had notified your sister that you were coming to see us, she would have told you that we were not at home and had not let her know when we might be returning."

"Wait," I said, struggling to catch the discussion which had left me far behind. "Sister?" I looked more closely at our companion. "I think that I see it now. Are you *Mrs. Hudson's* sister?"

"Yes, I am," said the woman, a friendly smile now fully lighting her face, such a sharp contrast to the closed expression that she had previously assumed, one that all travelers wear during a journey at one time or another.

"The resemblance is obvious," said Holmes, "the shape of the ears and eyes, and the skull, if you will forgive me for saying so, madam. The unique ways of speaking certain words, indicating a distinct northern regional dialect, only confirmed the matter once our conversation began. I'm sure if your hands were ungloved, there would be similarities there as well."

"But how did you know to begin with?" asked the lady again. "That it was *you* that I was journeying to see?"

"It was no great feat, I assure you, and I'm rather loath to spoil the effect from such simple reasons. I had observed one of the papers protruding from your book," said Holmes. "I can see from here that, along with your railway ticket, you have written in precise and artificially neat letters, '221 Baker Street' on that long slip of yellow paper, no doubt to have at the ready, should you find a non-English-speaking cabbie at the train station. That, in itself, might indicate that you were simply going to visit your sister. However, below the address, and still partially tucked into the book, is what appears to be the top of a capital letter 'S', followed shortly by a capital "H" as well. As both these letters are also followed by what appears to be the tops of the other lower-case letters in my name, the conclusion was inescapable. And in addition, if you were simply going to visit your sister, you would not have needed to write out my name along with the address for the benefit of a cabbie.

"I must confess," he added, "that modesty prevents me from elaborating on the fact that the particular address you have inscribed is generally known to many of the London cabbies who transport people needing my special skills and abilities.

"Thus, seeing that you had taken care to write it all out ahead of time, including what appeared to be my name, before departing on your journey, I made the conclusion that you were coming to consult me about some problem. I then made a closer examination of you, and was startled to see your quite notable resemblance to our good landlady. A rather circular series of confirmations, as one led to another, confirming it, and returning again to the first.

"You see, Watson," he said, glancing my way, "there really is a place in the world for coincidence."

"Or Providence, as you so recently pointed out," I said, my earlier sleepiness entirely dispelled.

"Exactly," said Holmes. "And now, Mrs. – ?"

"Grimshaw," said the woman. "The widow of Mr. J.A. Grimshaw."

"Mrs. Grimshaw. How may the doctor and I help you? As I said, it is obvious that you did not consult with your sister before departing for London, or you would have realized that we were not at home, and had not indicated when we would return."

"That is correct, Mr. Holmes. Martha has always been the most sensible sister of us all, in every sense of the word, and she might have tried to talk me out of relating my story to you. After all, she would say that it was a just a ghost story, but I know what I've seen. Therefore, I decided to journey up to London, as if I were simply a client, and then listen to my sister's sharp criticism on the matter after the fact."

Holmes glanced out the window as the train slowed for the next station. "Perhaps, if you do not wish for your sister to know about the reason for your trip, it might be better for us to leave the train here, at the next stop, and discuss the matter, instead of traveling on up to town. That would also have the benefit of putting us closer to your home, should we decide to return there, rather than going all the way up to London, simply to come back again."

"That would suit me admirably, Mr. Holmes. There is a small tea shop near this station where we may talk, and you can tell me whether my fears have any merit, or are simply caused from living alone for too long. Although I will tell you," she added, "I am not a woman given to fancy!"

As the train huffed to a stop, we gathered our things and departed, moving awkwardly around the sleeping behemoth sprawled by the door. He sputtered and blew out his moustache several times, but never awakened. I hoped that he roused himself in time to disembark at his destination.

"Do not worry about our friend, the salesman," said Holmes softly, reading my thoughts. "He is obviously from London, and is returning after a successful week or two roaming the Midlands and the West Country. He will awaken at the end of the line and make his way home to his wife and three young children, the youngest being the only boy, who will all be glad to see both him and the small trinkets that he is bringing to them."

Before I could ask how Holmes had determined these facts about the man, he had left me, hurrying to catch up with Mrs. Grimshaw as she turned in her ticket and walked out of the station, never looking back, and rightly assuming that we would be following smartly behind her.

After a short left turn, and then a right into a quiet lane, we found ourselves seated in one of those little tea shops that occur with great regularity throughout the country, crowded with dainty furniture and tea-related appurtenances. It was not too heavily occupied at that time of the morning, and we made our way to a quiet table along a side wall, not quite in the back, but close enough to the front to have the benefit of the morning light without being too visible from the street outside.

We ordered a strong pot of tea and a selection of cakes, although something more substantial, such as coffee and sandwiches, would have been more to my liking, following the night that Holmes and I had just faced. After the comestibles were placed on the table by the shop's apparent owner, a scrubbed-looking and doughy woman in her sixties, Mrs. Grimshaw began her tale.

"As I said, my sister Martha has always been the sensible one of us girls, and I do not doubt that she would have tried to discourage me from asking your advice. However, while I don't like to think of myself as any less sensible, I know what I've seen, and I finally decided that I must speak to you.

"I'm fortunate to know so much about you already from Martha's letters, and also from what I hear from time to time from one of our other sisters, Mrs. Turner, who lives nearby, and who I understand occasionally helps Martha when needed."

I nodded. "We think a great deal of both of your sisters."

"The others are just as sensible as well," said Mrs. Grimshaw, taking my comment to refer to their Scottish pragmatism.

"As we grew, we all went our different ways. I married Mr. Grimshaw, who was a soldier at the time, but he was soon invalided out, which suited us both just fine. He had good reference from one of the officers for whom he had done a turn once, and we found positions at a house and grounds north of Sudbury, him as the handyman and groundskeeper, and me as housekeeper.

"I need to describe things so you'll understand me when I tell what I've seen. When we went to work there, over twenty years ago, the house was already mostly empty and closed off, and owned by a retired broker named Mr. Felton."

Holmes's eyebrows slightly lifted. "Clifton Felton?" he asked.

Mrs. Grimshaw smiled. "I see that you remember him. I'm not surprised."

"Well, I'm not ashamed to admit that I have not made his acquaintance," I interrupted.

"All in good time, Watson," said Holmes. "Let Mrs. Grimshaw continue with her narrative, and I'm sure Mr. Felton's relevance will become obvious as we go along."

With a smile, Mrs. Grimshaw continued. "At the time that my husband and I went to work for the man, he was a widower, living a very quiet life amongst his papers and books. He had a young son, still a boy, Theodore, or Ted as he was called. After about ten years or so, Ted grew up and moved away, only visiting on occasion. I believe that he held a job somewhere around Oxford. The two seemed to get along well enough with one another, on the occasions when Ted came to visit.

"My husband and I never had very difficult duties. Mr. Felton did not entertain, and great portions of the house were permanently shut up. The grounds, which consisted of several acres enclosed by a wall, did not require a great deal of work, as Mr. Felton did not have formal gardens. Rather, he simply wished for the natural intrusion of the trees and other plants to be kept at bay, instead of completely tamed. Therefore, my husband usually had his work well in hand each day, and did not require any assistance from other employees, unless he had to bring in an occasional day helper, if a tree fell, for instance, or something else along those lines, that was too much for him.

"In the main house, we had a cook and a maid that came in by day, but left in the evenings. My husband and I did not live in the big house – in fact, no one lived there but Mr. Felton. He allowed us to live in a small cottage on the western side of the grounds and its surrounding quarter-acre at that corner of the property, which has come to be known locally as the Kerrett's Rood. The overall property has always been known as Kerrett House, in reference to the rich shipping agent who first built it early in the century. Although there have been several owners since that time, the original name has stuck.

"We existed in the same routine for many years. Cooks and maids would come and go, but naturally, without any great drama. Day in and day out, I would make my way up to the house in the morning and my husband would carry out his tasks outdoors, and we would return to our little cottage at night, leaving Mr. Felton in the house.

"All until September of 1878," said Holmes, with a knowing look.

"Exactly," said Mrs. Grimshaw. "Suddenly, Mr. Felton's quiet life was exposed as a lie, and as it all tumbled down, it shook what my husband and I had with it for a while, despite our complete ignorance of what had happened."

I struggled to remember what had occurred during that time, before quickly realizing that I had not been in England then at all, and could not be expected to know. Earlier that year, I had taken my degree as a Doctor of Medicine at the University of London, and had left London to begin a series of events that eventually took me to the other side of the world and back, before depositing me again in that great metropolitan cesspool, where I would have probably foundered and died if not washing up on the friendly steps leading up to 221b Baker Street.

Holmes noticed my chain of thought, and interrupted. "You would not have known anything about what happened, my friend, although you might have heard me mention it once or twice in passing. Perhaps you recall a reference here or there to the Reckless Goings-on at the Suicide Club?"

I did remember hearing of it, but no details of this case had ever been provided to me. Mrs. Grimshaw nodded in agreement. "That was it. That's what the papers called them. That all took place about the same time that Martha's husband was killed in a railway accident, and she decided to take in boarders. Is that when you first moved there?"

Holmes shook his head, and I added, "Holmes and I met on the first day of January, 1881, when he had learned of the available rooms, and was introduced to me afterwards upon realizing that he needed a fellow lodger to share expenses."

Holmes smiled. "By that point in time, your sister had already been renting the rooms for a year or so, and believed that she understood what was involved with being a landlady." His eyes took on a mischievous glint, and he added, "That was before I moved my little practice there."

We laughed, Mrs. Grimshaw included, and the owner of the shop used the opportunity to approach our table. Mrs. Grimshaw indicated that another pot of tea would be welcome, while I expressed a desire to switch to a cup of strong black coffee instead. The owner quickly returned, and after our cups were filled, Holmes indicated that Mrs. Grimshaw should continue her story. She glanced at me, and then back at Holmes, who said, "Tell us why you have decided to seek me out in London, braving possible discouragement from your sister, whom to my knowledge you have not visited since Watson and I became tenants."

"Because I have seen Mr. Ted Felton, the son, in the window of the big house at night, staring down the hill toward my cottage."

I could see that the statement meant something to Holmes. "And why should that be unusual?" I asked, feeling that I was still very much in the dark.

Holmes answered. "After the events of 1878 were concluded, and Clifton Felton, the father, died, Ted Felton did away with himself."

Mrs. Grimshaw nodded. "I see that you still remember it, Mr. Holmes. After Mr. Clifton's death, and what followed, it was said that Mr. Ted couldn't bear the shame, and that he drowned himself in the Thames."

"Where his body was never found," added Holmes. "And his 'ghost' has contented itself with a peaceful rest for over four years until recently, when suddenly it has returned to haunt his father's former home. I can see why you believed that your sister might discourage you from bringing this story to my attention."

His statement seemed to rub Mrs. Grimshaw the wrong way for a moment, as I could see her eyes tighten, resembling more the grim woman who had first entered our train compartment that morning. But then she seemed to sense what I already knew: Holmes was not dismissing her story outright, and was in fact interested in what circumstances could have led her to believe that a young man had returned from the dead.

26

"How," said Holmes, "has this manifestation of Ted Felton made itself known?"

"By showing himself in the great window of the big house, that is centered in the very front of the building. It was two weeks or so ago that I first looked up and saw him. I was out in the small garden behind my cottage, seeing what needed to be done for the spring planting, when I glanced up and there he was, framed in the window. As you might recall from before, Mr. Holmes, the land slopes up to the east from the back of my cottage, toward the big house. That main west-facing window looks down toward me. It is several hundred feet away, but I could see him as plain as day, as the evening sun was shining full on the front of the big house. He was always a lanky lad, and he had a unique way of standing, leaning back on one leg as if he were propped on a shooting stick. That first night, I admit, I was so shocked that I just stood and looked. He was there for another minute or so, and then he seemed to vanish."

"How many other times has he appeared?

"Oh, five or six, I suppose. The next night, after I first saw him, I stood around outside at sunset, waiting to see if he appeared again, but he did not. I haven't been out every night since then, but I've tried to see if he reappeared. A few nights he has."

"And did you only watch from the back of your cottage, or did you investigate further?"

"I must admit that I did not want to know anything about why he was there. At least not at first. But last night, when I saw him again, I finally got up my nerve and took the old key and made my way up there."

"And the house has stood empty since the tragedy to which you have referred took place in 1878?" I interrupted. "Who is the current owner of the property? Are you the caretaker?"

"After Mr. Clifton Felton died, and then Mr. Ted followed soon after, I was visited by the old family solicitor, Benjamin Weekes. His office is located in the village, in the High Street. He had known the Felton family for many years, and I believe there was some gossip that, when they were all young, Mr.

Weekes had set his cap for the woman who later became Mr. Clifton's wife. Of course, this was long before I knew any of them."

"I heard something of it at the time, during that day or so when I was in the village," said Holmes.

"Mr. Weekes explained that, while Mr. Clifton's affairs were tangled because of the events that led to his death, Mr. Ted had inherited his own separate income from his mother, and that the father's will had indicated that after his death, my husband and I were to inherit Kerrett's Rood, which would be sectioned off as its own property, and that the residue of the money would go to pay the taxes on the remaining estate for as long as it would last. Mr. Weekes told me that the amount of money left by Mr. Ted would last a long time.

"My husband, while he was still alive, worked out an arrangement with Mr. Weekes to continue to keep up the estate. He would maintain the grounds in a limited way, and check the house on a regular basis. After my husband passed last year, I've hired some day jobbers to work in the grounds as needed, but the house has stood empty this entire time, although I do walk through it once a quarter or so to see that everything remains the same. It is a solid old place, and may sit there for many years as it is, dark and quiet and still inside. I take in work as a seamstress now, and Mr. Weekes still sends me something each month for keeping an eye on the place, but I don't have the time or the authorization to keep the house clean inside. So there it stands, and will continue to do so, I suppose. Which is why I was so surprised to see Mr. Ted's spirit come back."

"And you've only seen it manifest itself at sunset?" said Holmes. "It is a curious spirit indeed that eschews the haunted midnight hour to reveal itself during daylight. You say that he only first appeared a couple of weeks ago. Around the twenty-first day of March?"

Mrs. Grimshaw nodded, and Holmes continued, "Around the first of spring, then. Had you been outside much before that in the evenings, or was that an activity that you had only recently resumed, upon the return of warm weather, and the need to begin preparations for this year's garden?"

"Just about then, I should say," replied Mrs. Grimshaw. "Everything was all tucked away tidily enough last fall for the winter, and there was no need to go out back until recently."

"Just so," said Holmes. "And the big windows where you saw this spirit face toward the west, so they are directly looking at the setting sun, whose path across the earth is progressing northwards this time of year. Our ancients understood where to look for the rising and setting of the sun against the horizon on different dates, and it still has an effect on our activities as well."

"Do you mean," I said, "that the springtime sunset was in such a location as to fully highlight the large windows where the figure was seen, whereas in the winter it might have lit the house from a different direction?"

"Exactly," said Holmes. "The spirit, or whatever it is, might have been standing there in that location for weeks or even months before Mrs. Grimshaw first spotted it − or him − but it was only the combination of her desire to examine the area behind her house, along with the exact angle of the sun on those windows upon those dates, that made him visible. In fact, I would wager that the figure, man or spirit, who was standing in those windows looking down the hill, did not see you at all, Mrs. Grimshaw."

"But how could that be?" she asked. "It is only a few hundred yards away, and I was right there in front of him. The lawn slopes between the two buildings, and there are no trees or bushes between to block his view."

"Yes, but he was facing into the setting sun," said Holmes, "and you were in the shadow cast by your cottage, as the sun was setting behind it. That is why he probably felt free to return to the window on subsequent nights. He did not believe that he had been observed."

"You sound as if you already have a theory, Holmes," I said.

"And so I do," he replied. "Let us make our way back to the station, and we will journey with Mrs. Grimshaw to Kerrett's

Rood. I'm afraid that your visit to your sister will have to be postponed," said Holmes. He then lifted his teacup, which had been mostly ignored during the conversation, and swallowed the entire contents in two gulps.

I could see that that owner of the shop had been watching us with some impatience as we continued to occupy space, although there did not seem to be any great influx of patrons as the morning progressed. Happy to accommodate, we paid our bill and stepped out into the quiet street.

We made our way to the station, and only had to wait a few minutes for a down train to arrive. While Mrs. Grimshaw and I stood about, Holmes sent several wires, without revealing their destination or contents. There were far fewer passengers waiting to travel away from London, and we quickly found a private compartment. I noticed with a suppressed grin that Holmes, always the gentleman when circumstances allowed, made an effort to lead us to one that did not accommodate smoking.

After we had seated ourselves, Holmes said, "While we make our way, perhaps we can elaborate for Doctor Watson the tragic events of 1878, so he will have some context of what I expect to discover when we arrive."

Mrs. Grimshaw nodded and began. "As you mentioned earlier, it was late September, 1878, just another month in just another year. Mr. Felton's son, Ted, was away at the time, as he usually was, probably in Oxford, but I couldn't say for sure.

"I need to further explain how the estate around Kerrett House is laid out, for the doctor's benefit. It is a walled enclosure of about five acres. As I have said, the grounds were managed by my husband, but not strictly controlled and landscaped, if you understand my meaning. The house itself sits in the middle of the property, on a slight rise that drops off in all directions. There are a few small outbuildings at the back toward the eastern wall, but they are still quite a distance from the walls.

"The only building that is adjacent to the wall is the cottage in which I live, on the West Road. In fact, the front of the cottage is part of the wall, so that my front door opens directly into the street, and the first floor windows look down into it. There is only one door in that whole wall, front or back, other then the front door to my house, and it is the great gate that also opens onto the West Road. This is located some little distance from my house, in the same side.

"This gate is probably twenty feet wide, in two ten-foot sections that swing wide when something big goes in or out. Set into one of these sections is a smaller door for regular in-and-out foot traffic. That is what we used when we needed to enter or leave on any normal day."

"We?" interrupted Holmes. "Who would have used that gate, or visited the Felton house?"

"Why, the cook and maid would come in by the regular door in the gate, as would my husband or myself if we had business in that direction. That was where Mr. Felton's son would enter as well, when he was home. Tradesmen would use it when they brought supplies to the big house, although sometimes they would deliver in a wagon. If that was the case, arrangements would be made for my husband to unlock and open the big gate."

"So the large gate was normally kept locked, but the regular door there was not?"

"During the day only. And at night, the smaller door was locked as well, by my husband. Of course," she added, "my husband and I used the front door in our own house, which opened through the wall into the street, to go in and out as we felt like."

"Did Mr. Felton leave specific standing instructions that the gate be locked?"

"He did," replied Mrs. Grimshaw. "He greatly valued his privacy, and did not really see anyone during the day but me or my husband. The cook and the maid stayed out of his way, and he kept to himself. At night, when the small staff would leave, he wanted the gate locked. He told me that, living as he did in that big house, he did not like the idea of people getting in at night and roaming the grounds, and him up there alone. It did not seem to be unusual to either me or my husband, and locking the gate was simply one of the few duties in my husband's day."

"Thank you," said Holmes. "I quite understand."

Mrs. Grimshaw smiled and continued. "September 1878 was like any other month, until that early morning when the police knocked us up, showing us papers and demanding to be let into the grounds. For it turned out that Mr. Felton, the man that we had believed was asleep in the big house, was dead in the cellar of a London warehouse. And as if that were not enough, it turned out that he was the leader of a criminal gang that had been in existence for years."

Holmes nodded, and Mrs. Grimshaw said, "I believe at this point, Mr. Holmes, you might be able to tell us more than I can of what was behind Mr. Felton's mysterious past. Even after nearly five years, come this September, I'm not sure that I understand it all."

As Holmes gathered his thoughts for a moment, and then said, "At the time these events were going on, I was living in Montague Street, beside the British Museum, dividing my efforts unevenly between investigations and my unique studies. When I became involved in this investigation, I had no idea that it would lead to exposure of the Suicide Club as well, of which we have recently spoken."

"But not explained," I said. "I am anxious to hear about this grim-sounding group. Did it have anything to do with Stevenson's story, first published about that same time, if I recall correctly?"*

"I believe that around the time these events first came to light, some clever member of the press remembered the title of Stevenson's book and appropriated it. Otherwise, there were no connections.

"Without taking too much of our time with this tale, I was approached in early September of that year by the banker, Sir Wilton Cole, whose house in Surrey had been burglarized a week or so before.

* Editor's Note: See *The Suicide Club* (1878) a collection of three related stories by Robert Louis Stevenson.

"Most of the silver plate, as well as some minor artworks, had been taken. It was not a substantial loss to Sir Wilton, but he was nevertheless quite angry, and did not enjoy being taken advantage of without making some effort to fight back.

"He informed me that it was the opinion of the authorities that the crime seemed to be the latest to have been perpetrated by a group known as the Bracknell Gang. They had come to be given that colorful title throughout Surrey, and areas to the north and west, not because of any known fact about them that would affix the name to them, but rather because Bracknell was the first location that one of their robberies had seemingly taken place.

"The crimes were all very similar in method, location, and what was stolen. They had been occurring for several years at that point on a sporadic but predictable basis. The loot would eventually turn up in London, having been sold and resold, untraceable, and long after the actual robberies. I must admit that, in my more-than-adequate time to study London crime during those periods between clients in my Montague Street rooms, I had found several occasions to look into the activities of the supposed Bracknell Gang and ponder their methodologies. Since this is another story for another time, and without elaborating too much, which I am sure is a disappointment to the doctor," he said, smiling in my direction, "I will simply say that I had been able to form a theory or two, and I was glad of this opportunity to test them first hand."

"I traveled to Sir Wilton's Surrey home, with a letter in my pocket informing his staff to provide all cooperation that I would need. In short, I saw evidence, underneath the trampling of the police, that three men had been involved in the crime. I tracked them across the grounds to where a wagon had been secured in a nearby copse at the rear of the estate, alongside a small and little-used farm road. The wagon had a crooked left rear wheel, and the footmarks of the horse had their own unique characteristics, especially in the poor way in which the right rear shoe had been attached. The wagon had been there for an hour or so, unattended but with the horse tied, based on the evidence on the ground. Also, the wagon was heavier leaving than it had been when it had arrived. If Sir Wilton had waited one more day to seek me out, the clues would have faded away.

"I managed to follow the trail to a nearby village, where I located both the wagon and the horse at a stable. They had been rented on the day of the robbery. I obtained a very accurate description of the three men, since it was quite unusual that the wagon had been returned so late at night. With this description in hand, I also discovered that these same three men had been at the local railway station an hour or so before returning the wagon, where they had arranged to ship a number of sealed wooden crates on the last train of the night, the very same train that they themselves used. It was relatively easy from that point, based on the descriptions and carelessness of the burglars, to track them back to an area north of Sudbury. The crates were to be delivered to that station, where they would be held until retrieved.

"They had become rather arrogant after several years of successful robberies, and had not bothered to take the time to adequately cover their trail. An hour or two of asking questions identified the three men, two of whom were locals who had taken delivery of the crates, Amos Sykes and Steven Wells. The third, as you will have determined, my dear Watson, was our reclusive Mr. Clifton Felton.

"I made my way to the local constabulary, well aware that my youth and small reputation at the time would require some little extra effort on my part in order to convince them that the three men were in fact the Bracknell Gang. In particular, from what I had learned, this Mr. Felton, a retired broker who seemed to live a quiet and reclusive life within his walled estate, would seem a most unlikely villain.

"I made my initial explanations, and was soon passed along to an Inspector Ross, since deceased, who tolerantly allowed me to explain my reasoning. He listened with increasing interest as I made my case.

"Finally, he said, 'I am convinced, Mr. Holmes. At least enough to follow up on what you have brought to me. But there is one thing, one small factor that you should know. Perhaps, being away from London for a day or so as you trailed these three men, you have been prevented from hearing the latest news.'

"He handed me a wire from London sent that very day, revealing the death of Mr. Clifton Felton, just the night before. He had killed himself in the basement of a London warehouse. Although we did not know it yet, not having any idea of the true nature of the crime, Felton's would turn out to be the last of the deaths connected to the reckless 'Suicide Club'."

Mrs. Grimshaw nodded, while I sat up straighter, interested in learning more of this sinister and intriguing organization.

Holmes, however, veered away from it, instead stating, "Inspector Ross explained that he was expecting a representative from Scotland Yard on the next train, whereupon they would go to the house to break the news to the staff. My information relating to the robbery added a new layer to the problem. By the time the London man had arrived, Ross had a warrant to examine the property, looking for stolen goods. He had also sent out men to take Amos Sykes and Steven Wells into custody for further questioning.

"And so I set out for Kerrett House with Inspector Ross, along with Inspector Plummer from London, whom I previously knew." He turned to Mrs. Grimshaw, "I do not know if you recall that I was accompanying the police when we searched Mr. Felton's house."

"You'll forgive me, I'm sure, that I did not notice you. I was understandably not very observant that morning," she said. Turning to me, she explained, "The day had started like any other. My husband and I were up very early, eating our own breakfast before he was to leave, in order to unlock the small gate for the cook and maid, and I to go on up to the big house. The cook and maid were never required to arrive particularly early, as Mr. Felton always slept until mid-morning. Only later did we realize that he was probably sleeping so late because he was often out far into the night, and he was not home in bed as we had always believed.

"We did not know that the police had arrived and had been pounding on the main gate for quite some time before one of them got the idea to knock on our door."

"Actually, I was the one who knocked on your door," said Holmes. "However, Inspector Ross had followed me down the wall to your house, and by the time you opened it, it was he who took charge, with great authority."

"As I said, I'm afraid that I don't recall you," said Mrs. Grimshaw. "In any event, we were told that there was evidence indicating Mr. Felton was the leader of a long-standing burglary ring, and there was a warrant to search the house and grounds. In addition, the inspector mentioned, almost as an afterthought, that Mr. Felton was dead by his own hand."

"You can imagine, gentlemen, that this news fairly astounded me and my poor husband. Mr. Felton, who never left home – or so we thought then – was accused of being a criminal, and he had been found dead as well, on the far side of London. And there was every indication that the police believed that we were somehow involved in his crimes along with him."

"The police mind," said Holmes, "first looks at everyone with suspicion, assuming that all involved are initially guilty, and then sorts out the wheat from the chaff later, so to speak, hopefully successfully. When I first presented my theories to Inspector Ross, I could tell that he was even weighing my own possible involvement and guilt in the matter, as if my accusations were part of some too-clever plan to implicate one of my fellow gang-members and thus take over the operation for myself. As you know, it was soon established that neither you nor your husband had any knowledge of Mr. Felton's night-time activities."

Mrs. Grimshaw nodded. "And for that I'm grateful, Mr. Holmes. After the police were let in, the house was searched, and a great deal of the stolen materials were found hidden in a locked room in the basement of the big house. But one great mystery was that there was never any explanation as to how they had actually come to be there. My husband always locked the only gate every night, and surely we would have noticed something

36

suspicious during the years that the gang was going about its business. We never saw any signs of anyone leaving or entering at night, let along carrying in heaps of stolen property. We truly believed that Mr. Felton stayed inside and had no visitors."

"And you may not have been aware that no key for the gate was ever found in the big house, or on Mr. Felton's person. The only key that we could locate was your husband's, which had remained with him the entire time. How the loot came to be in the basement of the house, as well as the other indications that the two other gang members were frequent visitors down there, remains a mystery to this day. Inspector Ross theorized that somehow they came and went over the back wall, but I remain unconvinced, as the estate is surrounded by fairly well-traveled roads on all sides, and moving that amount of material back and forth over the walls, even in the dead of night, in order to carry it across the grounds and hide it in the house, seems unlikely and would have left some trace. And there was no indication anywhere that the walls had been climbed or breached, and no paths in the grounds leading from the walls to the house. Sykes and Wells were certainly never forthcoming with any useful information. They went to Dartmoor with the secret sealed within them."

"But surely," I said, "you must have theorized some other explanation."

"Ah, Watson, you must remember that I was younger then, only twenty-four years old. I was still learning my craft, and not as confident as I am now. Besides, Inspector Ross was not interested in finding out specifics. He had captured the Bracknell Gang, he had recovered some, if not all, of the booty, and he did not yet know the deeper connection to the sensational events of the Suicide Club, as it came to be called afterwards in the London papers. He was more than full with the meal that I had brought to him. He did not need to seek anything else."

"And this 'Suicide Club'?" I asked. "What was it? How did it fit in to this odd business?"

"Again, that should be another story for another time. Nevertheless – "

"But Holmes!" I interrupted, refusing to be denied the details of this intriguing story. "Surely it is relevant to Mrs. Grimshaw's problem."

"As I started to say," Holmes continued, "I will give a short précis of the events, so that Mr. Felton's death, and the subsequent suicide of his son Ted, may be better understood."

He glanced out the window and said, "I see by the slow progression of the quarter-mile posts that I should have time to tell you what happened next.

"Following the exposure of the robbery gang, and the arrest of the surviving members, I returned to Montague Street. I was not completely satisfied with the case, as there were several questions left unexplained. How had the loot made its way to the big house without any signs being left of its passage? What had prompted Clifton Felton to take his own life, on the very night before his long-standing criminal activities were about to be exposed? Was there a connection, or was it merely coincidence, which does happen more than I would like. I intended to see what could be discovered in London, at the other end of the matter, on my own time and for my own edification. Before I could begin, however, I was visited by Mr. Ted Felton, who had come up to London to hire me to answer the very same questions that I had been asking myself.

"Even then, I was learning to recognize the various approaches that a client might make as they made their way to my lodgings. Whether they forcefully approached the door and pulled the bell with great vehemence, or possibly stepped close to the doorway in a timid fashion several times, before veering off and then returning, finally overcoming great reluctance to meekly climb the stairs to state their business, each client was a great study for an up-and-coming consulting detective. I had observed Ted Felton from my first-floor window. He came straight on, with the look of a man walking with grim purpose to the gallows.

"When he was shown in, he took a few moments to get to the reason for his visit, a reason that I had already divined: He wished to know what lay behind his father's participation in the robbery ring, and more importantly, why had had killed himself.

"I could see that something else was on his mind, until he finally could not hold it in any longer. 'Mr. Holmes, do you think that word of your trailing my father from the robbery site in Surrey could have reached him, and he therefore chose to end his life before he was to be arrested?'

"I had been asking myself the same question, but I had already decided that I had been quite careful not to reveal any information during my travels, nor had I given my questions too much importance as I tracked the robbers. Clifton Felton could not have known that I was on his trail, and his suicide must have come about from some other cause. So I said to Ted Felton, and I think that he believed me. I agreed to examine the matter further.

"After he departed I made my way from Montague Street down to Scotland Yard, where I found Inspector Plummer, now long since retired. I questioned him about several aspects of the matter, including the whereabouts of Sykes and Wells on the night of the suicide. He had established without a doubt that both men were in the local pub near their homes, and had not been in London when Felton's suicide occurred.

"Inspector Plummer also revealed other specific circumstances related to the events of Clifton Felton's death. He told me that the body had been found in the basement of a warehouse, one of those brooding and dangerous buildings between Cannon Street and the Thames. The building had been standing empty for nearly a year, as the heirs to the previous owner squabbled amongst themselves, choosing to make no income in the meantime in order to spite one another. There had been no reason to believe that Felton would have been found anytime soon, perhaps not for weeks, except that a message had been left at the nearby police station, stating that a man, named specifically in the note as Clifton Felton, had hanged himself at that particular warehouse. A couple of constables had been dispatched to the scene, whereupon they confirmed the contents of the short note.

39

"Inspector Plummer had the note with him, in his file relating to the case, and he gladly let me examine it. I could see right away that it was not written by some civic-minded vagrant who had trespassed into the warehouse and discovered the body. It was on good quality paper, with better ink than one might expect from that area, and there were no instances in the note of either misspellings or punctuation errors. I asked Plummer if the quality of the note did not seem unusual to him, but he commented that he had not found it to be so. He expected that it was probably left by one of the children of the former owner, who had been inspecting the property and found the body. Rather than become involved in the matter, an anonymous note had been written. When asked how the writer had known that the dead man was Clifton Felton, and could thus name him in the note, Plummer dismissed my query by saying that the discoverer of the body no doubt knew Felton when he was a broker, before his retirement.

"I was filled with objections, as this theory assumed too much without proving anything, but to Plummer the case was closed. Thanking him, I departed and wondered what to do next. More to fill up my time than having any expectation of discovering a new fact, I made my way to the warehouse, in order to inspect the scene of the death. Something was preventing me, even at that point, of thinking of it as a suicide.

"Although the building was sealed, I had no difficulty in gaining entrance. I quickly saw that there was very little to be learned, as the building truly had been closed and empty for quite some time. There were no signs of any vagrants having obtained access, and the movements of the various policemen at the time of the body's discovery were quite obvious. The remains of the rope were still tied around a rafter, but it had been cut, certainly when the body was removed. I realized that I would have to return to Scotland Yard to ask if the knotted section from around the dead man's neck had been retained. It was something that I should have thought to ask about when I was there, showing that at that point in my career, I still had much to learn. If I had examined the knot on my first trip, the second would not have been necessary. I retraced my steps westward. I left Scotland Yard later that afternoon, having determined that the rope was knotted in a perfectly ordinary fashion, and not showing any signs of exotic origin, such as might have been tied by a one-armed Siamese sailor."

I could see that Holmes made the last statement with a twinkle in his eye, and Mrs. Grimshaw, who did not know him as well, appeared to believe that he was speaking in jest and that such an obscure clue could not exist. The irony was that, in spite of Holmes's subtle ridicule of such a thing, just such a knot had been relevant not three weeks before, although the matter had related to a complicated and grotesque fraud case, rather than a murder.

"Not knowing where to turn next," Holmes continued, "I decided to start over and look for a pattern, a system that has been of use to me in the past. Returning to Montague Street, I began to examine my scrapbooks, which even then were proving to be quite useful. It was there that I found the loose thread. I had been reminded of something while I was examining the warehouse, and I was sure that there was information about it back in my rooms.

"And I was correct. Over the past eight months, there had been six seemingly unconnected suicides, all men of Clifton Felton's approximate age and station in life. Each was an older man, retired from a professional career. Each was a widower who, if he did have children, did not live with him. In fact, each of the men lived alone, with a minimal housekeeping staff. Each was believed to be the sort of man who stayed in at night, and each had been found in remote London locations, dead by their own hands, although by a variety of methods, including a couple of hangings, one who left the gas on in a rented room, two self-inflicted gunshot wounds, and one fellow who was suffocated by shutting himself up in a servant's bedroom in an empty house while burning a brazier full of charcoal. In each case, an anonymous note had been left for the authorities, telling where the men might be found, and specifically naming them to speed their identification.

"Those were the stories of the six men that I found, based on clippings that I had kept for my scrapbooks. It was my habit to docket news stories related to odd or unusual deaths, but I was not yet experienced enough to have noticed the pattern when I first clipped the stories, spread out as they were over a number of months. And even after identifying those six, I did not realize then how many others there were. However, surely six was enough to indicate further investigation was required.

"Even in those days, I was making connections within the police force, and no one was more obligated to me than our old friend, Inspector Lestrade. He was able to allow me access to the files regarding these various and seemingly unrelated suicides. As they had been spread out over a period of months, had occurred in different parts of London and the surrounding Home Counties, and had involved victims who lived in all the compass points around the capital, no one had associated any connection between them. I started with a list of six names, and by the time I had combed through the Yard's files, I had identified thirteen other probable and similar victims, going back for a period of several years.

"I shared my findings with Lestrade, who agreed that there was indeed a pattern. He also held my belief that this needed to be investigated quietly, so as not to spook whoever was involved in what was seemingly a large number of similarly suspicious suicides.

"I spent the better part of a week traveling here and there, cautiously interviewing servants, family members, train station employees, and cabbies, who might have remembered taking any of the men in question to any common locations. Eventually, one recurring factor became clear. At some time before their deaths, the men in question had been spending an evening or two a week at a pub in Hampstead, unknown to their servants.

"I had determined this by querying various railway employees in the stations near each man's home, determining through further questioning along the line that their destinations had been Hampstead. Once there, I was able to find one or two people who remembered the destination of this or that man. I assure you that what I have boiled down to a sentence or two was rigorous and painstaking work, and for every successful thread that I isolated and followed to its conclusion, I had to drop a hundred others. It was an excellent educational experience for a young consulting detective, I can assure you.

"By the end of my investigations, I had identified a common locality as 'The Dog and Wolf' in Hampstead. It will do you no good to look for it the next time you are up that way. It is out of business and gone, and both of the owners, a pair of brothers named Will and Edward Duval, are no longer there either, or with us among the quick at all, for that matter.

"Edward actually ran the pub. Will, who went by the more formal 'William' when he was in the City every day, worked for several life insurance companies over the course of his last few years. It was there that he managed to keep track of the various insurance policies that he and his brother had taken out in the names of the numerous dead men, naming fictitious individuals of their own invention as beneficiaries.

"It was never clear exactly how their scheme started, and obviously they were not very forthcoming in revealing how many men had fallen into their trap, beyond the number that we confirmed. Their scheme was simple. They had gained a reputation for running an establishment that seemed to attract older, retiring men of like backgrounds and disposition. By providing several less-than-salubrious activities to their hand-picked customers, they managed to keep these men returning on a semi regular basis. And every once in a while, when they had found out enough about this or that man to know personal information and forge signatures, they would apply for a life insurance policy, with a fictitious person as the beneficiary. Usually, Will would open an account at an out-of-the way bank in this fictitious person's name, so there would be a place for the insurance payments to be deposited. Then, once the funds were there, the account would be quietly closed and the money funneled back to the two brothers.

"Ordinarily, this scheme could not succeed. However, Will Duval had worked for a number of years as a trusted employee of some of the larger insurance firms in the City, and he was able to slip the policies through the cracks in the system at each of his employers. Then, after each of the victims died, he would process the claim himself, while making sure that any mention of suicide did not show on the official books, as that would invalidate the policy. However, when the Duvals killed their victims, they had to make it *appear* as a suicide so that there would be no ongoing murder investigations. And it was the two of them who left the anonymous notes, so that the bodies could be discovered quickly, speeding along the death payment from the insurance companies.

"None of the policies were ever very large, and therefore did not attract attention from anyone higher up at any of the firms. During the course of their activities, Will changed employers three times, always welcome at his new location, and always careful to leave the previous employer before anything unusual was noticed.

"It seems likely that they were working this system for a while before eventually attempting to take a big prize, one that would perhaps allow them to leave the country. However, their last victim, Clifton Felton, was, to their misfortune, also identified at the same time as the leader of a burglary ring. It was, as it turned out, a coincidence that Felton had been murdered while he was being scrutinized and pursued for his crimes.

"The arrest of the two brothers was surprisingly a quiet affair. The police, led by Lestrade, closed upon the pub, catching both brothers unaware. Their records were easily found, as they had become quite careless due to the ongoing success of their schemes. A few other names of victims were revealed as well, bringing the total number of murdered men to nearly two dozen. It was believed at the time that there may have been even more, before they began to document their records in such a helpfully systematic way.

"Lestrade received a commendation of some sort that turned out to be of value to him, and I subsequently received his gratitude. The insurance companies were both embarrassed at the way the two brothers had used the weaknesses within their system in order to hide their activities, and they were also grateful that these same weaknesses had at last been exposed. They have since tightened up many aspects of the way they do business. And the press, once it learned of the activities promoted at 'The Dog and Wolf' that had been used to attract the lonely old men and start them on the path to their early deaths, was happy to have a story with all the seamy aspects ready made that sell newspapers. The fact that Stevenson's story, 'The Suicide Club,' had appeared just months earlier, only helped to give them a peg to hang their hat upon.

"However, neither of us, Lestrade nor myself, could ever figure the complete story behind Clifton Felton's relationship to the events. No doubt he had heard about the place from someone or other, by word of mouth. He may have been leaving his home at night for years. His visits to the pub were verified as having started a month or so preceding his death. His movements were traced from the station near his home to Hampstead, and then back again in the early hours. But after all was said and done relating to the matter of his murder, we never learned how he departed from his property to either go out at night or to commit the robberies, any more than we could determine how the burglary ring was able to enter or depart the premises, leaving a mound of stolen loot in the basement.

"But there was one final chapter left in the story, or so I thought until today. The part about Ted Felton, and his death following the revelations regarding his father."

There would be no time to hear this part of the story now. The train was pulling into the station. We stepped down to the platform, but instead of moving toward the exit, Holmes walked over to a man standing off to one side, wearing a stiff-looking glove on his left hand and a noticeable red scarf around his throat. The fellow handed Holmes a packet of documents which turned out to be a collection of telegrams. Holmes and the man in the scarf shook hands, and the fellow turned and left without another word.

"That was Sacker," said Holmes. "He sometimes acts as my unofficial agent up in these parts. Lost most of the fingers on his left hand, back in '79, during a gelignite accident while trying to blow one of the Cox & Company safes. If I hadn't arrived there in time, his compatriots might have blown up the rest of him, as well." He started reading through the telegrams.

"And the scarf?" I asked.

Holmes shook his head, almost testily. "Do I have to explain everything, Watson?" Then, realizing his tone, he lifted his head and smiled. "It was so I could spot him easily in the station and save a few moments."

As if Sacker wouldn't be able to spot Holmes first, I thought, looking at him, reading the telegrams in his Inverness and fore-and-aft.

Finally, Holmes completed his perusal of the messages and said, "Let us be off." He led us outside, whereupon Mrs. Grimshaw gestured to the left. "The West Road is this way, Mr. Holmes."

"We are not going to your cottage, or to Kerrett House," said Holmes. "At least not immediately. Our way first leads us to the offices of Mr. Weekes." He tapped his pocket, where the telegrams now rested. "He is expecting us."

Five minutes later, we had traversed the typical village high street to arrive at the door of Mr. Weekes's small but well-kept law office. Holmes turned to us and said quietly, "Perhaps it might be best to allow me to do the talking." Then he led us inside.

Mr. Weekes's law office was on the first floor above a sweet shop. The incongruity of this made me smile, but only to myself. I sensed that there was a grim purpose to this visit, and that Holmes was not simply stopping here to ask a few questions, or from a feeling of good fellowship.

Upstairs, the clerk appeared to have been expecting us, and appeared to be nervous in Holmes's presence. As he led us into Weeke's office, he kept glancing anxiously toward Holmes.

Weeke's office was a room that must have taken up most of the space on that floor. There were a number of old legal tomes filling fine-looking shelves around three of the walls, while the fourth wall was a large window overlooking the street. Weekes's desk was centered before this window, and at a different time of day, the sun would have been behind his back. Holmes had used this trick before, placing his chair in the Baker Street sitting room with its back to his chemical corner and the window behind, allowing him to watch visitors in the basket chair while he appeared to them to be shadowed.

Fortunately, the sun had not yet crossed to the point where it would shine in our faces, and I could see that Weekes was a wiry fellow, probably in his fifties. He stood and came from behind the desk, offering us his hand. While we found chairs, he stood beside the desk, and I was shocked to see that as he waited there before resuming his seat, he leaned back on one leg, as if – one might say – sitting on a shooting stick. It is not often that I can anticipate Holmes's thoughts move for move, but on this occasion, I saw that Holmes had noticed it as well, and I began to have some inkling or intuition about at least one thing that might be discussed or revealed in this room very soon.

Weekes settled himself behind the desk and moved some papers away from him. He seemed to be rather fidgety, but I did not know if this was his usual manner of existence, or if it was related to our visit.

"I received your wire, Mr. Holmes, and I've had my clerk pull the files relating to the unfortunate Felton family." He clucked his tongue and pulled the papers back in his direction. He looked down and turned over the top two or three sheets. "Most unfortunate."

"I have been relating some of the history of the events of 1878 for the doctor, who was not previously aware of any of it," said Holmes. "Mrs. Grimshaw knows about some aspects of the matter, as you are aware." Weekes nodded but did not speak. "Perhaps," said Holmes, "you recall our conversation in these rooms some four-and-a-half years ago, following the suicide of Ted Felton." Weekes nodded again. "Would you care to relate the details of that suicide for Doctor Watson and Mrs. Grimshaw?"

"Certainly, certainly," said Weekes, again glancing at his papers. Then he pushed them aside again, laced his fingers, and began to speak. "It was a few weeks after the facts regarding his father's murder, as well as the separate incident of his implication in the burglary ring, first came to light in the press. As you may recall, it was a nine days' wonder. The group of men who had been murdered, those who came to be known as 'The Suicide Club,' were all considered together as a group, and as such were simply names that were quickly forgotten. But Clifton Felton came under a special and intense scrutiny, as his story was augmented and made more interesting due to the related account of the burglaries. This too was soon forgotten, at least by many, although it was obviously still a subject of talk for a longer time around these parts.

"Ted shouldn't have let himself be bothered by it. He had inherited a substantial income from his mother, who was a fine woman, if I may say so. A fine woman indeed. Her money was set aside in her will for Ted, and had been kept separate from Clifton Felton's finances. Young Ted could have chosen to return to Oxford, or anywhere else, with no difficulty at all. But he was always a sensitive lad, very intelligent. Much too sensitive for the burdens that the discovery of Felton's crimes placed upon him. He took after his mother in that respect, poor woman. Finally, when it all became too much for him, Ted left a note in his Oxford lodgings saying as much and threw himself into the Thames. The river isn't very intimidating at that point, but if a man is set on ending his life, he won't let that stop him."

"I understood at the time that he was working in town there, and attempting to carry out studies as well," said Holmes.

"That's right," said Weekes. "However, he never seemed to be able to settle on exactly what field of study would suit him best. He was always interested in the sciences, and particularly physics and astronomy, but he just did not have the mathematical aptitude to get started. Time and again he would plunge off in some new direction, only to be disappointed. I had hoped he might return to this part of England and read for the law, but he wanted to remain in Oxford. He only returned here to visit

Clifton Felton on a very irregular basis. I believe that they did not get along all that well with one another, and that living in this area pained him somehow."

"Not true," interrupted Mrs. Grimshaw, speaking for the first time in a while, and forgetting Holmes's injunction to allow him to carry the conversation. "Mr. Clifton and Ted were warm enough to each other. In all the years I dealt with them, I never saw any signs of disagreement. And if he didn't have any feelings for his father, why then would he feel the need to do away with himself upon his father's death?"

Weekes seemed nonplussed at Mrs. Grimshaw's argument. "I, um, well, based on my experience, I – "

"I believe that we have had enough of this charade," said Holmes impatiently, reaching into his pocket for the telegrams that he had received at the station. "Were you aware, Mr. Weekes, that Ted Felton is back at Kerrett House? That he has been back for at least several weeks, if not longer?"

Weekes's jaw dropped in surprise before he recovered himself. He straightened in his chair, and his gaze shot to the right as he stared into the distance for a few seconds and collected his thoughts. He cleared his throat several times, and then said, rather weakly I thought, "Not possible. Ted committed suicide. That is an established fact."

"Nonsense," said Holmes. "After the full truth about his father was revealed in 1878, it was obvious that the young man was under a great deal of stress. That much is true – I observed it myself. As obvious as it was that he was a rather weak young man – like his father – who might break as you have suggested." Weekes bristled at this statement, but Holmes continued. "When he disappeared, I could not believe that he would actually kill himself because of what had happened. You are correct when you state that the matter was quickly forgotten, even in Oxford. I made some inquiries of my own at the time, and determined that a man closely matching Ted's description left Oxford on the night of his supposed death and made his way to Belgium. I was satisfied then that he had *not* killed himself, but had simply chosen to escape from the attention he was receiving related to his father's crimes and subsequent death.

"I had a few quiet words with the police, and they tended to agree with me, although with no hard evidence to the contrary, such as tracking the young man down and dragging him home, the suicide verdict still stood. No one, myself included, felt that it was worthwhile to go and find the young man on the Continent, since he had committed no crime. I was content to let the matter rest, and wish Ted Felton good luck with his decision to begin a new life elsewhere, even if that new life began with a faked suicide.

"Today, Mrs. Grimshaw came to me with the story that she has seen Ted Felton staring down from the windows of the great house for the last couple of weeks. She truly believed that he had died over four years ago, but I knew that in all likelihood he still lived, and had simply returned home, although choosing to do so in secret, without telling his father about his decision. That is, without telling *you, Mr. Weekes*, he had done so, as it is highly unlikely that he knows you are his real father."

Weekes was folding and unfolding his fingers, shaking his head. "I don't understand. I simply don't understand."

"It's time to come clean, Weekes," said Holmes. "You aided Ted Felton when he left the country after Clifton Felton's death, because he is your son, whether he knew it or not. I heard something of the matter in '78, about how you had first loved Ted's mother years ago, before she eventually chose another and married the much older and wealthier Clifton Felton. As it wasn't relevant at the time, I saw no need to pursue it, but I did not forget it. Perhaps, if I had questioned you then, I would have learned that you had helped Ted in his quest to leave the country. But I had moved on to other matters.

"While supposedly carrying out the terms of settling Ted's estate, you arranged for the small cottage, Kerrett's Rood, to be transferred to the Grimshaws, and for the rest of the estate to continue to be kept up as well, should Ted ever decide to return. Using his money that he inherited from his mother, you paid the bills, and you provided funds as necessary to Ted, who I presume was still in Belgium until recently."

"But why would he come back? Why now? And why wouldn't he tell me?"

Holmes slapped another telegram onto the desk. "I believe this is why. Steven Wells, one of Clifton Felton's partners in the robbery ring, died while in Dartmoor, but the other, Albert Sykes, was released from prison two months ago, early as it turns out, for good behavior. Tell me," he said, "how much of Ted Felton's current *vitae* is contained in that file?" He pointed to the papers by Weekes's trembling fingers.

"Nothing too specific," he replied. "But enough to find him if I need him. His current address. The name that he is using on the Continent. There is nothing specifically saying that the alias is Ted's but the fact that it is in the file would be . . . suggestive, as there is no other clarifying context with it, should anyone happen to look with the idea that Ted is still alive and living elsewhere under another name."

"Have you had any signs of a break-in in the last month or so?" asked Holmes. "Has there been any reason to believe that the information in that file has been compromised?"

Weekes shook his head with some confusion. "No, no, nothing like that."

"And what of your clerk? Is he completely trustworthy?"

"Who? Sykes? Why, he is – Oh, my God."

"A relative?"

"Albert Sykes's cousin, I believe. We are a small village here, Mr. Holmes."

"I believe that we should call him in."

It was only the work of a moment to break down the story of the nervous young clerk. He was, in fact, the cousin of Albert Sykes, who had been released from prison in February of that year. Sykes had not returned to the village, but had arranged to meet the clerk, Josiah Sykes, in a neighboring town, where he had revealed that he believed Ted Felton to still be alive, and that if he was, Weekes would know how to find him. Albert Sykes had then pressured the clerk into finding out Ted's true location.

Josiah was surprised, as he had, like everyone else in the village, believed that Ted had committed suicide years before. However, Albert Sykes seemed convinced, and would not take no for an answer. All that Josiah had been able to discover was an unconnected name and address in the Ted Felton file. That had been enough, however, to please Albert Sykes, and he had gone on his way.

While I kept an eye on the clerk, Holmes stepped out and summoned a constable. After identifying himself, the constable snapped to with a smart, "Yes, sir!" Holmes explained that Josiah Sykes had vital information in a case and needed to be kept incommunicado for the time being. It was a tribute to Holmes's increasing fame and notoriety that his wishes were carried out without question.

"There is no doubt," added Holmes, "that Albert Sykes contacted young Ted, and did something to convince him to return to this country, where he has taken up residence in Kerrett Hall."

"But why?" asked Weekes.

"I believe that if Sykes is involved, it must relate somehow to the old burglary ring. Perhaps Sykes knows something that he is using to blackmail Ted. We will only find out by asking him."

"But what do you suggest, Mr. Holmes," said Weekes. "We cannot just go up and knock on the front door."

"I still have the key," interrupted Mrs. Grimshaw.

"It does not matter," replied Weekes. "If he is in there and does not want to be found, he will bolt, and we won't find him."

"By way of the house's secret?" asked Holmes. "How much did he reveal to you before he left the country."

Weekes swallowed once or twice, and then said, "Not everything. Just that he had found how Felton was able to leave and return without detection, and how the stolen items had been moved the same way into the basement. It seemed to add to his shame, as if, by discovering it, the facts of the matter became more real to him somehow. But he never told me what it was. He said . . . he said that it would die with him. I was sure that he meant that the secret would go with him when he faked his death. Could he mean . . . ?"

"Mr. Weekes, that unfortunate young man, who was so shamed by the one that he believes to be his father – he *does* still believe that Clifton Felton is still his father, doesn't he?"

Weekes nodded. "I could not harm my precious Emily's reputation by revealing the true facts of the matter, and the . . . bargain that she made with Felton when she chose him over me at the end of it all."

Holmes continued, "Then Ted Felton, who was somehow pressured by the criminal Sykes to return from his exile, has been living alone in that house for weeks, caught in what he perceives to be a trap. I am certain that Sykes is somehow trying to force him to either restart the burglary ring, or give him access to something that is still hidden in the house. In any case, we have to speak to Ted Felton immediately."

"But I repeat, Mr. Holmes, that if we approach it, he will simply hide or bolt."

"Then we will have to gain entrance from the other side, from his escape tunnel."

"Escape tunnel? What do you propose? Do you know where this tunnel is located?"

"I believe so." Holmes laid the final telegram on the desk. "I know a great number of people who owe me a great number of favors. It was relatively easy to get a line on exactly what is involved in the property owned by Ted Felton. Or should I say, properties. Mr. Weekes, doesn't Ted Felton also own an empty house, located some little distance to the east of the property, on a dead end lane running away from the eastern perimeter of the Kerrett House estate?"

"Why, yes. Yes, he does! Is that it? Is that where the secret entrance is?"

"I believe so," said Holmes. "Mrs. Grimshaw!"

With a start, the sister of our landlady sat up straighter and turned toward Holmes. "Yes?"

"Will you serve as our beater? Will you, at the appointed time, enter the great house and begin to call for Ted Felton, explaining that you know he is there? It may be that he will come out and speak to you. But if not, we three will be approaching silently from the other end, through the tunnel that surely begins in the empty house, and will bottle him up somewhere between us. Then we can learn what hold Albert Sykes was able to exert over him, and let him know that he has nothing to fear with our assistance."

"Certainly," said Mrs. Grimshaw.

"And we can count on you as well, Weekes?"

"Of course, of course."

The rest is quickly told. With a time agreed upon, we separated, Mrs. Grimshaw to return to her cottage, and Holmes, Weekes, and I to the empty house. Weekes had a key for the place, but before he could use it, Holmes examined the outer premises. He called us over to a window on the south side, shaded by overgrown bushes, and opening into the dining room. "This has been forced open, fairly recently," he said. "This is how Ted gained access when he returned from the Continent."

Weekes quietly opened the door, and we crept in, pausing a moment to listen for any sounds. Holmes had previously warned us to move softly, watching where we stepped in case Ted had left anything rigged to make a loud noise if disturbed. However, in the afternoon light, we saw nothing.

It did not take a Sherlock Holmes to find the entrance to the secret tunnel. Making our way through the house had revealed nothing, but in the cellar, there was a different story. By the light of several candles that we had appropriated upstairs, Holmes silently indicated the dust on the floor, previously disturbed by numerous footprints leading both ways between the stairs and a seemingly blank wall on the western side. It was but the work of a moment for Holmes to find an unusual knot in a board. We heard a small click, and a wide segment of the wall swung noiselessly open. I realized that the cellar was particularly and unusually clear in front of the path of this door, while the rest of the room was cluttered with old and broken furniture.

There was another candle in a sconce, just inside the secret door. Holmes lit it, and we could see an arched stone passage leading off into the darkness. It was at least eight feet wide, and nearly as tall. There was no need to stoop at all as we started down the tunnel.

As Weekes later explained to us, these houses had been built outside the estate wall by the original Kerrett, long before the road which lay atop the tunnel had been constructed. No doubt there had been some reason, possibly illegal, for the two to be connected, back in the early part of the century. It was never known how Clifton Felton had learned the secret, although Weekes was able to confirm that it was a good five years after he bought Kerrett House that Felton suddenly felt moved to buy the empty house at the other end of the tunnel, indicating that perhaps it was only then that he learned of the terminus of the passage leading from his own home, and he wanted to own both ends, for whatever reason.

The floor of the tunnel remained level as we progressed, and the stones lining the arched walls appeared quite solid. However, there were a number of roots hanging from the ceiling, indicating to me that the structure was perhaps not quite as stable as it might appear. I, for one, would be quite happy to reach the other end.

As we progressed, we occasionally came across other sconces hanging on the walls, all with fairly new candles within them. As we would pass each one, Holmes would pause to light it, increasing the visibility in the gloomy tunnel. With each candle, I could perceive that the air in the tunnel had more dust, or perhaps vapor, hanging in it than I had first noticed. I began to be aware that my breathing was rather labored, and as there was no climb associated with our traverse of the tunnel, I concluded that it must be from breathing the poor-quality air. Beside me, I could hear Weekes begin to wheeze, and as I glanced at him, I could see that he was breathing through a cloth clenched to his nose and mouth.

None too soon, we reached the end of the tunnel. We could all perceive a greater degree of brightness ahead. There was no door or separation. The walls simply widened out into a greater area, lit by a lantern standing on a rough deal table off to the side. A cot was located beside it, and there were several empty crates along the opposite wall. Across from us, as we stood quietly in the entrance to the tunnel, was a young man, ignorant of our approach, his face and hands pressed against a wooden partition that had been built across the width of the stone chamber.

He was listening intently to the sound of Mrs. Grimshaw's muffled voice, calling in the distance, asking him, for I assumed that this was indeed Ted Felton, to come out, as all was known, and he would be safe. He listened for another moment, and then with a small sob turned away from the wall, only to discover the three of us in the tunnel entrance.

"Mr. Felton," said Holmes, only to be interrupted by Weekes.

"Ted," said the man gently, stepping forward, his hand stretched forth. "It's all right. We now know that you are here. There is no need to keep it secret any longer. Everything will be all right."

Mrs. Grimshaw continued to call from the other side of the wall, in the cellar of the great house, where Holmes had sent her. Ted looked over his shoulder at the wall, and then back toward Weekes. He seemed to vibrate, as if he were a string that had been stretched too tight for too long.

"Ted," said Weekes again, and the string broke.

Ted sank to the ground, saying to himself, "I couldn't find it. God help me, I couldn't find it."

Weeks and I rushed toward him, while Holmes moved to the wall, only taking another moment to discover the method to open the connecting door. While Mrs. Grimshaw stepped through, I knelt by the bed, pushing Weekes away as I commenced an examination.

"He is malnourished, and has suffered a great deal of mental anguish, but he will make a full recovery," I said. "However, we need to remove him from this place. May we take him to your cottage, Mrs. Grimshaw?"

"Certainly," she replied.

We managed to get the young man to his feet and through the connecting door into the larger cellar. Holmes stopped me for a moment to indicate how the hidden door appeared on the tunnel side, nearly invisible once the door was shut. He quickly found how to open it on the side of the great house cellar. "I was not able to discover this door when I looked several years ago," he said. "It is no self-flattery to state that my skills have improved, and I would have been able to find it, if I had been given the task today. Do you need any help taking him down to the cottage?"

I indicated that between us, we should manage all right. Holmes nodded, and said he would go back through the tunnel to blow out the candles, and then join us in a few minutes.

We managed to get Ted to his feet, and he climbed upstairs on his own, although he paused once or twice going up. I stood behind him, ready to catch him should he collapse. Outside, the sun was just starting its descent toward the cottage, and was shining full in our faces as we walked down the slope. Looking beside me, I could see how pale Ted was, while Weekes's shown with tears at the condition of his son.

In the cottage, Mrs. Grimshaw made a place for Ted on the settee, and then bustled out of the room, only to return in an unbelievably short amount of time, carrying a hot drink that appeared to be heavily laced with spirits. Ted coughed at the first sip, and then cautiously took another. Mrs. Grimshaw nodded, and then left, muttering about warming up some of the beef soup.

Holmes had entered during all this, and I saw that he was not wearing his Inverness or hat. Rather, the Inverness was rolled over, and he placed it on a nearby chair before centering the hat on top. "How is he?"

"He will be fine," I said. "He has simply used himself up much too freely by living in that dark, foul-aired cellar, with insufficient food for too long. I imagine that his expeditions to look at the setting sun were the greatest joys that he had during that time."

Ted cleared his throat, took another sip of the drink, and said, "You are right, sir. I tried to stay hidden, but sometimes it was just too difficult to remain in that dungeon. I wanted to get in and get out, but day after day I looked and couldn't find it, and I knew what would happen if I didn't. Sometimes I went up in the morning as well, but the evening sun was best. I could feel the warmth upon my face before I went back downstairs to resume my search. Was that how I was discovered?"

"It was," said Holmes. "Mrs. Grimshaw noticed you. She thought that you were a ghost."

"Not really?" said Ted, with a glimmer of unexpected but welcome amusement.

Mrs. Grimshaw returned with a bowl of savory-smelling soup. "Yes, I did." She handed him the bowl. "You were thought to be dead. Eat that, young man."

Holmes pulled a chair closer and sat down, facing Ted. I realized that Ted and Holmes were about the same age, each in their late twenties, but two men could not be more different. Holmes was hawk-like and alert, while Ted seemed uncertain and hesitant. I knew that it was not just the recent deprivations that gave this impression.

"We understand from Mr. Weekes how you came to flee to the Continent, leaving the impression that you had thrown yourself to your death in the Thames. But why have you come back, and put yourself through all of this misery? Is there a connection to the recent release of Albert Sykes from prison?"

"He had never believed that I truly died," agreed Ted with a nod. "He thought that I got away with his treasure, and went to start a new life. A month or so ago, he found out my address from his cousin, who works for you, Mr. Weekes." Weekes hung his head, but did not interrupt.

"Sykes showed up at my home in Ostend over a month ago. I wouldn't let him in, but made him stay on the doorstep. That only made him angry. But how could I let my wife and son – "

"You are married?" said Weekes with wonderment. "I have a grand – That is to say, you have a son?"

Ted nodded, unaware of Weekes's near slip. "I met Sykes at a place by the water. There he told me what he wanted. He told me a great many things. He said that if I did not help him, he would rake up the whole scandal once again. He would reveal that I was still alive, and make sure that I paid for my father's crimes." He closed his eyes. "And he threatened my family."

"What exactly was it that he wanted?" said Holmes.

"He said that during the course of their last robbery, he, James Stevens, and my father had inadvertently found, along with their other loot, a chest full of gold coins. They had brought it with them, and my father had hidden it in a secret place somewhere in the great house, with the idea that it would be split in a few days. However, before this could take place, Sykes and Wells were arrested, and my father was found dead in London.

"Sykes and Wells did not mention this gold, and he was greatly surprised that the man from whom it had been stolen did not mention it either."

"Sir Wilton Cole," said Holmes. "I wondered why he was not very grateful at all when his stolen property was recovered from the cellars of the great house. Now I understand. He was most interested in the recovery of the gold coins. I would expect that he had himself gained them in some illicit or illegal manner, and could not report them stolen without implicating himself. He must have believed that they were still hidden, as it turned out, or that I had found them myself and chosen to keep them. But he could say nothing."

Ted nodded. "Sykes told me that Sir Wilton visited him in prison, trying to get Sykes to admit that he had taken the coins. He offered to assist Sykes in getting a reduced sentence, but Sykes told him nothing. Sykes knew that the coins were still in the house, and after his release, he went there on numerous occasions, searching for them himself. He came in through the tunnel which leads to the empty house on the other side of the road. When he couldn't find them, he became convinced that I knew where they were. He sought me out, told me about the tunnel, and forced me to come and search." He swallowed. "What choice did I have?"

"But you could not find the coins."

"No."

"How did you search?"

"The same way that Sykes did, I suppose. I knocked on walls, and looked up and down the tunnel. I went through my father's papers in his desk, seeking a clue, but to no avail."

"I believe that your weeks of effort, combined with those of Sykes, who was just as desperate as you, indicates that there was a good chance that the coins were not in the house after all. My quick examination while you were being brought to the cottage proved that as well."

"So . . . so this was all a waste?" said Ted. "Sykes will not believe me. He will reveal the truth to my wife, and to everyone else. It was all a waste."

"Not so," said Holmes, standing and retrieving his folded Inverness. "When we found you, you said that you had been unable to find 'it,' whatever that was. I decided that you must have spent the last few weeks looking in the wrong place.

Unfolding the coat, he revealed a wooden chest, about the size of a large family bible, its dark wood bound by ironwork at the corners. There was a broken lock in the hasp. "Instead of looking in the cellar of the great house, I examined the empty house at the other end of the tunnel. It was only a few minutes work to find a sliding panel in the woodwork near the tunnel entrance."

He raised the lid of the box to reveal a small fortune in gold coins. They seemed to shine in the afternoon light penetrating Mrs. Grimshaw's front window.

Holmes plucked out one of the coins, looking at it front and back, before turning it on its edge. "Look here, Watson. At the inscription on the side of the coin, showing a mint mark. That was a new thing that was tried back in the mid-70's, but soon rejected. A box of them was stolen and never recovered." He shut the lid. "Until now. I anticipate some interesting questions for Sir Wilton Cole before the week is out."

He set the box aside. "How were you to reach Albert Sykes, once you had found the box?"

"He has come in the night on several occasions, but not lately. I have an address where I'm to send a letter. It was too risky to send a wire. Someone might recognize me. Instead, I was to write, and slip the letter into a local box. He will come within a day."

"Then we must send him an invitation to join us."

And so we did. Holmes dropped the short letter, written by Ted, into the village postal box, arranging a meeting for the very next night. We were there, Holmes, Inspector Lestrade, and myself, when Albert Sykes made his way in through the empty house and found us in the chamber under the great house. His attempt to turn and flee was blocked by the two burly constables who had silently followed him down the tunnel. His return to Dartmoor was swift and uncomplicated. Lestrade was quite pleased to return the missing coins to London.

The afternoon of the discovery of Ted Felton and the missing gold coins, we still sat in Mrs. Grimshaw's parlor, waiting for Holmes to return from his postal errand. Ted had progressed to eating some cold slices of ham, but not too many, as Mrs. Grimshaw felt that any more might put a strain on his digestive system. Weekes sat by Ted's side, asking and repeating questions about Ted's wife and child. At one point, Weekes looked up and caught my eye. I glanced meaningfully at the weakened young man lying on the sofa beside him, as if to say that it was time to tell him the truth. Then I stood up and excused myself, taking Mrs. Grimshaw with me into the kitchen.

We did not hear their conversation, but in a few moments we perceived the sounds of both men breaking down, and by the time Holmes returned, the truth was known to Ted, to his great amazement and happiness. Mr. Weekes was overcome, planning a visit to Ostend in order to meet his new family, while Ted promised to return to Kerrett House and reopen it, making it a showplace once again, as it must have been early in the century. It turned out that Mrs. Grimshaw had been wrong, and Mr. Weekes right. Young Ted and his supposed father, Clifton Felton, had not been very close after all. Mr. Clifton, as Mrs. Grimshaw called him, had long felt a certain resentment toward his wife that he passed on to the boy, although they had maintained civil relations. Following the revelations about

Clifton Felton's secret life, Ted was more than happy to have found his real father.

Holmes cautioned that Ted Felton should remain hidden until the capture of Albert Sykes, and it was arranged that he would stay with Mrs. Grimshaw. Weekes agreed to tell no one. Holmes indicated that, while he had been out to mail the letter to Sykes, he had also conferred with the police, revealing something of the story to them, and making sure that Josiah Sykes could not notify his cousin of the fact that his activities were discovered before he could step into the trap on the next night.

As we stood at the door to Mrs. Grimshaw's cottage, on the stoop leading to the West Road, Holmes said, "We must be getting back to London. Mrs. Hudson will be looking for us soon. And we did tell the inspector this morning at Stoke Moran that we would be available later today in Baker Street for any questions that he might have. He probably believes that we have fled the country.

"Might we expect, Mrs. Grimshaw," he continued, "to be formally introduced to you by your sister sometime in the next week or so?"

"I believe that would be likely," she said. "I would enjoy seeing Martha again, and this time it would be without any criticism that might come from bothering her lodgers with a ghost story."

"Mrs. Grimshaw," said Holmes, "feel free to bring us any little problem that might cross your path at any time, with no fear of recriminations from your sister. If your next visit provides something as interesting as this one, it will be most welcome, and if you have no story to tell us at all, that will be fine as well. However," he added, "I suspect that soon you will be too busy to visit very often, as Kerrett House, and Kerrett's Rood beside it, will soon welcome a new family and the new vitality that comes with it."

And so it proved. The next week, Mrs. Grimshaw was "introduced" to us by Mrs. Hudson, who never suspected that her sister had been a client. If Mrs. Hudson wondered why we got on so well so quickly with her sister, she was too canny to say so. Mrs. Grimshaw visited off and on over the years, but on a rare basis indeed, as Kerrett House became a vibrant home for Ted Felton, that is, Ted *Weekes*, along with his wife and – eventually – his eight children as well.

Sir Wilton Cole's future after the clearing-up of the affair of the stolen gold coins was not so bright. But that is another story entirely.

The Curious Incident
of the
Goat-Cart Man

It is sometimes easier to believe a man from Bedlam than in coincidence. In the case of the following narrative, my friend Sherlock Holmes and I believed both.

Like his older brother Mycroft, whose great mind served as something of a great clearinghouse for the various departments of Her Majesty's Government, Sherlock Holmes had created a special and unique niche for himself, acting as a resource for those in need, while forever seeking to improve and increase his knowledge and awareness of crime in the great tapestry that is London. He liked to believe in the order of his system, as reflected by the hard work that he put into it. It is certain that without his specialized knowledge, allowing him to make connections from one disparate set of events to another, the curious incident of the Goat-Cart Man of Meadcroft might have gone forever unresolved, or at least it might have concluded in a more tragic manner. And yet, it was only through coincidence, which Holmes was always loathe to credit, that the matter was placed before him at all.

In recording these varied sketches, I have attempted to balance the fantastic with the prosaic, relying neither upon the involvement of important and well-known figures, nor upon the rehashing of events that are already familiar to readers of the daily press. Rather, I have tried to present those matters that best illustrate the gifts and skills of my friend. This particular adventure occurred as something of a pause or detour in the midst of a larger investigation, taking only an hour or so. However, no record of my friend's activities would be complete without it.

It was on the last Saturday in September of 1890, only a day or so after Holmes and I had returned from Dartmoor, and specifically King's Pyland. We had journeyed there regarding the matter of a missing race horse and its murdered trainer, whose body had been found on the Moor. Our return to London had followed Holmes's confident assurance to the horse's owner, Colonel Ross, that the great beast would be found in time to participate in the Wessex Cup, to be run on the subsequent Tuesday. Colonel Ross had seemed less than confident in Holmes's assurances as we departed, but had reluctantly agreed not to withdraw the horse's name from competition. Although I had been privy to Holmes's masterful discovery of the horse's true location, and his reluctance to share it with Colonel Ross, I did not as yet know the murderer's identity. However, I was certain that the matter would be resolved to everyone's satisfaction, having seen Mr. Sherlock Holmes do this sort of thing before.

Early in the afternoon of that particular day, I had been finishing my lunch with my wife, following a light morning of rounds and seeing patients. I think that neither of us was surprised when the abrupt ringing of our bell led to the maid's announcement that Holmes was calling.

He refused anything to eat, as was to be expected, but he did agree to a hurried cup of black coffee. He was there to request my assistance on what he described as a "long shot." After a concise explanation, I made to get my coat and hat. Holmes graciously and sincerely thanked Mary for sharing me in this way, to which she simply smiled and laid an affectionate hand on his shoulder.

The matter which required my participation that afternoon is neither here nor there in relation to the events that I propose to recount. They simply served to place us where the current narrative began. At that time, Holmes was engaged in following the series of steps that would culminate the next spring at the top of Reichenbach Falls. Holmes had finally managed to find a narrow crack in the armor of that master criminal, Professor Moriarty, and had slowly been wedging it wider as the weeks and months progressed. That day, he had learned of a diary that was supposed to contain incriminating information of an explosive nature, and was to be carried back to London from Exeter by one of the Professor's lieutenants, whereupon it would be delivered to the Professor himself. Holmes and I, along with Inspector Patterson and a number of plain-clothed detectives and constables, had made every effort to track the diary and arrest the courier, but alas, on this day, it was not meant to be. The identified courier was successfully followed and detained, but when the trap was sprung, on one of the platforms in Paddington Station, no diary was to be found.

After it was clear that there would be no victory on this occasion, most of the Yarders had dispersed from the station, while Holmes and Patterson remained in quiet conversation to one side of the great and noisy waiting room. I was standing beside them, watching the ebb and flow of the crowds as trains arrived and departed. It was then that I noticed one of the porters talking to two men and pointing them in Holmes's direction. They nodded to him and then began to walk our way.

Interrupting Holmes's conversation, I spoke in a low voice and made him aware of the approaching men. He and Patterson turned, and we all separated slightly, almost instinctively, in case either of the strangers should pose some threat.

It was quickly obvious that neither man presented any sort of danger. The man to my left was tall and fit, wearing a fine overcoat, perhaps a little heavy for the unseasonable warmth of the evening. He kept one arm protectively about the other, a smaller fellow, draped in clothing that was more worn than that of his companion, but still thoroughly respectable.

I could see that the second man had recently been ill, and possibly ill-used as well. His face was pale, with bruised-looking smudges under his deep-set eyes. An unsuccessful effort had been made to comb his hair, and there were stains upon the knees of his trousers. His shirt was pulled to, but a few of the buttons were missing. I could see the outline, barely visible underneath his hair, of a contusion above his left temple. He carried himself with that pulled-in and self-aware look that illness brings to a man, when he evaluates every movement to see if it will be tolerated, or if it will worsen whatever condition is being suffered.

"Mr. Holmes?" asked the stronger of the two men, instinctively facing my friend. Holmes nodded his head, and the other continued. "My name is Walter Forsythe, and this is my brother, Henry. We were walking down the street outside just now, arguing whether to continue onward to my home or instead seek medical attention for my brother nearby at St. Mary's, when we heard a group of departing constables mention your name. I was for continuing on, but my brother, as weak as he is, insisted that we come inside to see if we could find you in the station."

Patterson had looked surprised, and then angry, when he heard that Holmes's name was being discussed by his men out in the street. "This was supposed to remain confidential," he muttered, before turning to Holmes. "If I may, I will call upon you later in your rooms to discuss our strategy, Mr. Holmes." Then, without waiting for Holmes's response, he turned and made for the exit, in that peculiar gait when a man wants to run but is forcing himself to remain at a dignified, although accelerated, walking speed instead.

"Really, Henry," said Walter Forsythe, turning to the other man as Patterson departed, "we should not bother Mr. Holmes. After all, you've been ill. What you recall may not have really happened at all!"

Henry Forsythe flashed an angry glance toward his brother.

"I am a doctor," I interrupted. "Perhaps I can be of some assistance."

"We will be fine," replied Walter. "My brother simply had a fit last night. I just need to see him home. Please excuse our imposition."

"Hearing your name mentioned outside seemed like a sign, Mr. Holmes," said Henry, in a weak voice. "You are just the man to get to the bottom of this situation. But we must be quick about it. The old man may already be dead!"

Holmes glanced at me with a flash in his eyes, as if to cry, *"The Game is afoot!"* Then he turned toward Patterson, who was just disappearing out of the station and into the sunlit afternoon. "Perhaps," said Holmes, "you would be more comfortable relating your story while we sit. With a cup of tea? Or would you rather return with us to my rooms in Baker Street, to share the details of your recent travails?"

"Let us be on our way!" cried Henry, a shrill tone rising in his voice and attracting the judgmental notice of a pinch-faced matron passing by.

Holmes nodded, and spoke to me. "I will get a four-wheeler. Can you help our new acquaintances outside?" And then he was off in that way of his that never seemed hurried but covered ground at an incredible pace when he wished.

As Holmes walked away, Walter continued to insist that none of this was necessary, and that he should not have indulged his brother's whim to enter the station after hearing Holmes's name. Nevertheless, Walter Forsythe assisted me as we maneuvered his brother out of the station to the street. Henry seemed quite weak from whatever he had experienced. I began to ask a few general questions, in order to ascertain the nature of his condition, but Henry stopped me, explaining that it would become known what had happened to him when he could tell his story to Holmes.

Outside, there was no sign of Patterson or the loose-lipped Yarders. Holmes was standing with his hand upon the door of a four-wheeler. Up top, I could see the grinning face of our old friend, Bert Deacon, the former Houndsditch ramper who had been falsely accused of a particularly brutal murder, back in '82. Holmes had proven his innocence, based on the reversed obverse of a shilling found clutched in the dead man's hand, as well as the inward twist of Deacon's left foot. Holmes had then found him steady work as a cab driver, much to the relief of Deacon's wife and six children. His former line of work had not paid nearly as steadily as driving a cab.

I nodded at Deacon, and we boarded the growler. I noticed an odd alertness had come into Holmes's eyes, but I did not presume to question him about it in front of the two brothers. We all settled back as the cab lurched into motion without any instructions having been given as to our destination, and I realized that Holmes must have already told Deacon to take us to Baker Street.

"Where are we going?" cried Henry Forsythe, sitting up abruptly, looking from side to side. I could tell that his nerves were stretched to the limit, and I was concerned that the mere effort of telling his story might propel him into brain fever. "We must go back to Meadcroft! The old man may already be dead!"

"Calm yourself, sir, and you may tell us of the danger to this old man," said Holmes, in the soothing tone that worked so well in situations of this type. I was amazed yet again to see the hypnotic affect that Holmes's voice could have on someone. While he often insisted that the problem itself was his only interest, and that people were simply factors in the equation, he had an amazing ability to empathize with their troubles when needed. "We are going to my rooms in Baker Street," he said softly, "where you can tell your story. Then we shall decide upon a course of action."

"We should get you home, Henry," said Walter, but in a resigned way, as he realized that his brother was set on relating his story.

"My tale is easily told right now, here in this cab," Henry replied. "Once you hear it you will agree that we should make our way to Meadcroft at once."

"Henry," interrupted Walter, "all of this may have just been the result of your fit last night. There is no need to take any more of Mr. Holmes's time."

Ignoring him, Holmes said, "My knowledge of London is fairly exact. Is that the Meadcroft that is located by Kennington Park, on the South Side?"

"It is," said Henry. Holmes's display of omniscience seemed to calm him further. "It is where I have leased a house since early this year, attempting to improve my craft."

"You are a writer, then?" asked Holmes. I glanced at the man's hands and sleeves, and could see, from the collection of unique callosities and shiny right cuff, the source of Holmes's deduction.

"Yes," he said. "My stories are in the manner of Sir Walter Scott's, although I have not yet duplicated his mastery of the form, or believability. I must admit, I'm afraid, that I have also yet to duplicate his ability to have anything published. Perhaps, if I went out and experienced life, rather than simply trying to write about it – "

"Now, now," said Walter Forsythe, "you will achieve your goal! I am certain of it. But you do not have to live apart from your brother to do so."

We were traveling down Praed Street, nearing the Edgware Road crossing. I glanced up and to my right. I did not know if Mary would be watching as we passed, but I looked forward, as always, to telling her of the day's events. Hopefully this new and unexpected adventure would have a better and more successful conclusion than that upon which Holmes had initially summoned me.

"In January," said Henry, shifting in his seat to a more upright position, "I had resolved, with the turning of the new year, to move out of my brother's home, where I had lived for the past two years, and find a place of my own."

"You were no bother to me at all, Henry," interjected Walter. "You are my brother." He glanced at me, and whispered, for no reason, "I have a position in the City."

Henry continued as if he had not been interrupted. "I intended to give myself a year in which either to master my craft, or abandon it. My brother and I have both inherited money, and I could afford to indulge in this quest – or folly – for a little while. I found a small house of rather new construction in Meadcroft, arranged terms with the landlord, and settled in to my routine.

"In case you don't know it, doctor," said Henry, shifting to address me, "Meadcroft is a new set of houses by Kennington Park, east of The Oval. It was once part of a larger estate of several acres, but eight or ten years ago, the owner, Sir Giles Gidley-Hall, was forced to sell everything but the main house to cover some long-standing debts, after some mysterious circumstances depleted his funds."

70

"The Threadneedle Scandal," interrupted Holmes. "I was able to satisfy myself at the time that Sir Giles had no part in the matter, although his own personal honor compelled him to make restitution." Turning to me, he said, "It was before your time, Watson."

Holmes looked back at Henry, and said, "You were telling us about the construction of Meadcroft? I assume that it is relevant to your story?"

Henry Forsythe nodded. "New houses were built in rows stretching out to the left and right from the front of the main house, and a large open area in the front center was left as something of a park for the residents.

"It was into one of these houses, near the main house, that I moved last winter. And it was not long before I became aware of Sir Giles's strange eccentricity, which has become a source of great amusement – and sometimes irritation – to the entire neighborhood.

"You must know then that Sir Giles, after being forced to sell the land adjacent to his house, became something of an eccentric recluse. It is rumored that he has still managed to retain quite a bit of money, but he released all of his staff, and lives alone in the big house, making do for himself. At night, one can see that the entire building remains dark, but for one room on the front right corner of the ground floor.

"Although the grounds stretching in front of the house serve as the common park for the new houses, Sir Giles still seems to feel some attachment for them. During the daylight hours, when people make use of this open area, Sir Giles ventures forth from the house on a regular basis, approaching his neighbors in a manner stopping just short of harassment. What makes this situation almost comical, rather than criminal, is that Sir Giles's defense of the common green is done from atop a small wagon, pulled by a large goat."

Holmes's eyes twinkled at this revelation, and I felt a smile tug at my mouth at this ludicrous image. Even Walter Forsythe, concerned for his brother as he was, smiled as well.

"If just hearing about him makes you smile, imagine actually seeing him as he charges his way across the green, with a thin cane rod held high overhead, serving to encourage the goat if it slows down. I must admit that the first time I saw him, I thought I was dreaming, or going mad." He paused, and the humor which had lightened his face for a moment and seemed to chase away his illness drained away. "After last night, however, I should never joke about my sanity again."

He fell silent for a moment. Traffic was thick during that time of the afternoon, and our progress was slow, even with Bert Deacon's best efforts. Still, I wondered if Henry's tale would be completed before we reached Baker Street.

As if reading my thought, Henry continued. "Sir Giles is a small, withered old fellow, and the burly beast does not seem to strain at the burden, although it certainly displays no enthusiasm for it, either. Sir Giles harnesses it each morning, leaving it tied by the front door with something to eat and drink. As the day progresses, he will burst out of his front door and sally forth whenever he sees someone enter the park, riding toward them as fast as he can go, before suddenly reining in the goat and then pausing to examine the trespassers critically. Then he will circle away, before returning again, sometimes approaching three or four times before he is satisfied. I do not know if he is trying to intimidate them, or simply to examine them for some unknown reason at close range. He doesn't speak, and the residents are tolerant of him, even the mothers with their young children.

"I cannot tell you the number of days when I have been distracted from my writing as I would look up and see Sir Giles go flying this way and that across the green. And I myself have not been ignored by him, either, during my times outside. Perhaps this is what led to my unfortunate experience. If I had not repeatedly encountered him, then he and I might not have formed a wary friendship, if I may call it that, and his disappearance would not have mattered to me one way or the other. Certainly, I would never have ended up here today, or where I found myself this morning after the events of last night.

"Sir Giles and I met in this way. One day a month or so ago in the hottest part of summer, I had taken myself outside to walk and think my way through a point in my plot. It was then that I became aware of the unsurprising approach of Sir Giles. He circled me once, and again, when finally I impertinently asked him the name of his goat.

"I cannot believe that no one had asked him that before, but he seemed surprised that anyone would speak to him. Not as surprised as I, however, when he replied back to me that the goat's name was Tommy.

" 'Not Billy?' I returned with a smile.

"He started to scowl, and then chose to reply instead. 'Tommy after my dead brother,' he said. 'He was my only family. He's gone now, and he looked like the goat.' And then he laughed, a harsh bark of a laugh, and I could not help but join him.

"After that, we would talk sometimes when I was taking a stroll. It was not every day, by any means, and it never progressed to the point where we socialized in each other's homes. I suppose that I cannot even say that we were any more than passing acquaintances, rather than friends. But I think that he enjoyed the experience of our occasional conversations, as did I, and when I would appear on the green, his charge toward me on the goat-cart did not seem as aggressive as it must have appeared to others who were his targets.

"I have never spoken to any of my other neighbors during the entire time that I have lived there, and have in fact never revealed any of my reasons for choosing to live in the neighborhood to Sir Giles. I did not explain about my labors to become a better writer, and I never mentioned any of my family to him. From small things that he said, as we stood and talked for odd random moments on the green, I believe that Sir Giles was alone in the world, and certainly he must have believed that of me as well.

"Several days ago, when I went out for my afternoon constitutional, I was mildly surprised when Sir Giles did not appear. This led me to observe that, over the next day or so, he d the goat did not make their usual inspections whenever anyone else walked the green. I did notice, however, that the usual light was showing in the front corner room of his house at night. Unusually, however, there were also lights burning in other parts of the building, something that had never happened during the time that I have lived there.

"Finally, the day before yesterday, my concern grew, and at dusk, I hesitantly made my way over to Sir Giles's front door, with the intent of checking to see if he was all right. I knocked, and after long quiet moments, hearing nothing but the wind sighing in the great trees behind me surrounding the green, I knocked again.

"As I was looking back toward the green, and thinking how abandoned it was at that time of night, I heard footsteps within, and then the door opened. Two men faced me, one tall and heavy-set, about forty years of age, and the other a decade or so older, with a pointed beard and a sharp expression.

" 'Well?' said the younger man.

"I explained my concern for Sir Giles, as he had not been seen in the last few days. The younger man gruffly replied, 'I'm his brother. He's been ill, and I've come to take care of him. This other man here is a doctor. Now clear off!' And he slammed the door in my face!

"I made my way back home, puzzled by this encounter, and trying to reconcile the idea that the man, clearly much younger than Sir Giles, could be his brother, when Sir Giles had intimated to me that his only brother, Tommy (who had looked like the goat) was dead. I continued to brood over the matter, and by the next evening, yesterday, I had decided to go back and inquire more forcefully as to Sir Giles's condition. We were not truly friends, you understand, but I felt some responsibility for him, as I was obviously the only person in the neighborhood that ever had any true interaction with him.

"Knocking as I had during my previous visit, I realized that it was later in the evening than when I had been here the day before. In the distance toward the Park, the gaslights were already lit, but they had always been markedly absent around the green, having been left out by the builders when the place was constructed. My surroundings were quite dark.

"When the door unexpectedly opened, this time without the necessity of me knocking a second time, the light from the inside hall momentarily blinded me. I had the impression that the same two men were standing there. Events subsequently proved this to be true. This time, however, there was no conversation between us whatsoever. The younger man simply reached forward, grabbing my arm and pulling me inside.

"The door slammed shut behind me, and there was a muffled thud as my head was hit with a hard object. That is how I received this." He lifted a hand to his left temple, gingerly brushing back his hair to reveal the contusion that I had noticed earlier.

"This served to further obscure my vision, as my eyes had not yet adjusted to the bright lights in the entrance hall. Still trying to regain my balance, I was shocked when my coat was roughly pulled down from behind, thus trapping my arms at my sides. Then, as I was completely pinned from behind by the younger man, the older man stepped forward into the blurred field of my vision and pulled open my shirt, baring my shoulder. He stepped back for a moment, fumbling with something on a side table, as I uselessly struggled against my larger captor. Then the older man returned into my line of sight, holding a hypodermic needle before him, reflecting the lamplight.

" 'Are you sure,' asked the man who had been identified the previous night as the doctor, 'that he is alone and has no family?' His accent was unusual. It was American, but in a flat way that I have never heard before. 'This could be a mistake, and we're not ready to move on yet.'

" 'That's what the old man said,' replied the younger man. 'He lives alone across the green, and never has any visitors.'

" 'Then,' said the older man, 'let the doctor take care of this.' And he plunged the hypodermic needle into my arm."

We crossed Upper Montagu Street, and Henry Forsythe took a moment as he breathed deeply and recalled the next portion of his story.

"I cannot say for certain what happened next. I recall the impression of swirling colored lights, and having difficulties breathing, and hearing loud noises that seemed as if they almost made sense as words, but were beyond my comprehension. I sometimes felt that I was hanging suspended above the earth, with a weightless sensation that I have never experienced before. I also had the sense of motion, and long periods of darkness when all that I could hear were the sounds of my own pulse in my head. It would get louder and louder until it sounded like the roar of a cataract, before I would suddenly be plunged into stretches of stark silence, the loneliest emptiness I have ever experienced.

"I had no idea how long this went on. I could not have told you anything about myself if you had asked me. The next thing that I knew for certain was when I awoke this morning and was being examined by a stranger who subsequently identified himself as a doctor, asking me if I knew my name.

"I did not know the time or even the day or year when I first recovered. It was only when my senses had cleared that I finally realized I had only suffered from my breakdown for only a single night.

" 'Where am I?' I asked, ignoring the doctor's question.

" 'You're in Bethlem Royal Hospital,' " he replied.

"His response puzzled me for a moment, as I attempted to reconcile the pieces of my memory that were trying to stitch themselves back into a whole cloth. Finally, the meaning of his answer seemed to resonate somehow with more meaning.

" 'Bedlam,' I whispered.

" 'We don't like to call it that,' the doctor said. 'You were brought here last night by two men after you went mad in the street and became a danger to passers-by. You continued to exhibit the symptoms that your rescuers reported for several hours after your arrival here. You broke an orderly's arm, and ruined the night director's coat in a way that I do not wish to describe. This evaluation is to determine if you are any further danger to yourself or others.

" 'Now,' he asked again, 'what is your name?'

76

"I told him, and he began to question me more closely. I could tell that he did not believe my story at first, of the attack and the use of the hypodermic syringe, thinking instead that I was suffering from a delusional episode. As my mind cleared, however, and I was able to consistently provide further details that matched my basic story, he admitted the possibility that what I was saying was true.

"The doctor indicated to me that my admission by the two strangers from off the street was unofficial, and that there was no reason that he could keep me here without further orders. He finally decided that, except for my disheveled condition, I appeared to be functionally sane, and he agreed to send a message to my brother, who obtained my release."

"The least I could do," murmured Walter. "We should get you home, Henry."

"The doctor offered to summon the police to hear my story," continued Henry, ignoring Walter's latest interruption, "but Walter refused. We were making our way to Walter's home when we heard your name mentioned outside the railway station. Having heard of you before, and your ability to bring light where there has been only darkness, I insisted that we find you inside the station and relate my story, in the hopes that you will return with us and help rescue Sir Giles, should he still be alive."

"I believe," said Holmes, "that he was probably still alive as late as yesterday, at least. Otherwise, how would the younger man have known from him that you had no family, as he mentioned when you were attacked? Obviously, they had questioned Sir Giles after your first visit to obtain information as to your identity."

Henry nodded, and Holmes continued, "Did you happen to ask the doctor at Bethlem if the two men who brought you in for admission matched the descriptions of your attackers?"

"I did," replied Henry. "He did not know, but he asked an orderly at the front and confirmed, at least superficially, that they were in fact the same men. They did not leave their names, simply saying that they were concerned citizens who had discovered me nearby in the street."

"Describe these two men in Sir Giles's house in more detail, if you please."

As Henry closed his eyes for a moment, the growler lurched, turning into Baker Street. Finally, Henry looked up and said, "The younger man was wearing a plaid waistcoat, which seemed rather gaudy. He has a long head, wide at the bottom as if he habitually clenches his jaws, and rather narrow at the top. His hair, what there is of it, is cut quite short and parted in the middle."

"Did he have a mole on his right temple?" asked Holmes.

Henry stared straight ahead for a moment, and then looked surprised. "Why, yes he did! I recall being surprised by it on that first night, when he turned his head while shutting the door and the light caught it just so."

"And the second man," said Holmes. "Was he rather short and narrow, with thin legs, and an unnaturally substantial paunch that stretches his waistcoat? And does he have sandy hair that is combed straight forward onto his forehead, and trimmed across in a straight line an inch or so above his eyes?"

"Why, Mr. Holmes, it is as if you know them already! But how could you describe them so well?"

"Because I have been expecting them to arrive back in London for some time," Holmes replied. "I just did not know exactly when or where they would wash up."

"Two-twenty-one, Mr. Holmes," growled Bert Deacon from atop the four-wheeler.

"Wait here, Bert," said Holmes, jumping down. He leaned back into the vehicle and said, "I will only be a moment." Then he dashed inside, leaving the door ajar as he went.

After a moment, Mrs. Hudson leaned out, looking left and right before spotting our cab. I waved from within, and she wearily smiled and shook her head knowingly. As she started to close the door, I could hear Holmes return as he descended the seventeen steps from the sitting room, crashing down two at a time. He danced around Mrs. Hudson, said something to her that I could not hear, and climbed back into the cab.

"Scotland Yard, Bert, if you don't mind."

"Right, Mr. Holmes," Bert replied, and we made a lurch into motion, heading south.

"Is this really necessary?" asked Walter, only to receive a glare from Henry.

Holmes did not reply to Walter's question. He was holding a small clutch of papers, which he proceeded to sort on his lap, keeping some of them carefully hidden. I could see that it was a mixture of cables and photographs, as well as a large envelope holding additional sheets. Finally, he held up two of the sheets, both photographs, and asked, "Are these your attackers, Mr. Forsythe?"

I could see that the images were of the two men that Holmes had previously described while questioning Henry, who simply nodded wordlessly as the memory of the attack was obviously replaying itself in his mind.

"The younger of the two," said Holmes, glancing at one of the cables in his other hand, "is named Jack Gables, a career criminal and most recently a bank robber, originally from Manchester. The other is known as Layton Carr, which may or may not be his real name. He is an American, and originally from Chicago, which may explain the flat American accent which seemed unfamiliar to you. Carr is often a crony of Gables, and he fancies himself a doctor. I believe that he did have a form of medical training at one time in his life, but not to any meaningful completion. This has not prevented him from making dangerous use of the little knowledge that he has.

"I received a notification regarding Gables and Carr several months ago from my friend Wilson Hargreaves, of the New York Police Bureau, following a violent bank robbery that the two men had pulled off there. Both of them managed to gain illegal entrance to one of the larger New York banks, and using a chemical devised by Carr, overpower the guards. Things were touch-and-go, as they were discovered during the robbery, but they managed to escape, and haven't been seen in the United States, or anywhere else for that matter, since. Hargreave believed that they would make their way to England, and his initial message notifying me to keep my ear to the ground, as they say in America, was followed by this more extensive packet of information including these photographs. Hargreaves has also notified Scotland Yard, in case the two fugitives are spotted here, but he also wanted me to be on the lookout, as he put it."

"These men did make their way to England, as Hargreaves suspected they might, and for some reason have gone to ground in Sir Giles's home. Gables may be related to Sir Giles in some way, in spite of your impression that the old gentleman had no family. There may be some other connection of which we are as yet unaware. In any case, they must have decided to hide out there, thinking that Sir Giles had no friends or family to inquire after him. Your return on the second night must have prompted them to take action."

"I'm lucky that I was not killed, then, I suppose," said Henry.

Holmes shook his head. "They are not killers, at least so far. Even during the American bank robbery, when it would have been far easier for them to kill the bank guards who interfered with them, they took great effort simply to bind them, in spite of the fact their identification was assured, and also that it delayed and nearly ruined their escape. But," he added, "you have been lucky, nonetheless. Their decision to place you in Bedlam is unique in my experience, and could have been disastrous for you, if a different doctor there had decided to keep you for further evaluation, believing that your story was part of some greater delusion. No doubt Carr, the amateur doctor, assumed that the effects of the drug that he administered to you would last much longer, and that your incarceration in the asylum would be of an indefinite duration, rather than just for one night."

Traffic had thinned as the afternoon waned, and we were soon rounding Trafalgar Square and approaching Scotland Yard. Upon our arrival, Holmes decided that we should wait in the four-wheeler while he went inside, rather than waste the time it would take for all of us to go in and explain our purpose. With a bound, he carried his documents within.

It was less than ten minutes later, as I was wishing that we had all chosen to evacuate the hot cab and wait inside the

80

imposing building, that Holmes returned to the pavement with Inspector Youghal and three burly constables. Youghal nodded toward me, and then raised his arm, summoning a second four-wheeler from a short way up the street. When everyone was aboard both cabs, we set out.

Crossing Westminster Bridge, we turned along the south side of the river, before making a series of turns, working our way ever closer to Kennington Park. "It is fortunate that Youghal was at the Yard this afternoon. He has a particular interest in renewing his acquaintance with Gables. Watson, have you ever noticed that reddish scar across the back of Youghal's left hand?"

"From an old knife wound, I think he said," I replied. "Did he get that from Gables?"

Holmes nodded. "Years ago, back when Gables was just beginning his illustrious criminal career. Gables escaped, and he has since risen to greater heights, within certain circles. Youghal is anxious to congratulate him."

The distance to our destination shortened rapidly, Holmes changed the subject entirely, discussing our planned excursion to the Wessex Cup on the following Tuesday. Without mentioning specifics about either the missing race horse or our client, he speculated as to what set of circumstances during a horse race could cause an owner to be permanently warned off the turf for life. Neither Walter nor Henry Forsythe felt the need to contribute to this conversation.

Soon we were pulling up at one of the outer boundaries of the Park. Henry indicated with a gesture that Meadcroft was not far away, but our current location was not in direct sight of Sir Giles's home. The Scotland Yard men emptied from their four-wheeler, and Youghal dispersed his troops in different directions to surround the house.

There was still an hour or so of sunshine left in the sky, so our approach could not be entirely hidden. Walter and Henry stayed with the cabs, while Holmes, Youghal, another plain-clothed detective named Benton, and I walked down the side of the green, showing no interest in the great house that stretched across one end of the common.

The old house was a big and double-fronted affair, gone to seed. However, it had been built in a time when workmanship was solid, and it might still remain standing when the newer houses around it have fallen into decay.

As we neared the old house, having been walking in an oblique and indirect way toward it, we abruptly changed direction and mounted the steps. Standing to one side, in case someone fired a weapon through it, Youghal pounded upon the door with all the authority of the Yard behind him, demanding that the occupants open in the name of the law. After a few seconds of silence, he pounded again with a bellow. In a moment, we heard scrabbling sounds from the right side of the house, followed by a blow and a cry. Leaving Benton at the front door, we ran to the side to find both Gables and Carr, struggling in the hands of some of Youghal's men after their unsuccessful and awkward attempt to exit a side window.

The matter was quickly sorted out. A search of the house found the bulk of the New York bank robbery loot, still packed in the men's cases. More importantly, we discovered Sir Giles Gidley-Hall, gagged and bound hand and foot on a sofa in one of the interior ground floor rooms. I ordered that he be carried out into the fresh air, where I began to administer what aid that I thought necessary. He was a tough old man, and was soon on his feet, as mad as blazes, although he seemed to calm himself when one of Youghal's men reported that Tommy, the goat, had been discovered well-fed and watered in his shed behind the house.

While I was assisting Sir Giles, I was unable to hear the exact exchange between Youghal and Gables, but I did see that Youghal was holding his scarred hand in front of Gables's face and explaining something in a very precise manner. Gables, who had attempted a belligerent attitude up to that point, seemed to collapse when he realized that his story was completely known, and that there would be no escape this time.

Holmes asked a few questions of Gables and Carr, chiefly to confirm his explanation of the events. It was revealed that Gables was a distant cousin of Sir Giles, and he had long been aware of the old man's hermit-like existence. Upon his and Carr's return to England, the house in Meadcroft had seemed like a good place in which to hide. They had initially been left alone there, waiting until they deemed it safe to move on, but then Henry Forsythe's concerns had led him to check on his neighbor, thus causing the fugitives to become irrationally fearful of discovery.

Neither man had wanted to kill Henry Forsythe, but they had not wanted to have him remain as a captive in Sir Giles's house either. They believed that if someone had arrived and had insisted on examining Sir Giles, they could have drugged the old man and explained that he was under a doctor's care. But a persistent neighbor was another matter. He might talk, and then more people might investigate. It was decided to do something about Henry Forsythe, sooner rather than later. Keeping Henry there in the house, along with Sir Giles, was deemed too great a risk, as Henry might escape, or someone might have seen him visiting the house on two successive nights and suggest that as a location to examine if someone noticed that he was missing as well.

It was Carr who decided that they should drug Henry and have him hospitalized in the Bethlem Asylum. He had mistakenly believed that his concoction would last for much longer than it had, and that Henry would be held incommunicado at the hospital until long after Gables and Carr were gone. It was much better, in their opinion, than drugging him and simply leaving him to be found in the street. After Henry's capture, they had made sure that Sir Giles was adequately bound, and then they had taken Henry to Bedlam, telling the cab driver that they were transporting a sick friend.

After Gables and Carr had been taken away, Walter and Henry were brought up to the house, where Henry and Sir Giles were able to speak to one another. It was difficult for the old hermit, but he managed to express his thanks to Henry in a gruff way. Henry then introduced the old man to his brother, Walter, who seemed relieved that the whole matter was at an end.

83

As Youghal was making motions that he was prepared to depart, Holmes spoke. "By, the way, Youghal, there is one other little matter that should be taken care of while we have the opportunity."

"And that would be?" asked Youghal, in a jovial tone.

"Would you mind having a couple of your men take Mr. Walter Forsythe into custody?"

A shocked silence fell upon the group for just a moment, before Walter bolted. Youghal's men were not close enough to make any sort of attempt to stop him, although there is no doubt that they could have soon run him down. Walter made as if to dash toward the open green, in a perpendicular path away from the front of the great house where we stood. As no one else was in a position to intervene, I stuck out my right leg into Walter's path. He tumbled and fell hard, skidding into a pile of autumn leaves. Youghal's men were on him in an instant, dragging him to his feet.

"Well done, Watson," murmured Holmes

Gone was the mild older brother. Instead, a raging, foul-mouthed beast stood between the two officers, cursing Holmes in every way imaginable. Henry Forsythe seemed to shrink within himself, and took a step backward. Sir Giles, without thought, put a fatherly hand on Henry's shoulder to calm him.

"Well, we've got him," said Youghal. "Now can you tell me why?"

"Certainly," said Holmes, reaching into his coat and pulling out the sheaf of papers that he had brought from Baker Street. As he thumbed through them, pulling previously hidden sheets from the envelope, he said to Benton, who was one of the men holding Walter, "Would you mind pulling back his left sleeve to expose the inside of his wrist?"

Walter began to struggle all the harder, but to no avail. Benton roughly pulled back the sleeve and turned Walter's hand to reveal a tattoo. It was about two inches long, blue, and rough-looking and faded. It was a short, segmented serpent, and each of the three segments contained a number: 7, 4, and 2. The number seven was crossed in the Continental manner.

Holmes plucked out two sheets from his bundle and held them out for Youghal. I stepped over so as to observe them as well. The first was a document, dated nearly a decade before, from the Manchester police, describing the activities of a sophisticated gang of thieves. A sketch of the same tattoo was included on the sheet.

"It is a gang symbol," said Holmes. "An amateur tattoo. It is the house number on the street in Manchester where they were initiated. This other sheet from my scrapbooks," he said, holding out the second piece of paper, "is more specific."

It was written in Holmes's close script, describing one Walter Forsythe, late of Manchester, and now a mid-level cog in the machine of Professor James Moriarty. "I noticed the tattoo when Walter's sleeve pulled up, as he was helping Henry into the cab. I verified it when I went into my rooms to retrieve Hargreave's information about Gables and Carr.

Holmes faced Walter, who had slightly calmed himself as the evidence against him was revealed. He kept looking toward Henry, whose head was down and would not look back.

"Did you come to London after the Portland Street robbery in Manchester turned into a hanging job?"

Youghal looked up from the paper. "He was involved in that one? Then we're very glad to find him, and make no mistake about that!"

"I do not know if Moriarty planned the Portland Street business, and made a place for Walter Forsythe and the others after they had to flee Manchester when it went wrong, or if he came to the Professor's attention after he arrived in London. Nevertheless, he has been an important and rising part of the Professor's organization since then. From his position in the City, obtained for him by the Professor, he has been able to carry out all sorts of interesting chores." Holmes tapped the second sheet of paper. "This is a partial list of some of Walter's activities since he came to London, on behalf of his employer. I was not planning to try to land him yet, as I was waiting to net all the fish in one great haul, but as Walter has placed himself unavoidably on my hook this afternoon, the opportunity was too great to ignore, and I reeled him in."

"Well, to extend your metaphor, we'll fillet him and learn all about what he's been up to, and more, I assure you," said Youghal. "Take him away."

Walter kept trying to turn back and look at his brother as he was walked down the green and out toward the cabs. Henry would never glance his way. Sir Giles's hand had remained on Henry's shoulder throughout, and finally I heard him say, "Come inside with me, son. We'll have a little something." They turned and went into the great house.

Holmes and I were left standing alone on the green. The sun was finally dropping behind the surrounding houses, and shadows were rapidly lengthening from west to east.

"You know," I said, as we began to stroll back toward Bert Deacons's four-wheeler, "I have often heard you deride coincidence, but today had several of them. If you had not noticed Walter's tattoo – "

"That was not coincidence," interrupted Holmes. "That was observation."

"All right then," I countered. "If circumstances had not conspired to place Walter's tattoo before you, where it could be observed, and if the Forsythes had not been walking down Praed Street, and if Henry had not heard your name mentioned indiscreetly by one of Patterson's men outside the station, they would have never come inside and involved you, the one man in England with knowledge of these varied and wide-spread crimes at his fingertips, in these events. It is undeniably coincidence."

"Coincidence, Watson?" said Holmes. "Perhaps. But is it possible that it was simply an adjustment on the great scale of life in order to keep things in balance? We, on the side of good, were denied a victory today with Patterson and the matter of the diary. Score one for Moriarty. But perhaps it was only fitting that we then be allowed to achieve something on our side in order to keep things in equilibrium."

"It is a chess game, and you have taken one of Moriarty's pieces!" I cried.

"A pawn, possibly. But this is not a chess game where one player takes his turn, and then sits and waits patiently for his opponent to plan strategy before responding in kind. One does not wait for the other side to take its turn in this game. You can be sure that Moriarty will already be thinking of his next move, and the next. So it is up to me to plan my next move as well, and the next, and for three moves past that, and so on, until the end of the game."

"A game you will win," I said.

"That is my plan, Watson," said Holmes. "But I must have time – I must have time!"

We strolled together in silence back to the cab as the sun set and the wind picked up.

The Matter of Boz's Last Letter

Part I: The Client

"Make a long arm, if you would, Watson, and hand me my index for the letter 'R'."

I had been standing behind my chair, near the fireplace, when Holmes made his request, and it required no great effort to retrieve the volume in question. It was a large black thing, roughly matching its brothers lining the wall shelves to the left of the mantel, and it required careful handling, as numerous loose scraps of paper protruded from various pages, some newspaper clippings, and some of more obscure origin. Here and there across the slips were various notations in Holmes's careful fist. One caught my eye as I passed Holmes the book: *The most vilified man in Marylebone.* I had my own ideas as to whom that might refer, and I resolved to look it up at some later date, when the scrapbook had been returned to its resting place.

I turned toward the door, when Holmes stopped me. "Are you going out?"

"I had not planned to do so."

"That is fortunate, then. I have had a note from a prospective client, and I would value your opinion. He is due to arrive at the hour."

I glanced at the mantel clock and noted that it was nearly a quarter of nine. I informed Holmes that I would return momentarily, and continued on toward my room, one flight above.

I returned to the sitting room moments later, having retrieved the book which I sought, as Holmes laid aside his "collection of R's," as he often referred to that particular volume. He maintained that it was a fine one, but not so fine as his "M's." I saw that he had tossed a note into my chair. Lifting it, I sat and read the contents:

Mr. Holmes,

I propose to call upon you this morning at nine o'clock to discuss a matter of great importance to both myself and my business. It concerns the auction planned for the ninth of this month, less than a week away. As the affair is of extreme importance, I trust that you will make yourself available, and devote your full attention to this affair, in spite of any other matters which are currently engaging you.

Regards,

Leonard Rathham

"Rathham?" I said. "Of New Bond Street?"

"The same," replied Holmes, gesturing toward the index. "You are welcome to see for yourself, but my information on the man is limited. He is in his early fifties, has never married, is the sole proprietor of Sefton's, which he purchased from the Sefton family some fifteen years ago after working his way up from the bottom. It is a story that would be inspiring if not for the tedious and workmanlike way in which he accomplished it. The man is capable, wealthy, and most uninterestingly honest."

I laughed. "He also seems to feel that he can assume your complete willingness to set aside whatever you are working upon at the present time in favor of his own case." I paused, and then asked, "What do you have on hand at the present time?"

"Some ten or twelve other little matters, none of which present any points of interest. Let us hope that Mr. Rathham can remedy that."

We spent the next few minutes in desultory conversation, speculating on the origin of our prospective client's unusual surname. I was not aware of ever having encountered it before. Holmes felt that in spite of this, it seemed somehow fundamentally British. Soon, we were interrupted by the sound of footsteps on the stairs, followed by a pause on the landing as the man, presumably Rathham, paused for a moment to catch his breath.

"He is in poor condition indeed," said Holmes softly, "if seventeen steps can conspire to defeat him so easily. Perhaps, when he has settled, a drop of medicinal brandy?"

I nodded as there was a knock on the door.

Holmes called and invited him in, and a more English looking fellow we had yet to encounter. He was short, not much over five feet in height, and not heavy at all. In fact, if not for the grayish pallor of his skin, I would have expected him to show a great deal of boundless energy, and not the breathless weakness that presented itself. His clothing was well-made and expensive, but not ostentatiously so.

Shepherding him to the basket chair in front of the fireplace, between Holmes's chair and my own, I offered him some medical spirits.

"No, thank you, Doctor," he replied. "I am a lifelong teetotaler. I have no doubts that, were I to sample something right now, I would be asleep before I could convey to you the seriousness of my problem."

I acknowledged his refusal and made my way to my own chair. Holmes began by asking him to state his business.

Taking a deep breath, Rathham began "No doubt you gentlemen are aware of the auction to be held on the ninth, featuring a great number of fine pieces, a mixture of artworks and various examples of fine furniture with historical interest."

Holmes glanced my way. I shook my head, and he turned back to Rathham. "I am afraid that, while I try to stay aware of notable upcoming auctions, especially those related to works of art, I have not acquired any previous knowledge of this particular event."

"I suppose that is no surprise, after all," said Rathham. "It is not one of our more important auctions. At least, it did not start out that way. The offerings are certainly of fine quality, but the seller is not, shall we say, *first tier*. The furnishings and artwork have been in storage for ten years, prevented by a legal dispute from being sold. Only recently was it determined that the owner has true legal title to them, allowing him to offer them for sale. In all honesty, the auction would have merited no special interest, since it is only to provide needed funds for the current owner of the properties. Rather, what has elevated this auction to a position of rather more interest than it would have ordinarily generated is the item that was discovered by my staff, hidden in one of the pieces of furniture to be sold."

"And that would be . . . ?"

"Many of the furnishings, as I previously stated, are of historical interest. For example, there is a chair, collected by the owner more than ten years ago, and before his legal troubles began, that belonged to King George III, the Queen's grandfather. It is rather worn, but its provenance is unquestioned. And the bureau that came down from – "

"Are any of these furnishings that you have mentioned relevant to your problem?" asked Holmes, trying with great courtesy to keep Rathham on the track.

"No, they are not," replied the auctioneer. "I apologize. To stay on the point, I will tell you that one of the items is a desk that belonged to the late author, Charles Dickens, at the time of his death."

"In 1870, as I recall."

"Quite right, Mr. Holmes. The ninth of June, as a matter of fact. It was because of the interest in that particular desk that we chose to schedule the auction on the same day as that of the anniversary."

"But," I interrupted, "surely Dickens's desk, while interesting in and of itself, is not any more interesting or worthy of note than some of the other furniture, such as that which once belonged to a king."

"Dr. Watson, it was the item that was found *within* that desk that generated a greater interest in the sale. While the desk is now more of a curiosity than it was before the discovery, it is the item itself which is now the featured property in the auction."

"And that would be . . . ?" asked Holmes, with a small amount of vexation that only his closest friends might perceive.

"Dickens's lost ending to his final unfinished novel, *The Mystery of Edwin Drood.*"

Holmes and I were silent for a second or two, each pondering the implications of such a statement. I personally had more of an appreciation of one of the country's greatest writers, much more than Holmes. However, we both recognized the value of such a document.

"Such a thing might be worth a fortune," I said. "How is it that the discovery was not immediately announced in the press?"

"Perhaps I overstated the exact nature of the discovery," said Rathham. "The document is not the *definitive* lost ending. As far as we know, Dickens died without completing the book, and the version that is published ends where he stopped. What was discovered in the desk, pushed back behind one of the drawers, was not the legitimate answer to the mystery presented in the novel. It was not even an outline indicating what his planned ending would have been. Dickens was still working on the book up to nearly the hour that he died, and whatever solution he planned for the mystery that he had devised is still a secret that he took with him. Rather, this discovery is a letter that he wrote on the day of his death, outlining a 'false' solution, for the purposes of amusing, or perhaps appeasing, his correspondent."

"So," said Holmes, "the document would have some interest to a Dickens scholar, but that is the limit of its importance."

"If that were all it was, then you would be correct, Mr. Holmes. However, the nature of Dickens's false solution is quite . . . well, one would have to say that it is *incendiary* at best." Rathham fell silent then, pondering his own thoughts.

"Would you care to elaborate?" Holmes finally said, interrupting Rathham's reverie.

"Um? Oh, certainly, certainly. At the time of Dickens's death, he had been estranged from one of his greatest friends, fellow author Wilkie Collins, for a number of years. It seems that by June 1870, both men were making attempts to restore their friendship. In the letter, Dickens refers to other missives that had passed between the two in recent weeks, and it is clear that

Collins was informed of the nature of Dickens's latest novel. Dickens, with almost a whimsical tone, replies that the murderer – and this is what gives the document such an explosive power – was the Queen herself, carrying out first-hand crimes with the assistance of her ministers, family, and other associates, all of whom are identified by name. Various outrageous motivations are also given as well.

"After the document was found in the desk, it was brought to me for examination. Frankly, my astonishment at the discovery was balanced with my feelings of revulsion that one of our greatest writers could have made such offensive statements, even in jest. It goes beyond satire. Dickens mentions one or two events from the later completed parts of *Drood*, and then he spins a web from that point consisting of all sorts of depravity, laying the whole matter at the foot of the Crown.

"I called on several men of letters who have assisted me in the past, and they felt that the work was certainly written by Dickens. One of these men tried to dilute the importance or influence of the document, indicating that Dickens was simply being *whimsical* in order to amuse Collins, as well as to play up to Collins's strong feelings regarding social injustice, which had been increasing over the years."

"Dickens had a concern regarding society's ills, as well," I said. "It is revealed all through his books. But I'm not aware of him ever putting anything such as you have described to paper before."

"So said my experts," replied Rathham. "They felt that it was an ill-conceived impulse on his part, and either the letter would have been sent to Collins and kept between the two of them, at least until Collins's death, when it would have been discovered, or possibly Dickens would have chosen to destroy it before it was sent. However, neither outcome occurred, as Dickens's death took place that same day, and the letter was somehow lost in the desk until its discovery a few weeks ago."

"And yet, despite your obvious revulsion at the document, it was decided to proceed with the plan to auction it?" said Holmes.

"It was. After all, Mr. Holmes, I have an auction house. If I did not do it, someone else would. In my own way, I have directed matters so that only scholars who will be discreet with the document are even aware of it, or will be bidding on it. The current owner of the desk simply wants to accumulate funds, and does not care to whom the letter is offered, as long as he makes a profit. There have been certain scholars as well who have encouraged suppression of the document, or at least a temporary loan to various seats of learning for further study, but the owner insisted on an immediate sale, and the impending date of Dickens's death, as well as the anniversary of when the letter was written, was chosen as the day of the auction.

"And there the matter stood, with the letter being revealed to a limited number of buyers, all learned men or collectors of Dickens ephemera, every one. The seller had at least agreed to that much, that is, to keeping the matter out of the press. Then, this morning, events conspired to send me here, to plead for your help, Mr. Holmes."

"Then the logical conclusion," said my friend, "is that the letter has disappeared."

"Stolen!" cried Rathham. "I'm certain of it. It was kept in my own safe, to which only I have the combination. When I opened it this morning, the letter was gone."

"Are you certain? Might it not have simply become mixed with some of the other papers in the safe? Such things have happened once or twice before, in my experience."

"I assure you that I would not be here now in such a state if that were so," replied the little auction master. "There are very few papers in that safe, and the letter, a fairly thick packet of nineteen heavy-bond and folded sheets, was not there."

Holmes was silent for a moment, and then surged to his feet, peeling off his dressing gown as he made for the doorway to his room. "Then we must examine the scene for ourselves, Mr. Rathham. I assume that the safe to which you refer is located at the auction house?"

"It is. My carriage is outside."

"Excellent." Holmes left the room for a moment, and returned fully clothed, having exchanged dressing gown for acceptable outer wear. "Have you informed the owner of the desk that his property is missing?"

"Not yet," said our client. "After my initial shock, I wrote to you, and soon after made my way here. I am hoping that the matter can be resolved before I need take such action. I can assure you that the owner, who had hoped to realize some profit on the original items in the sale, has speedily become accustomed to the idea that he will receive a much greater amount of money with the inclusion of the discovered letter."

"And who is this man?" said Holmes, swinging into the Inverness that he insisted on wearing year-round, in city or country.

Rathham sniffed. "Not my usual clientele, I can assure you," he said. "Truth be told, if some of the items that he wishes to sell had not been of such fine quality, I would not have involved myself with him. I understand that he collected them all a number of years ago, before his imprisonment. Between ourselves, gentleman, I have heard more than one whisper that he is not really a Baron at all."

Holmes paused, reaching for his fore-and-aft cap, hanging on the peg behind the door. "And you say that this Baron's possessions were legally tied up for ten years?" he said. "May I inquire as to the Baron's name?"

"Maupertuis," replied Rathham. "You may have read of him. He was released from prison a month or so ago, after serving ten years at Princetown. Some financial scandal, as I recall."

Part II: The Auction House

We settled into Rathham's elaborately decorated four-wheeler, and set off south for New Bond Street. Rathham kept up a running chatter about his work, veering toward the current matter, but following conversational tangents without providing any further insight to the present affair. He told tales and gave sly hints regarding other scandals related to auctions over the years, both relating to his clients and those of his competitors. I politely nodded as necessary, but I kept my eye on Sherlock Holmes, who sat quietly and peered unseeing out the carriage window at the passing street. I knew that he was thinking of the name that he had just heard, and the events of the spring of 1887, just over ten years earlier, during his first meeting with Baron Maupertuis, and the resulting crisis that had overtaken him then.

I had reason for concern, as the events of the past few months had mirrored in some crucial ways those that had taken place in 1887. In that current spring of 1897, ten years after Holmes had defeated the Baron and resolved the dreadful scandal associated with the Netherland-Sumatra Company, I had been more aware than perhaps ever before of Holmes's high-strung nature, as he raced pell-mell towards a collapse of the sort that I had already seen once or twice in the years of our friendship. During the early years of our association, when I first met him and shared rooms in Baker Street, I had gradually become aware of Holmes's habit of dosing himself with weakened solutions of cocaine or morphine whenever he was bored, between cases, and, as he liked to put it, when he was "like a racing engine, tearing itself to pieces because it is not connected up with the work for which it was built."

Gradually, his chosen methods of making use of the substances, particularly cocaine, changed so that he was using it in order to provide himself with extra bursts of stamina and clarity of thought during particularly difficult cases. This was rare and infrequent, to the best of my knowledge, until early 1887, when he was taxed for several months during his successful investigation into the Netherland-Sumatra business, and the Baron's machinations. At the conclusion of that affair, Holmes's health was shattered, and I was called to Lyons to bring him back to England and help return him to his former strength.

But the devil that was Holmes's addiction was only sleeping, and not dead. After the death of my first wife, Constance in late 1887*, I moved back to Baker Street, and my presence, I believe, helped keep Holmes's attentions focused on his affairs and not on the siren call of the syringe. However, 1888 turned out to be a year necessitating massive efforts from my friend. That fall, while involved in one of Holmes's investigations, I met the woman who would be my second wife, Mary Morstan.

Following our courtship, I remarried in mid-1889, and my absence from Baker Street allowed the reliance on the evil drug to return, as Holmes required more and more stamina during his ever-increasing battles with Professor Moriarty. Fortunately, I realized in time what was happening, and intervened by seeking help from an expert physician in Vienna during the fall of 1890. Holmes and I traveled there, and when we departed, I believed that he had found a path, albeit a shaky one, toward what he needed to do.

The following spring, Holmes was believed to have died at the hands of Professor Moriarty at the Reichenbach Falls. After his miraculous return to Baker Street three years later, in 1894, he seemed to have no need for the drug, having learned several calming techniques during his travels in the East. My second wife, Mary, had died during the years that Holmes was missing and presumed dead, and following his return to London, I again began to share rooms with him. I must confess that it was several years after that before I began to see, once again, evidence of the dark intrusive tentacles of the opiate that Holmes seemed to need, at first just a little here or there, winding their way into his very existence.

As the carriage crossed Oxford Street, I watched my friend, even as he looked at the passing street views, and tried to see if the return of the Baron was causing any unhealthy reaction, as I

* Editor's Note: See Chapters 7-10 of William S. Baring-Gould's *Sherlock Holmes of Baker Street* for further information regarding Constance Watson.

did not want a relapse of his recent condition. For he had only recently fought his addiction, yet again, and at that time I was uncertain as to the complete reliability of his recovery.

By late 1896, it had become dreadfully obvious that, if somehow he were not stopped, Holmes would be unable to shake the grip of the drug, progressing to a steady and steep decline that would almost certainly lead to his death. Eventually, in a long and painful process that need not be recounted here, Holmes was finally persuaded to abandon London for a time and travel with me to the furthest stretches of Cornwall, where he and I obtained a house at the sea, and he set about bravely purging the drug from his system. It was not an easy thing for him, or for me, but as his friend and physician, I knew that we had to see it through or his life was forfeit.

After our return to London, a month or so before the events of the present narrative, he had some difficult moments, and he often fell into deep brown studies. But he had finally found the strength and understanding to rouse himself from them without the need to seek the drug. As I write this, now some thirty years on from the events of that June, I can affirm that he has never made use of the drug – or any other substance of a similar nature – again.

But I did not know on that day whether or not Holmes had truly defeated the demon. I had seen him slide back too many times before. So I kept a sharp watch, knowing well that a shock, such as learning of the involvement of his old enemy, Baron Maupertuis, might be the very thing that would bring about some new disastrous craving for the drug.

Rathham's carriage had turned into Brook Street, and so on until we reached New Bond Street. Not long after we turned the corner, we stopped in front of that austere building which had become noted in recent years for the nature of its auctions and for its discreet conduct. Rathham's man in livery at the door ushered us inside. We passed through an ornate lobby, and on through to the auction rooms themselves. Tapestries hung from the walls, and heavy chairs with golden trim lined the room from side to side, facing the short dais at the front. The great space was fairly well lit, and I knew that a closer examination of the room's various *accoutrements* that adorned the surroundings would show that they were indeed as fine as they looked. There would be nothing of a theater about this place, where the magic and illusion of the darkened room are revealed to be shabby and threadbare once the lights are turned up.

But after passing through the finely decorated public space, where nothing was too good for Rathham's patrons, it was something of a shock, although not altogether unexpected, when we went through a tasteful and heavy white door, and thus into the inner chambers of the great auction house. For here there was no decoration, and no need to impress anyone. The place resembled nothing so much as a warehouse, or perhaps more appropriately fitted to my earlier metaphor, the well managed backstage area of a theater.

Deep shelves were stacked far above our heads with all sorts of items, including works of art and furniture. Smaller cabinets, many appearing to be locked, held finer objects, each cluttered together so that it was impossible to tell at a glance exactly what one was seeing. However, I was certain that Rathham had everything organized, and could walk immediately to this or that location and lay his hands on any specific item that he wanted without a moment's delay

Our host led us past numerous bustling workmen and supervisors, all of whom continued to carry out their tasks, but gave us surreptitious glances along the way. We reached a plain door at the rear of the building and passed into Rathham's office.

It was a working space, with no signs of luxury. I felt that Rathham would reserve meeting the public, or clients or buyers, in more luxurious spaces near the front of the building. This was the man's inner sanctum, as evidenced by stacks of documents and materials waiting for his attention. In some ways the room looked like what happened when Holmes was allowed to pile objects and papers related to his investigations around our sitting room in Baker Street, following some obscure filing system that he kept to himself. It was only by the stern intervention of Mrs.

Hudson or myself that we were not eventually overrun by Holmes's archives.

Holmes immediately made his way across the room to the rather modest safe, standing alone beside a chair stacked with catalogs.

"A Victor safe," said Holmes, softly. "Combination lock only, no key." Slightly louder, he said, "Would you mind opening it, Mr. Rathham?"

"Certainly, certainly," said the small man, stepping forward. The safe was quickly opened, and Rathham showed no hesitation at revealing the contents. It was as he had said earlier: the Dickens letter was not there.

"When was the last time that you saw it?" questioned Holmes.

"About five o'clock last night. I always keep the safe closed and locked unless I am specifically taking or replacing some of the contents. I never walk away, even for an instant, with the door open. As you can see from the remaining contents, these items are highly confidential. Yesterday afternoon, I opened the safe to replace an estimate that was being consulted by one of my trusted employees. I laid the estimate on top of the Dickens letter. I specifically recall doing so because the letter itself is an unusual color, brought about by the discoloration that has occurred within the paper, and also because the estimate was slightly smaller than the folded letter, and I was able to center it exactly on top of the larger document."

"Who else has the combination?"

"No one."

"You are sure?"

"Absolutely."

"Do you have it written down somewhere that could have been discovered, in case you forget it?"

"No, Mr. Holmes. It is a number that has personal significance to me from a time in my youth. No one could guess it, and I would have no need to write it down, as it is something that I will not forget, at least as long as I retain my faculties."

Holmes was silent for a moment, before saying, "How many employees do you have?"

"Nearly thirty," replied Rathham. "Of course, many are laborers, or delivery people. About ten who work with the clients, and have knowledge of the business side of things."

"And how many of them knew about the letter?"

"Internally, just two. Angus Menzies, my chief assistant, and my secretary, Mr. Addison."

"I will need to speak with them, and possibly other members of your staff as well," said Holmes, looking around. "Will it be possible to make use of your office?"

"Certainly, certainly. I will just – "

Rathham was interrupted before he could finish by a knock at his office door, followed by the entrance of an average-looking man in a brown suit. "Mr. Holmes?" he said, looking toward my friend.

Holmes nodded, and the fellow stepped forward, holding an envelope in front of him. "No reply is expected," he said, stepping back, turning smartly, and departing the way that he came.

Holmes opened the envelope and removed the simple folded note. Opening it, he quickly read the short handwritten message, and then seemed to read it again, more slowly this time.

Shoving it into the pocket of his Inverness, he barked a short, "Ha!" and turned to our client. "It will not be necessary to interview your staff at the present time," he said. "New information has come to light that will require our presence elsewhere."

"But . . . " said Rathham, with confusion, "but how could there be any new information if you have only learned of the letter's theft just a short time ago in your rooms, from my very lips?"

"Nevertheless," said Holmes, nodding toward the door. "We must seek answers elsewhere. We shall be in touch, never fear!"

With that, we left the small man and made our way outside. My last view of Rathham was a study between puzzlement and anger, with the latter winning.

101

Outside, a smart-looking private hansom was waiting, its driver looking toward us expectantly. Without hesitation, Holmes entered, and I followed. As I sat back, he handed me the note.

Sherlock,

Your time will be better spent joining me for lunch to discuss the matter of the Dickens letter. Questions will be answered. A carriage awaits.

Mycroft

Part III: The Diogenes Club

The vehicle gained momentum, rolling through the crowded throngs of New Bond Street. I said, "Your brother? What could he know about this? And why should he care?"

"Possibly there is some government interest in this document that smears the Royal Family, written by such a noted author. That is the only theory that I can advance at the present time without more data. Data, it would seem, that we shall have in a very short period of time."

Indeed, the skillful maneuvering of the driver brought us along to Piccadilly quick enough, where a sharp right and then a left had us rolling down St. James and thence into Pall Mall. Halfway down that illustrious avenue, we drew to a stop between the Diogenes Club on one side of the street, and Mycroft Holmes's lodgings on the other. Holmes cast an interrogatory glance toward the driver, who nodded his head toward the Club. We went up the short flight of steps and inside.

In spite of what I knew to expect every time I entered that curious place, the vast silence still seemed overwhelming. The rustle of cloth as we removed our coats and handed them off seemed deafening and almost embarrassing, feeling as if it were something for which I should apologize, akin to bursting into laughter at a funeral. Holmes did not appear to suffer such concerns – he never did – as he turned and briskly moved deeper into the place, making for the Stranger's Room, the only place in the building where conversation was allowed or tolerated.

We found Mycroft, standing in front of one of the tall windows, resembling a great lion on its hind legs as he looked down at the street. It was the same stance that he had been making when I had first met him, back in the fall of '88, just hours before we were so deeply involved in the affair of Mr. Melas's problem.

"You were followed," said Mycroft. It was a statement, not a question.

"I was aware of it," replied his brother, joining him at the window. "The man across the street, two doors down."

I looked to see him. He was leaning in a doorway, looking up and down the street in every direction but towards us.

"He is an Australian by birth," said Holmes, "wounded in the left leg at some point in the past. In his early-to-mid-forties. He has recently had his unusually pale hair cut, and is wearing a false moustache."

I peered at the man, feeling safe to do so since he was conspicuously not looking our way. "I believe I can see the evidence of the hair cut, since the skin at his hairline and above his ears is noticeably paler than that of his face and hands. And he stands awkwardly on one leg, which reveals his injury."

"Very good, Watson. And his Australian background?"

After a moment's silence, with no answer from myself forthcoming, Holmes said softly, "His tie bar, Watson, although you might be excused for not being able to see it clearly now. As I circled behind the hansom after we arrived, I was able to glance at it. Although he is a street's width away, it is still visible, illuminated as it is by the sun. Although you may not have recognized it, it is definitely a stylized symbol of a kangaroo."

"Indeed," said Mycroft, "you are correct, Sherlock. But you would do well not to forget the tattoo of a kangaroo in the bend of his right forearm as well."

103

Holmes straightened slightly and smiled with a look of enlightenment, but I was confused. "Ah," said Holmes.

"This is surely too much," I said. "How can you know of any tattoo, hidden beneath his shirt cuff and coat sleeve?"

"Simply because," replied Mycroft Holmes, "he is one of *my* agents."

"Was, perhaps you mean?" asked his brother. "If he was following me on your orders, perhaps for my protection, or possibly to see where I have been and will be going, you would not have felt the need to point him out to us. That fact, coupled with that ridiculous false moustache, makes me think that for some reason, this agent is no longer under your control."

Mycroft sighed and turned away from the window, moving toward a table at the rear of the room, set for luncheon. "You are right, Sherlock. I fear that this man, one of my most trusted, for a while at least, has gone rogue."

"But why the obviously false moustache?" said Holmes. "Surely your agents are not so careless as to display such patent amateurism."

"I believe that he is sending me a message, although its meaning escapes me. Perhaps a taunt that, even with such poor protective coloring, he still believes that he is now beyond my reach."

Holmes nodded toward the window. "Why don't you simply send word to block up the street and catch him, then? I have half a mind to go do it myself, and I don't even know the full story yet."

"It is not that easy," replied Mycroft, dropping heavily into a chair. "Join me, please," he gestured to the seats beside him. "I am not certain of his plans, and until I have a better understanding, I must let him play his own game, though time grows short."

"From the fact that you knew how to find Watson and me at Rathham's auction house, I must believe that this rogue agent of yours has something to do with the stolen Dickens letter, and the auction in just a few days."

"He has everything to do with it," sighed Mycroft. "For he is the man that stole the blasted letter in the first place."

"That simplifies matters," said Holmes. He sniffed. "Curry?"

Mycroft nodded, and indicated that we should help ourselves. "I, for one," said Holmes, ignoring the offer as I lifted the lid of the serving dish with pleasure, "was not looking forward to tediously interviewing Rathham's employees, one by one, to eliminate the innocent and terrify the guilty. To the expert, there is a strong family resemblance about crimes, and if you have assembled for questioning a thousand witnesses at your finger ends, the thousand-and-first is very much like the first thousand."

"Perhaps, brother, when you hear more about this matter, you will admit that this is a little different than your usual inquiries."

I could tell that there was something about this situation that amused Holmes. Mycroft could see it as well, but he did not choose to let it rile him. "The fellow out on the street," said the elder Holmes, "who probably got onto your trail at the auction house, is named Julius Shipton. As you observed, he is Australian. He was raised without a father, and I gather that he ran rather wild during his youth. He managed to obtain passage to this country in his early twenties, and after his arrival, he pursued higher learning in a rather haphazard fashion, first at Oxford, and then at a few of the lesser establishments. At some point he drifted north into Edinburgh, where he fell into an acquaintance with a reporter who had chosen over time to make personal use of the facts that he uncovered while gathering information for his stories, rather than providing this information to his newspaper.

"Between the two, this reporter and Shipton, there evolved a rather systematic way of achieving payment from the subjects of their inquiries."

"Victims, you mean," said Holmes, finally deigning to take a serving of curry. "He was a blackmailer."

105

"Yes," said Mycroft, "and I am aware of your feelings regarding such creatures, and I am in complete agreement as well. But Shipton showed great finesse, and when one of the victims finally shot and killed the reporter, there were enough indications about what had truly been going on that my local representative in the Scottish capital was able to identify Shipton, and more specifically his skill and finesse at carrying out his chosen activity, albeit a dark one. I could make use of these skills, as well as the man himself, and I recruited him as an agent. I must say that it has generally been a satisfactory arrangement, at least up until now. While he certainly has not been the most patriotic chap to ever carry out an order, he has shown great initiative with a certain measure of luck in the bargain, and had earned a degree of trust."

"Until this matter of the Dickens letter," said Holmes.

"Yes. We first became aware of it a few weeks ago, never mind how. There was obviously some concern about such a thing possibly becoming common knowledge, just a short time before the Queen's Diamond Jubilee is to take place. There is already enough criticism in the press regarding the costs associated with the celebration, and so on. If it became known that Dickens himself had written such a volatile and critical letter regarding the monarchy, and about the Queen in particular, it could ruin the celebration, and have long-lasting consequences."

"Old Boz's last letter could never cause that much of a sensation, and you know it," countered Holmes.

"You should know better than that," said Mycroft. "It was you who prevented the same sort of scandal from occurring in August of '89, with the matter of 'The Bridal Night'."

I did not immediately recall the matter, and said so, asking if Holmes had investigated the case without me, due to my marriage.

"Yes, Watson," said Holmes, who seemed to recall the matter with some distaste. "Just another instance where the monarchy was saved from embarrassment."

"She was quite grateful, and you know it," said Mycroft. "That case could have been the making of you."

"As you said at the time. I have been 'made' quite well on my own, thank you."

"What was this matter of 'The Bridal Night'?" I asked.*

When Holmes made no effort to explain, Mycroft said, "In short, 'The Bridal Night' was a pen-and-ink illustration drawn and distributed by an American, Charles Leslie, in 1840, the year of the Queen's marriage. It consists of a man and woman in night clothing, standing in a bedchamber, and quite obviously the young Queen and Prince Albert on their wedding night. Nothing overtly distasteful, you understand. Husband and wife, perfectly legal. This drawing has resurfaced several times over the years, including a period during the last Jubilee."

"I do seem to recall something of the matter now," I said. "You were summoned on several occasions during the course of events to meet the Queen."

"And I managed to fulfill my commission regarding the suppression of the illustration. Now it is all water under the bridge."

"But," said Mycroft, "it illustrates my point that such things are a very real threat to the Crown. This newly discovered letter, indicting the Royals for all sorts of social ills, could gain real traction in spite of its outrageous nature, especially with its threatened revelation so close to the current Jubilee, now only a few days away."

"And what was your initial response to the perceived threat of the letter?"

"We initially sent Shipton to surreptitiously retrieve it during the night so that it could be examined. Obviously, Rathham's safe proved to be no difficulty at all, no matter how secure he believes it to be. I'm sure you made the same observation for yourself.

* Editor's Note: The events of "The Bridal Night" are recounted in Chapter 17 "At the Queen's Command" from *I, Sherlock Holmes* (1977), by Sherlock Holmes, and edited by Michael Harrison.

"After Shipton took the letter, he carried it a short distance to a rented room nearby, where it was carefully photographed. He then replaced the letter in the safe, and Rathham never knew that it had been taken.

"Upon reading the document, it was quite obvious that it was much more incendiary than you are willing to concede, brother. It was also obvious, but only to certain experts, that it was a clever forgery as well."

"A forgery? By the Baron?" asked Holmes with a wry smile. "Imagine that. Salting the mine with a gold nugget?"

"Quite."

"So this letter was never real at all," I said. "Dickens never wrote a document on his last day that would end up threatening the crown."

"That is correct," said Mycroft.

"Well, I must admit that I am relieved," I said. "This letter has the possibility of besmirching the Queen and soiling the reputation of one of our greatest writers."

"It still can, doctor, if we do not retrieve it," said Mycroft. "This scheme must have been in preparation for some time. I do not know if a subsidiary part of the Baron's goal was primarily to inflame the public against the Crown with the contents as it became more widely known, or if the shocking content of the letter was simply to increase its interest and notoriety, thus raising the asking price at the auction. Any damage to Dickens's reputation is probably only a secondary effect. One thing that is certain is that the Baron had assistance from someone or some organization. This scheme must have been started long before he left prison a few weeks ago. The forgery would have taken longer than that to accomplish."

"I would assume, then, that he has been working for Colonel Moriarty since his release, performing such deeds as he did for the Colonel's brother, the Professor, before his arrest and conviction in '87."

"Indeed. As you have been aware, the Colonel has been working to rebuild his brother's criminal network for several years now, although without the total success that he craves. The

108

conflicting actions of the youngest Moriarty brother, the former station master, to also declare himself the heir to the throne and take over the organization have served to stifle both their efforts. However, the Baron is *not* doing the same tasks for the Colonel that he did for the Professor. As you will recall, in '87 he fronted an incredibly complex scheme devised by the Professor that defrauded countless people of their money, some fatally so. Now, since his release from prison, the Baron is working as a simple collector, dealing with the riff-raff milling at the bottom of the Colonel's ladder. Still, he puts up a good front, dressing and living as well as the Colonel will allow him."

"And the false letter? What did you decide after you had examined it?"

"I did not want to steal or destroy it outright, as Rathham's outcry would give it too much attention – as has almost happened, as a matter of fact. We didn't want to bring Rathham into the circle of knowledge at that point in time, because he might have refused to cooperate and balked at participating in our scheme. Rather, I conceived the rather unique solution of forging a copy of the original forgery, but of such obvious clumsiness and false quality that it would be more easily denounced as a fraud, thus preventing a protracted debate about its authenticity, stopping it from ever being auctioned, and leaving it quickly forgotten without giving it any undue emphasis or importance. Plans are in place to make sure that the fraud reflects back upon the Baron, having the added benefit of embarrassing or ruining him as well. After all, he forged the letter to begin with. This simply made the identification of such a forgery that much easier.

"The new forgery was carried out by one of our experts. After its substitution, Shipton was to be finished with his involvement in the matter, and one of my more polished agents would have approached Rathham and explained the situation, attempting to enlist his participation. If that did not work, I would have then made an effort as well, and I must admit that Rathham's agreement would have been guaranteed."

"All of this forgery and counter-forgery, and burglaries and more burglaries, seems a little complex, even for you, Mycroft," said Holmes. "Couldn't you have just burned the initial forged letter, and let its disappearance remain a mystery?"

"You know better than that, brother," said Mycroft. "We create contingencies here, and who knows what possibilities we could have tied to various loose threads that we picked out of this cloak. For instance, at some point in the future, we might have used the existence of the letter to bring pressure in a certain quarter, in ways that I cannot yet imagine."

"I have to agree," I said, "that the whole thing seems unnecessarily complex."

Holmes turned to me. "I am reminded of a time when I was seven years old, I believe, and thus Mycroft was fourteen. Our father asked him to locate Sherrinford in the north field and have the sheep driven toward the ford for shearing. Mycroft – "

"You were only six at the time," interrupted Mycroft.

"It makes no difference to the main thrust of the story. As I was saying, after delivery of the message, Mycroft was nowhere to be found. He was eventually discovered in the village, talking with men there about setting up a series of telegraph lines across the farm in each direction in order to relay messages to various communication stations he intended to construct, dotted here and there in the fields. When he was found by our father, he had exhausted the inexact knowledge of the locals, and was planning on catching the next train to Thirsk to discuss it with someone there."

"It would have worked," replied Mycroft. "I understand that something along those lines was used by the Americans during their Civil War, which took place soon after."

"At least it was better than your initial scheme of having the sons of local crofters remain huddled in sheds spread out in lines stretching in each direction, waiting until they were needed to run messages up or down to the next lad as needed."

"The system had many advantages, especially in certain seasons."

"You simply did not like going to the fields to find Sherrinford."

"What I did not like was – " At that point, Mycroft stopped, and noticed my amused countenance as I listened to the bickering of the two brothers. With a cough, he returned himself to the matter at hand.

"Whatever our future plans were and still are regarding the forged letter, we must not lose sight of the fact that Shipton has stolen it for his own ends *now*. Last night Shipton was to make the swap, before Rathham was to be approached this morning by another agent. However, instead of carrying out his orders, Shipton stole the original and kept the copy as well. And then he wrote me a letter, delivered by messenger this morning, announcing that he intends to address his grievances against Her Majesty by releasing the blasted thing to the press on the day before the Jubilee Celebration. Apparently he has had several points of contention with our government that have festered for too long in secret, and have reached the lancing point."

"And also apparently," replied Holmes, "you should have made a better investigation into the background of your agent. Or perhaps you should have avoided recruitment of a blackmailer in the first place."

"As you said a moment ago, it is water under the bridge, brother," said Mycroft. "What remains now is to get the letter back. Shipton will know that you are involved, since he followed you here. It is possible that he had already expected you to take an interest one way or another. It will work out well, as your movements will serve as a distraction for him while my men work in the shadows to trap him."

"So I am to understand that I will simply be a decoy? Or a staked goat? Do you have no faith that I can resolve the matter satisfactorily?"

"I am sure that you could do it," replied Mycroft. "However, Lord Salisbury has been consulted, since he is expected to resume his post as Prime Minister any day now, and it is customary to begin briefing the new man in order to make for a smoother transition. At present, he is down in one of his troughs where his opinion of you is reflective of the events of late '88, when you pointed out his passive complicity in that vile matter which so occupied our attention at the time."

"I care not a farthing's worth about Salisbury's opinion of me. Ask him next week what he thinks about me and his comments will be glowing. The man is – "

" – still very influential," interrupted Mycroft. "And in any case, he has raised a valid point or two. Word of your . . . illness last March has reached his ears, and he has expressed concern whether you are now fighting fit, especially against an old foe such as the Baron, no matter how diminished are the man's current circumstances."

"I can assure you – "

"Additionally, he pointed out – and he was not the first to think of this, although he was the first to say it aloud – that you might not be willing to put forth your best effort to restore a piece of property to a former enemy, when that recovery would only seem to benefit him."

"Now see here," I interjected. "Holmes would never take a chance on endangering the Crown simply to vex the likes of Baron Maupertuis!"

"I agree, doctor, but there are other considerations, and at certain rarefied levels, one must go lightly. Therefore – "

"Therefore," said Holmes, rising from the table, his finely decorated china plate still holding the small serving of pristine and untouched curry, "we will go and serve as the distraction, while the pincers close on Mr. Shipton."

As he turned away, Mycroft added, "Brother, should you happen to find yourself in such a position as to effect a successful conclusion to this matter, to the satisfaction of *all* concerned parties, I am sure that no one, including our once and future P.M., would have any objections."

Holmes did not look back, but I saw the shadow of a smile cross his face. He understood the rules of the game, as did I.

Expressing my thanks for the meal to Mycroft Holmes, I took my leave in Holmes's wake, joining him outside in the early afternoon sunshine illuminating Pall Mall.

Down the street, about halfway between where we stood and Waterloo Place, I could see Julius Shipton, standing without a hat, his pale hair shining. Holmes tipped his fore-and-aft at the man, who returned the gesture by making a small bow. Then, he turned toward the Atheneum on the corner and in a moment was gone.

"I'm not sure but that we shouldn't follow him, Mycroft's wishes be d---ed!" I said.

"Not yet," said Holmes. "We need leverage. I must make a few inquiries." He turned from the east, where he had been gazing toward the site of Shipton's disappearance, and faced me. "Do you make your way back to Baker Street, there's a good fellow. I have an idea or two where to find the answers to my questions, and possibly start a few wheels turning in motion as well. I shall return in a few short hours."

And with that, he set off in the direction that Shipton had taken. I stood and watched for a few moments, but he did not turn right, as had the former blackmailer-turned-government-agent-turned-criminal. Rather, he continued onward, heading toward Trafalgar Square.

As he disappeared into the June haze, I turned and saw Mycroft Holmes, standing in the same window where we had found him upon our arrival. He nodded to me, and did not seem surprised at all to have been caught observing us. I nodded in return and set off walking, until shortly I found a hansom and returned to Baker Street.

Part IV: An Unpleasant Encounter

Fortunately, Mrs. Hudson had not prepared anything for lunch, as I was comfortably filled by the simple fare at the Diogenes Club. I settled into my chair by the fireplace to await Holmes's return, intending to catch up on my medical journals.

I had spent a fairly profitable three hours and a quarter when I heard the arrival of a cab outside our open windows.

Surprisingly, there came the sound of a second vehicle stopping almost immediately after the first, and then the sound of Holmes's voice. Although I could not make out the words, the tone was sharp. I was rising from my chair to have a look when Holmes called, "Watson! Can you join me on the street? And bring your Afghan friend!"

I knew that Holmes meant my old service revolver, which I had left on my desk following my earlier return. I had learned long ago not to cross the threshold without it. Holmes had many enemies, and by association I did as well. Several hard lessons had taught me the advisability of carrying that grim souvenir of my Army days.

Without bothering to look out the window in order to see what I was getting myself into, I dashed across the sitting room, down the seventeen steps, and out through the front door to find Holmes standing on the walk, in seemingly harmless conversation with a short, well-dressed man. There were two cabs beside them, as I had heard, but one was pulling away from the curb while the other, which had brought our visitor, paused as the path before him cleared. I looked more closely at the short man, and then recognized him with a shock. It was Baron Maupertuis.

Holmes was obviously tense, while the Baron seemed amused. I did not perceive any overt threat, but I kept my hand in my pocket and on the butt of my revolver.

The second cab was free to navigate, but Holmes held up a hand. "Wait," he said. "This man will not be staying."

"What?" said the Baron in a friendly tone. "Not inviting me in to reminisce about old times? The last time we met was in Lyons, when the British and French police took me in charge. You did not even appear at the trial. I was hurt."

"There was no need for you to mark my absence. The case was complete without my assistance."

"Oh, is that why? I had heard that you were ill."

"State your business," said Holmes shortly.

"My business," said the Baron, "is to make sure that you fulfill the task which you have taken upon yourself. Namely, to

114

retrieve my Dickens letter that has been stolen from Rathham's auction house."

"So Mr. Rathham felt the need to inform you of its disappearance, then?"

"Rather, I stopped in this morning, and when I wanted to see it, he was forced to admit that it had been stolen last night. But he was quite enthusiastic in telling me that he had taken the initiative to hire you, Holmes. England's greatest detective. I know you are proud of your honor, so I wanted to make sure that the investigation would be carried out in an honorable way. After all, I have paid my debt to society."

"As you were only released a few weeks ago, you must have been required to pay every single day of your debt," said Holmes. "I must admit that I lost track of how you were progressing through your sentence. I had heard that the authorities had to keep you separated from Colonel Moran, and that the mere threat of putting you in the same cell – nay, the same wing of the prison – with him was enough to make you a model prisoner."

This statement seemed to break through the Baron's contrived good humor, and he frowned for an instant before his face devolved back into a bland, amused mask.

"That is all past now," said the Baron. "I am simply another one of your beloved Londoners, appealing to you for assistance. I am even in a position to provide a little something extra to whatever you expect to get from Rathham. As you might imagine, the sale of that letter will mean a great deal to me, and my continued rehabilitation into society."

"Your rehabilitation might seem more genuine if you had not, upon your release from prison, immediately found employment within Colonel Moriarty's organization."

"Surely you are mistaken," said the Baron. "I have a small establishment set up near Mayfair, where I counsel a select group of individuals on various financial speculations. I did have a gift for that type of work, you might recall."

"Do you wear your gloves throughout these appointments?" asked Holmes, gesturing toward the man's hands. "In order to

115

hide the permanent darkening of your fingertips from picking oakum in Dartmoor?"

The Baron's pretense fell away. With a snarl, he turned back to the waiting cab. His sudden move caused the horse to shy before it was quickly taken in hand by the hansom driver.

At the cab, the Baron turned back and said, "I expect the return of that letter, Holmes. I have as much right to protection under the law as the next man. If I don't get it, Rathham's reputation, and yours as well, will be ridiculed from here to the sea."

"I will handle the matter according to my own lights, the way that I always do, Monsieur Petit."

I glanced at Holmes in puzzlement. The Baron seemed nonplussed as well, before asking, "What? What did you say?"

"I used your correct name," said Holmes, finally moving, taking a step forward as some of the tension fell away from his tall frame. He seemed to have attained the upper hand. "After your arrest in '87, I was ill for some time. Unraveling your scheme took two long months. It was only later that I realized that you had been backed by Professor Moriarty himself. I should have known – you were never intelligent enough to have constructed that unholy spider's web known as the Netherland-Sumatra Company.

"Although I did not need to attend your trial, I did keep an eye on you from afar, especially as the battle of wits with the Professor escalated over the next few years. And part of that was to delve into your background for additional information, should your piece ever be returned to the chess board."

"You know nothing," said the man, now named by Holmes to be Petit. "Lies."

"You think that because so much time has passed, that the truth cannot be discovered. Just because you are on the books at Princetown Prison in the 'M's' for Maupertuis does not mean the truth won't eventually come out. Your real name is Rémi Petit, and the closest you've ever been to legitimately being a Maupertuis was when the circus that employed your mother stopped near Saint-Malo nine months before your birth."

This last statement seemed to enrage the small man. He threw his cane into the cab and moved his hand toward the pocket of his waistcoat. Holmes, indifferent now and having said his piece, turned toward our front door, while I removed my trusted service revolver from my own pocket and held it low to my side, while still quite visible to Monsieur Petit. "Time to go," I said.

Petit stayed still for a moment as the anger held on. Eventually, however, it began to settle away as he realized that this encounter was over. While he climbed into the cab, I asked the driver, "Do you work for Colonel Moriarty as well?"

"I really couldn't say, sir."

"I see. Well, it would be a good idea to keep this man away from here from now on. He will only cause the same problems and embarrassment for the Colonel that he did for the Professor. Do you understand?"

The driver nodded, and when Petit, formerly Baron Maupertuis, had closed the doors, he gigged the horse into motion. They headed towards Regents Park and soon turned out of site.

Inside our front door, I found Holmes laughing silently to himself. "That was enjoyable," he said. "I've held onto that little nugget for some time. Spending it just now gave me every bit of its worth in return. Did you realize that the Baron – which I will continue to name him, as it amuses me! – the Baron must not realize that we know the Dickens letter to be a fraud? If he thought it was discovered, I do not think that he would still urge its recovery. He might just write off the whole thing as a bad investment. Mrs. Hudson!" he suddenly and abruptly called without warning.

She quickly appeared from her rooms at the rear of the house, while Holmes fished a piece of paper from his wallet. While he scratched a note onto it, he said, "Things are working out rather splendidly, and I find that I am in the mood for a bit extra with tea today, if it would not be too much trouble."

"Not at all," she said, with a twinkle in her eye. Holmes handed her the note and a couple of coins, instructing her to have the message sent from the Post Office as soon as possible. She took it, with an amused smile on her face. And as Holmes started up the steps, she even had the audacity to give me a wink!

Upstairs, as we settled into our chairs, I remarked, "You certainly seem to be in good spirits."

"I should think so. I believe that this matter will be wrapped up by this time tomorrow."

"That soon? What were you able to accomplish after we separated at the Diogenes Club?"

"Oh, a great deal," he replied. "As I previously indicated, we needed some sort of leverage. It seemed to me the quickest way was to see if Shipton has anyone that he cares about. With his recent actions, he has cut the lines to the dock and drifted quite a ways out from shore, so to speak. However, if he has anyone for whom he feels affection, he might be approached from that direction.

"I stopped and wired Mycroft, asking him a few questions that should have occurred to me while we were there in the Strangers Room, such as when Shipton first came to this country, what boat he came in on, and the like. With this information in hand, I went to the shipping offices and managed to find someone who had been on that ship. I was fortunate that this company frequently breaks up its crews, so the likelihood of finding someone from that sailing was not too small.

"At first the man didn't remember anything. However, careful questioning eventually helped him to recall Shipton, and more importantly, the other person who had traveled with him in an adjacent cabin, a young Australian woman with a unique feature. A return to the shipping office revealed that her name is Emily Smith."

"Smith, eh?" I said. "It might as well have been Jones, I suppose. And the unique feature about this woman?"

"Although she is quite attractive otherwise, she has the sad affliction of having a *talipes equinovarus*."

"A club foot."

"Quite. With this information, I then went to the area around Shipton's residence near Cannon Street Station, as related to me by Mycroft. It did not take long to determine that a Miss Smith of matching description worked in a nearby pub, and lived 'round the corner."

"And did you approach her?"

"No, I did not, although I did observe her for a bit, while having a pint of rather mediocre quality. After identifying her, I went to the Yard, where I spent a productive quarter-hour with friend Lestrade, going over recent unsolved murders in the Cannon Street area."

"Murders?" I asked. "Is there a murder mixed up in this affair?"

"Not until I did the mixing," replied Holmes. "Going over the records, we found where the owner of a stable on Garrick Street had been found early yesterday morning, his head crushed in by a piece of stove wood discovered on the ground near him in one of the stalls. Lestrade and I went there, and it was quickly apparent to me that the murder had been committed by the dead man's brother, who is a half-owner in the business. So after this was established, confidentially between Lestrade and myself, you understand, we promptly went to 'The Crown and Garter' on Cloak Lane where Shipton's sister was working and arrested her for the murder."

"You . . . you arrested this poor girl for the murder, when you knew that it was committed by the dead man's brother? I don't understand."

"It is obvious, my dear Watson," said Holmes. "Lestrade will make sure that the arrest is trumpeted in the papers. 'Emily Smith Accused of Murder by Sherlock Holmes.' The press is such a useful institution, if one only has the knowledge of how to use it."

"But your reputation, Holmes," I said. "It will be trumpeted that you have identified this killer, only to subsequently admit that you made a mistake."

"I care not about my reputation," said Holmes. "And this won't be the first time that I have done something like this. I have to say that Lestrade had your same misgivings, but he

119

quickly saw the wisdom of the plan, which seems like the quickest way to settle the matter.

"If Shipton doesn't find out at the pub about her arrest, he cannot fail to see it in the newspapers. He knows of my involvement. I'm sure he knows that his sister did not commit this murder. He will realize that this is a maneuver to flush him out, but he will have no choice but to come to me, knowing that I am essentially offering his sister as a trade for the documents. It was the leverage I needed."

"But the girl, Holmes! Put in cells for a crime that she did not commit!"

"Do not fear, Watson," said Holmes, as Mrs. Hudson arrived with our tea, along with all the delicious things that went with it. "She was placed on a train and smuggled discreetly out of town. She is now residing at a very pleasant inn near Eastbourne. She is under guard, and cannot be held for long, but she has been given to understand that she is helping us in a matter of national security – which she is! – and she was quite willing to assist us. She does not seem to hold her brother's anti-government beliefs in the least."

After she set down the tray of food, Mrs. Hudson stepped across the room, fishing a telegram out of her pocket. Holmes reached for it and tore it open. He read it quickly and smiled before tossing it toward me. It was from Mycroft, and simply said:

No.

- M

I knew that he would explain it when he was ready. "So now we wait?" I asked, rising and moving toward the food.

Holmes remained in his chair. "We wait. And I do not believe that we shall have to wait for very long at all."

He settled back and reached for a pipe. Clearly he meant to think for a while, and more importantly, he seemed to have forgotten about the tea that he requested. Mrs. Hudson's good humor slowly neutralized and then evaporated, and she looked at the ignored food, then shook her head and departed. Did the door perhaps close with a little more force than usual? If so, it did not intrude whatsoever on Holmes's three-pipe cogitations.

Part V: At the Old Roman Wall

We did not have long to wait. It was not more than an hour later that a boy arrived with a handwritten message. Holmes asked Mrs. Hudson to bring the lad up, and he waited by the door, looking as if he might bolt at any second, while the message was read.

"Are you empowered to deliver a reply?" Holmes asked. The boy simply looked confused, so Holmes tried again. "Tell him we will be there. And tell him to bring the letters."

The boy nodded and slipped through the door. I heard his feet land solidly on approximately four of the seventeen steps before he was gone. "He wishes to meet in an hour, just north of the Tower, at that segment of the old Roman wall where one can cross through into the City."

"I know the place. Are you going to notify Lestrade?"

"No, we will go alone. He has no reason to harm us. After all, we all know that there is no case against his sister, but he must surely think that without me to free her from the spider's web, she might be convicted. He won't risk harming or angering me before she is free. The letters cannot be that important to him, certainly not worth the girl's freedom."

We left soon after, walking for a bit until we hired the third cab that we encountered. There was a late spring fog rising, and it was turning out to be a cool evening for June. I pulled my coat tighter.

We wound our way east and south through the thickening mist, and I began to think that an hour was not enough time to reach our goal. However, traffic thinned as we neared our destination, and visibility was not yet bad enough to substantially slow our cabbie.

We left the cab and went on foot from the north side of the Tower. I glanced at the ancient pile, thinking of other occasions that we had been there. The times – and there were more than one – when Holmes and I had prevented the thefts of the Crown Jewels. The instances when we had gone there to question men suspected of high treason. That terrifying period in '88 when we had hidden Mary there, as the men involved in the terrible crimes occurring nearby in the City had tried to find her for a different kind of leverage. And they *had* found her, leading to the shedding of their blood on the Tower grounds. But that is another tale.

Holmes led me north for a few blocks, before turning right. My eyes had adjusted to the ambient light, and I could see that we were approaching the ancient Roman wall, a part of the original enclosure of Londinium centuries before. Holmes veered slightly to the left, and we came to the opening in the wall that led through and into the City proper. There he stopped and said, "We are here."

A small, hatless man stepped out of the doorway to face us. His very pale hair seemed to glow in the near darkness, as well as making him instantly identifiable. It was Shipton. He was only about halfway between five and six feet, and couldn't have been more than ten or eleven stone. His coat was buttoned, outlining his slim and wiry frame. He seemed to bounce with a barely-suppressed energy.

"You know Emily didn't kill that man," he began. "Well, you got me where you want me, Mr. Holmes. I brought the letters. But surely you can see that what I'm trying to do here isn't all bad?"

"Exposure of evil is not a bad thing, Mr. Shipton. I have spent my whole life pursuing that purpose. But what you have chosen to do, your initial foray into this type of reform, is not the way to go about it. You have picked the wrong ammunition for the wrong target. You may think that the Crown is evil, although Watson and I will disagree with you. Each man is entitled to his opinion. But embarrassing the Queen for no reason will do nothing but rile her loyal men as if you had kicked over a bee's nest."

"But she represents what is wrong," said Shipton. "Surely you know how England has treated Scotland, and Ireland, and Wales over the years. And what about India? Why, even my home country has seen its share of abuse."

"Some of that was a long time ago," I said. "We are more enlightened now."

"Really, doctor? You can say that, after what you have seen?" He gestured behind him, to the east. "Would you care to walk with me for a quarter-hour in that direction? You've seen it all before, when the Ripper was there. I've seen some of the files. I know what went on then, and how some of the high and mighty were either the responsible parties, or else they stood by and let it happen. All under the skirts of this Queen.

"And I know what I myself have been ordered to do on occasion, Mr. Holmes, by your very own brother. He tries to justify it, saying that sometimes Britain needs a blunt instrument. I never wanted to be that, Mr. Holmes. But I never really had a choice."

"I, too, have occasionally had to be the 'blunt instrument,' Mr. Shipton. But I always tried to make sure that I was working for the greater good. Perhaps you did not have that option. You have been like a soldier, however much you were recruited against your will, and as such, you were expected to follow orders without question. It was the price you paid for an implied pardon to your crimes. But the fact that you were carrying out orders should also give you comfort in knowing that you were only doing your duty, and that the responsibility, or even guilt, lies on other men's shoulders."

"But what makes them any better to decide what is right or wrong? Who watches them? Do they justify it by simply passing the guilt on up to the next set of men?" He gave a weary little laugh and shook his head. "Well, it doesn't matter, and it's no use trying to explain it to you. It has always been that way, and it always will be. Right now it comes down to you and me, standing by this old wall, debating about the details of releasing my sister. For you know that I will give you the letters, and I believe that you will let her go. But then what? I trust you, Mr. Holmes, for it is known that you are an honorable man. Therefore, I know that there are no police here waiting to arrest me when you have the letters in hand. But what about tomorrow? What then?"

"My only brief is to recover the letters, both the original and the fake that you were supposed to plant in Rathham's office. After that, my work is done. I cannot offer you any assistance, but perhaps I could give you some advice. It might be prudent for both you and your sister to make your way to the Continent and leave England behind. Possibly to one of the neutral countries?"

Shipton nodded, and reached into his coat pocket. I tensed in spite of myself, although I did not believe that he was reaching for a weapon. In fact, he pulled out two folded packets and handed them to Holmes. "These are both of the letters," he said. "I would get them in your coat fairly quickly and examine them later, due to the dampness from the fog. You will see that they are what you are looking for. I wouldn't take a chance on risking my sister. You knew that. When will she be released?"

"Once I can look these over," said Holmes, slipping the documents under his Inverness, "I will send word to Lestrade to have her moved back to her lodgings. She is currently out of the city. Would you prefer her to be awakened and moved immediately, or in the morning?"

"The morning is fine. It will give me an opportunity to finalize my plans."

"I assume that you have funds squirreled away for such an eventuality?"

"Some. Also, I must admit that I came into another bit of money that gives me feelings of unease, but I suppose it's too late to worry about that now."

"Unease? And why is that?"

"Earlier this afternoon, before I saw that my sister had been arrested and I realized how this had to play out, I was not quite certain of my plans, including the disposition of the letter. In order to have another possible option, I sent a message to the owner of the letter, Baron Maupertuis, offering to sell it back to him. We met soon after, and I was careful that he wasn't able to identify me. Working for your brother has taught me several useful skills.

"The Baron gave me a substantial amount of money for the letter's return. I honestly told him that I did not have it with me at that time, but that I would let him know. I never intended that he should have the original, since I was going to have that published, but I was going to give him the forgery. Then he could auction it if he wanted, or not.

"He was not happy that he couldn't have the letter right then, as he had wanted to take possession of it immediately. I gathered that he had 'borrowed' the funds that he used to pay me from his employer without that man's knowledge, and he was understandably anxious to conclude our business. Having read some in the files about this Baron Maupertuis and his current employer, I could understand why he was nervous."

"Yes," said Holmes, "it does not pay to embezzle from one of the Moriartys."

"I feel no compunction to return the Baron's money, since it was dishonestly acquired by him to begin with, but if word gets to Colonel Moriarty about my having it, in spite of my efforts to hide my identity, I could be in for quite a bit of trouble. So that's an additional reason that I'm glad to be getting out of England."

"When you establish yourself in your destination and have time to ponder such things," said Holmes, "remember that there are better ways to accomplish what you tried to do here. A good government needs a balance of sensible limits and also to be able to take care of threats when necessary. We have seen when things are handled badly. Find a legitimate and helpful way to encourage things to be handled better."

Shipton nodded, and then to me as well. Turning, he slipped back through the passage through the wall and disappeared in the darkness.

Part VI: Conclusions

What remains is quickly summarized through a series of short epilogues:

A few days later, the auction of the Baron's furniture was held at Sefton's. The event was poorly attended, and the various bidders were quite unenthusiastic. Items of established historical significance went to people who would certainly appreciate them, but for very little money. Other lots with a set reserve amount were sold for that price and no more, and non-reserved items went for mere pounds.

At the side of the gallery, Baron Maupertuis, once known as Rémi Petit, watched with an increasing escalation of impatience, disbelief, and finally anger, as the possessions that he accumulated during his periods of affluence in the 1880's, those same items that he had managed to retain through legal twisting all during the years of his imprisonment, were sold for nearly nothing. And then, when it was announced at the end of the auction, that the Dickens letter had been withdrawn, there was no surprise in the room at all, except on the part of the apoplectic Baron.

For the whole matter had been explained to Rathham, who was more than grateful that the theft of the document had led to the revelation that it was a forgery. He had contacted those men who had been interested in purchasing the supposed Dickens letter, and they were quite happy to divest themselves of any connection to the matter as well. Somewhere in the whole process, no one had remembered to tell the Baron that the jewel of his crown was paste, and that not only was he not going to make a small fortune from the sale, but he wasn't going to make enough to return the money that he had stolen from Colonel Moriarty before it was discovered that it was missing.

As the auction concluded, the Baron surged to his feet, his rage directed toward Holmes, who sat beside me on the other side of the room. We were in shadows, watching the carefully contrived auction take place, but I had known from the time of our arrival that the Baron had been observing us. Now, he moved toward us, with murder written on his face.

Before he had taken more than three steps, two nondescript men that had been seated near him throughout the auction rose and took his arms, one on either side. They wore matching plain dark suits, and each had anonymous faces with small military moustaches. They were Mycroft's men, and they held the Baron motionless as if he were chained to the wall of a tomb.

Holmes and I approached him. "I was unable to find a genuine letter by Dickens that had been written on the day of his death," said Holmes, "although I did come across another document during my investigation. However, it turned out to be a forgery, and as a valuable and rehabilitated member of society, you certainly would not have wanted any association with anything like that, would you, Monsieur Petit?"

The man hissed a string of offensive words, until one of Mycroft's men shook him as if he were a rat in a terrier's mouth. "Here now, none of that." When the Baron had fallen silent, the same man said to him, "We've got orders to assist you home, or back to your place of business in Mayfair. What's it to be then?"

At the mention of the business location, the man's eyes widened with terror. He looked back at Holmes, as if he were going to ask him for help, before he realized that such a thing was outrageous. Finally, he swallowed once or twice and whispered, "Home." As the two minders led him out, he stumbled once, but they still had his arms and continued to propel him forward, his short legs working until they found the ground again. It was the last we saw of him.

Later than night, we had a visit from one of Holmes's agents, Shinwell Johnson. He had been given the task of keeping an eye on the Baron after the auction. His report was short and to the point. "If I hadn't known who he was, and hadn't been watching him right up until it happened, I wouldn't've been able to swear that it was the same man. But it was, all right. After he left the auction house, the government men took him home and left him there. He went in, and came out a quarter-hour later with a trunk. I heard him tell the cabbie to get to Victoria as fast as possible. I managed to get on the back of the cab, which is a skill from my boyhood that I continue to whet, as its usefulness never diminishes. I hopped off right before we got there, and found a place from which to watch.

"He was still opening his coin purse to pay the cabbie when the shot struck him, dead center. There wasn't any noise at all. He just went down, and at first I thought that a rock had hit him. But it took him centered on the bridge of his nose, and ruined most of his face. The bullet must have spread out something awful."

"A soft-nosed revolver bullet," said Holmes, "fired from an air gun. It's good to know, I suppose, that there was more than one of the cursed things built by von Herder. And now we know that Colonel Moriarty has it. It certainly didn't take him very long, did it?"

"Not long at all," said Johnson. Then he glanced at our open windows, and beyond to the other side of the street, toward Camden House. He had heard the story about another one of the air guns, and the time that it had been fired from there and into our sitting room. He stood up and took a step to shift himself between the windows. "I'll be off, then."

Holmes nodded. "Thank you, Johnson. I'll be in touch." The man touched his forehead and was gone. His feet made no sound on the steps, but I could hear his labored breathing as it faded away nonetheless.

The next morning, we met Mycroft at the Diogenes Club. Luckily Holmes had not expected any effusive gratitude, as there was none forthcoming.

"I suppose it was the best solution for quickly resolving the matter," said Mycroft. "I have just one question. Why did you cable me to ask if Shipton knew that the document in the safe, which he was supposed to take, was also a forgery?"

"Ah," I said. "the laconic 'No' telegram."

"I simply wished to determine if he knew the value – or lack of value – of what he had taken. If he knew that he was simply replacing one forged document for another, he would not place any value on it, and he would know that *we* did not really place any on it, either. But if he thought that he was holding a real letter by Dickens, with the power to shake the crown, he would believe that he held something that was valuable enough to use in order to redeem his sister from the police."

Mycroft nodded. "I do wish, however, that you hadn't taken it upon yourself to allow Shipton to go free. Not – " he said quickly, as Holmes attempted to disagree, " – that your solution isn't what I would have ended up doing myself. It was rather tidy, actually, with a simple elegance. After all, he had only made the *threat* of releasing the letter to spoil the Jubilee, he hadn't actually done it yet. His only real crime was stealing the document from the safe, and that was done under orders. He disobeyed me in that he didn't leave the false replacement where he was told, or bring the supposed authentic letter from the safe back to me, but that is more of an internal administrative issue, rather than breaking a law."

"So my solution, and letting the man escape, is not going to result in *my* arrest, then?" said Holmes with a smile.

"No, no. It had a certain *finesse*. Baron Maupertuis is no longer a problem. Shipton and his sister 'escaped' the morning after you met with him, without any hindrance. And you did resolve the whole thing rather quickly. I think that we may consider this matter successfully concluded.

"Now, is it too early for a sip of Tokay? The quality has been off the last few years, but I managed to acquire a certain amount back in '74, in gratitude for a little matter in which I played a helpful part. I highly recommend it – only twelve bottles remain from this vintage, and nine of them are downstairs in the cellar. Let me ring to have one brought up, and then you can tell me how you plan to avoid the Jubilee celebrations. If any of your ideas have merit, I may join you."

The Tangled Skein at
Birling Gap

On the southbound train from London that Saturday morning, I had been fortunate enough to glance up from my newspaper in time to spot the ancient chalk man carved into the hillside, westward towards Wilmington. I was closer to my destination than I had realized, and began to ready myself for arrival.

In no time at all, I was standing in the Eastbourne station, waiting for the inevitable confusion that follows an arrival to clear. I was surprised that there had been so many other people making their way down from London and in this direction, but that September had produced some quite pleasant days, and I supposed there was no better time for taking a holiday, as most of my fellow travelers were. I was not averse to spending some time at the coast as well, but in my case, I had been summoned to provide assistance to my friend, Sherlock Holmes, now living in supposed retirement on the Downs, only a couple of miles west of where I now stood.

A man wearing a driving hat, with goggles pushed up, was leaning against the wall near the open exit to the station. As he spotted me, he straightened and walked my way. "Dr. Watson?" he asked.

I acknowledged the fact, and he identified himself as Hipkins, down from London to act as Holmes's factotum during the upcoming matter, which had attracted interest from the highest quarter. His voice was odd, both flat and a little too loud. I deduced that he had type of damage to his hearing, either congenital or resulting from a later cause.

We stepped out to the street, where Hipkins had parked a disreputable-looking Rover, at least two or three years old. He reached to load my luggage, in this case a single worn portmanteau of black, dull leather. My travel kit is never elaborate due to my former military background, but in this case

I was journeying with somewhat more than usual. Hipkins pulled on a pair of driving gloves, and we set off slowly down the crowded street, picking up speed as we reached the road out of town toward Friston and East Dean.

I had a chance to study my driver as he fought with the automobile. He was a tall, thin man, with sallow skin and the look of a malnourished youth that gave me to believe he had grown up in one of the rawer quarters of London. Except for the fairly new-looking goggles, his clothing was worn and well-used, but clean. Before he had pulled on his gloves, I had noticed that his hands looked as if they had done their share of past work.

When we reached the first road that angled to the south, toward Beachy Head, I was surprised that we did not make the turn toward Holmes's residence, situated as it was on the road running parallel to the great chalk cliffs. It was there that he maintained the reclusive illusion of keeping bees. Oh, to be sure, there was an apiary there, and Holmes was quite interested in studying it. But his retirement had served multiple purposes besides watching the wee creatures (as Mrs. Hudson called them,) some of which I do not propose to relate at this time.*

One of the reasons for his move to this part of Sussex, back in October 1903, was to be able to surreptitiously increase the level of his assistance in the work of his brother Mycroft, who has been described broadly but accurately as sometimes being *the* British Government.

In those days, it had been feared by some, but not all, at the highest levels in government that a massive European war was inevitable, if not in a few years then certainly in a decade or so. Therefore, it had become imperative that someone of Holmes's intelligence and skill be available and at the forefront of the preparations, providing his own special abilities toward those matters that absolutely needed him – and only him. And that was

* Editor's Note: See "The Adventure of the Missing Missing Link" in *The Papers of Sherlock Holmes* Volume I (2013).

partially why I had traveled to Sussex that late summer morning in 1905. For a child had been taken, and even though no threats other than a ransom demand to the family had been made, it was postulated that the kidnapping might be used to pressure the child's father, a man of some influence, to make some move that would aid a future enemy.

Hipkins was not a talkative driver, possibly self-conscious about his speaking voice, and he simply gestured ahead of us along the Friston Road when he perceived my confusion when we did not turn directly toward Holmes's villa. I call it a *villa* because that is how Holmes refers to it, when he is not calling it a farm, but in truth it is a serviceable stone home, with a couple of acres of walled gardens, surrounded by the Downs and located just north and downhill from the highest of the chalk cliffs looking out over the channel. It is a site with a long history in that area, known locally as "H------- Farm." The house, consisting of a ground floor and cozy first floor as well, is surrounded by trees, and there is a barn of sorts on the eastern side of the property. Toward the southwest, the Downs slope gradually toward Birling Gap (which both Holmes and I have at times referred to by the less-identifying and anonymously British *nom* of "Fulworth.") Holmes had been given the property years before, following the successful conclusion to an investigation that we had conducted in the area*, and had joked in the years following, when the Capital had proved particularly vexatious, that one day he would retire there and keep bees. Little did I realize that when it was necessary for Holmes to leave both London and his practice at the unlikely age of forty-nine, he would ensconce himself in the beautiful southern Sussex countryside.

* Editor's Note: For more information regarding Holmes's acquisition in 1900 of his retirement cottage in Sussex, listen to "The Adventure of the Out-Of-Date Murder" from *The New Adventures of Sherlock Holmes* Radio Show (September 17, 1945), or read about it in *The Lost Adventures of Sherlock Holmes* (1989), transcribed by Ken Greenwald.

Hipkins's car traveled past the East Dean turn as well, with the small village on the left, and Friston rising above us on the right. I began to wonder exactly where we were going. The answer was obvious in mere moments, as we topped the hill, and the vehicle slowed and then stopped outside the stone wall of the ancient St. Mary the Virgin Church. Through the greenery growing over the stones, I could see Holmes walking in the graveyard, reading the markers, and pushing back the grass where it was long with his stick.

After I had retrieved my single bag, Hipkins dismissed himself, turning and driving back down the hill toward Eastbourne. I did not question this, trusting that he understood his own purpose and role in the matter. But I did realize that I was now a mile or two from Holmes's villa, and still in possession of my bag. I foresaw an uncomfortable job of carrying it.

"Not to worry, Watson," said Holmes as I entered the graveyard. "We will make a stop or two on the way back, and I will do my share of acting as a pack mule if the need arises."

I suppose that my thoughts must have been visible on my face, as had been the case so many times before. I was not surprised at all, only happy to see my friend, since I had not set eyes on him for several weeks. On that last occasion, he had been in London carrying out more of his secret business, and had stopped at its conclusion to share a meal with my wife and me in our Queen Anne Street lodgings. It frequently seemed to amuse him that my home and practice were located in the same building that in times past had been a residence of Boswell.

I looked back and forth around the peaceful graveyard. "A fine place to spend eternity," I said.

"I doubt," replied Holmes, "that this hillside will outlast eternity."

"Well, certainly, everything will fade away. That is the nature of things. One only has to look at some of these stones to see that even they cannot resist time. In terms of how long the church has stood here, in one form or another, they have barely been here for any time at all."

"In this instance, I was referring to the very land upon which we stand. At some point, this spot will crumble into the sea."

"It will be some time before that happens," I said. "We are surely a mile back from the edges of the cliffs."

"Yes, but a few feet gone, year after year, century after century, and eventually our descendants will have to redraw their maps. As our friend, Hatherley, the hydraulic engineer, told us when he made that unexpected visit four years ago to introduce his latest child, water is the great leveler. Given time, it will dissolve or wear away everything, even the very land that pokes its way above the oceans."

With this cheery thought, Holmes led me over to a wooden bench, one of several scattered about the graveyard. Some were tucked under the trees along the bordering stone walls, but this one was in the open, with a magnificent view of the Downs. Behind us was the church, parts of it nearing a thousand years in age. A hill rose to the south, and in the distance we could see a couple walking on one of the footpaths that crisscrossed the grass. The birds were flying to and fro, catching the late-season insects. It was hard to believe that somewhere, probably near by, a small boy was being held captive. I refused to believe that he might already be dead.

Holmes and I spent a good three-quarters of an hour seated there in the graveyard, going over his plans for that day and night. It was warm and peaceful, and there was nothing fearful about the place in that bright morning, although I must confess that it might have had a different atmosphere on a windy autumn night.

I listened as Holmes complained that his involvement in the matter, at the specific request of Lord Holdhurst himself, had seriously interrupted his observations of his bees. I smiled to myself, knowing that Holmes would never have refused his assistance in such an affair. I also wondered if he was starting to begin to believe more in the fictional picture of a hermit that he had so carefully created, primarily a solitary and dedicated beekeeper, and only rarely a specially-skilled consultant, currently put out to pasture.

Lord Holdhurst, now quite ancient, was a close friend of the boy's father, the Earl of H-----, and it was he who had involved Holmes in the matter. The boy had been taken undetected two nights earlier from his own bedroom. A note had arrived with the post the next morning, before the boy was even discovered to be missing, asking for a substantial amount of money, with terms of delivery to be arranged later. The note read that police involvement was forbidden, upon threat of the boy's life. However, Lord Holdhurst, when advising his old friend, had pointed out that there was no injunction against involving Holmes, who now lived in Sussex, not far from the Earl's estate.

Holmes had spent less than a day, in disguise, tracing the man who had sent the letter through the local countryside. "It was mere child's play, Watson," he had told me. "The letter was mailed from the local post office. I must admit that I had a bit of luck. A man had come in on the afternoon before the child was found to be missing, and dropped a letter into the outgoing basket just as the post office was shutting up for the day. This was before the child had even been taken. The postmistress started to tell the man that she had already gathered the outgoing letters, and that he was too late, but the man was gone. Then she looked and saw that it was a local letter, being sent to the Earl's home, which is very unusual in these parts, as the locals do *not* send letters to the Earl. She recognized the man as someone she had recently seen going occasionally into the local pub down the street. Upon further questioning, the woman's husband had seen the man there a few times over the last few days as well, but did not know him."

Holmes had not wasted time trying to determine how the kidnapper had entered the estate undetected, or had managed to get away with the boy. Rather, he asked around the villages until he found other people who had seen the man who sent the random letter. By working backwards along this fellow's route, Holmes had identified where he was staying, in a lonely and recently rented cottage a few miles to the north, and subsequently his identity, one Les Chetwood. Holmes had set quiet inquiries in motion, quickly learning what he could. But there was no immediate sign of accomplices, if any, or of the boy, and he did not want to take the fellow into custody without knowing where the child was being held, or if there were other confederates involved. The Earl was adamant that the ransom must be paid as demanded, to ensure the boy's safety.

Holmes had sent to London to request the assistance of Hipkins, whom he had used in the past for various matters. A second note then arrived from the kidnappers, also mailed locally, arranging for the daylight exchange of the money in a nearby inn, which was described as a "neutral location." At that point, Holmes had sent a wire with specific instructions, requesting my presence as well.

I glanced at my watch. The ransom exchange was scheduled to take place within the hour. It was to be in the open, where we would pass over the money, and then, after the man receiving it – presumably Chetwood – safely took it away, the child would be released. Holmes was not happy with the situation, and some aspects about it still puzzled him, but he agreed that retrieving the child safely was the most important consideration, and that it would be fairly easy to pull in his net with the kidnapper – or kidnappers – caught in it later.

Thus, it was due to this ransomed child that I came to be in Sussex on that beautiful morning. But very quickly, unrelated events intruded upon us after our graveyard meeting, unraveling the proposal to deliver the payment, as well as doing much to tangle Holmes's other plans.

I knew that Holmes was not telling me everything, but he had shared what he felt that I needed to know. Having come to the logical conclusion of our discussion, Holmes stood abruptly. "Now," he said, "let us make our way down to East Dean, where your arrival will be noted with interest by at least one individual."

I lifted my bag, and we started down the path, separated by a thick hedge from the road which I had so recently traveled upon. I noticed that, even this late in the year, bees were working with great energy all around us. Leaning in, I looked more closely at an industrious little fellow and joked, "One of yours?"

"Hardly," Holmes replied. "You will notice the slightly tapered abdomen. This is a type of hornet, with remnants perhaps of the European honeybee in its makeup. I hope that they do not encounter my bees, as I fear the outcome." I leaned back slowly in order not to alarm the hornet or to seem too concerned in front of my friend. Over the last year or so, I had become used to Holmes's hives, and had come to an uneasy truce with, and even appreciation of, their residents. I certainly appreciated the honey that they provided on those regular visits that I made to Holmes's villa. Once or twice he had sent jars with me back to London. But I had no wish to have any closer associations with these hornet-like chaps, here in this enclosed hedged path leading down toward the village inn.

We walked for a few minutes in silence, each appreciating the wide views through gaps in the foliage, and anticipating the meeting that we expected upon our arrival. As we approached the village green and the buildings surrounding it, I wondered how many other people on strange missions had met over the years at that inn, which had been standing there now at that location for hundreds of years, and had frequently been the haunt in times past of coastal smugglers. Our appointment today was just the latest in a long list of quiet arrangements there, and no doubt there would be many others to come in the future.

Stepping onto the green, Holmes indicated for me to wait a moment as he went into a nearby stone building. I knew that he had use of some space in the structure, as well as an arrangement to receive messages there, along with what little mail that might find its way to him from individuals who had worked out that he lived in this part of Sussex, while not specifically knowing where. Although he cultivated, with my assistance, the impression of being a reclusive hermit, he did still take on the occasional private consulting job, in addition to those affairs which were assigned to him by his brother. I had the impression that Mycroft did not discourage the private investigations, as they managed to give the impression that Holmes was in Sussex on a full-time basis, being . . . Holmes.

My friend stepped out of the house, holding an unfolded note. He informed me that the members of his household, including Mrs. Hudson, were still in London, staying in Baker Street, and that we would be making do for ourselves, at least for a few days. After Holmes's retirement, Mrs. Hudson had joined him in Sussex, but had retained the lease on 221. When Holmes went back to the Capital on one of his activities for his brother, he regularly used it as a staging area, rather like one of his other London hidey-holes, and often in secret. During the periods when it stood unoccupied, Mycroft made sure that the place was well-kept and cared for.

We reached the door of the inn, ducking our heads as we went inside. I am a fairly big man, having played rugby in my youth, and my friend is very tall. Neither was the common size centuries earlier when the Tiger Inn's doorway was constructed.

The room was cozy and clean, with a bar across from us, and sunlit rooms opening to either the right or left. Standing and sipping a cold beer was my driver and Holmes's agent, Hipkins, now missing his driving hat and goggles. He ignored us, and Holmes led me to a nearby corner table in the shadows along the front wall, opposite the bar.

I looked around the taproom, representative of the finest aspects of so many similar inns and gathering places throughout Britain. The great hooded fireplace across the room from our table would make the place very snug indeed on those cold winter nights so close to the sea.

We sat down, and I pulled my case back behind my feet under the table. It made a rough sound as I dragged it along the floor, and Holmes said softly, "Did you pack too many extra collars along with your toothbrush?"

"No," I replied quietly, "just too much ammunition to go with the service revolver in my pocket."

At that moment, a small man appeared from one of the back rooms, to the left of the door. Holmes gave a small nod. This, then, was our man, Les Chetwood, the kidnapper that Holmes had managed to identify. He had a pint of something dark gripped in his right hand, and he squinted as he came into the darker room. As he paused for a moment in the low doorway, I had a chance to examine him. He was dressed in wool from head-to-toe, buttoned up and looking too warm for this late summer heat. He had a pale face, with some color on his cheeks that did not seem normal for him. He had thin, sandy hair, brushed straight forward and down toward his eyes. A soft mouth gave an initial impression of weakness, but there was an animal cunning that brightened his gaze as he finally recognized us. As he was taking a step toward us, the front door flew open with a crash, and a tall man in a Coast Guard uniform stepped in.

As the new fellow stopped to let his eyes adjust, Chetwood froze, looking back and forth from the newcomer to our table. No doubt to him, the man just entering appeared to be dressed in some variation of a police uniform.

His eyes having adjusted, the man in uniform saw us and his eyes lit up. "Mr. Holmes!" he cried. "It is so fortunate that you are here! I don't doubt that you would have been summoned at some point."

Chetwood, frozen in the door to the side room, our only link to pay the ransom and retrieve the boy, quickly set his glass on the bar and moved toward the door like an animal escaping a trap. Sliding around the man in uniform, he pushed open the door and was gone.

Under his breath, Holmes said, "Blast!" He tensed, as if starting to rise, before changing his mind. Realizing that to pursue Chetwood might make things worse, he settled back toward his seat and said with a sigh, "What is the problem, Commander?"

"Murder, Mr. Holmes! Down at the Coast Guard residences atop the cliffs. I came up to find Constable Anderson. He is getting ready to join me now in his house across the road – he was out working in his garden, you see, it being a Saturday. He told me to wait for him here, and then we would go down together." The fellow was obviously overwrought, his words tumbling out, one atop another.

Holmes caught Hipkins's eye, nodding toward the door. Hipkins nodded and slipped out of the inn. "Hipkins will follow him," Holmes whispered to me. The sound of the Commander's voice had attracted attention in the back, and a girl appeared through a doorway behind the bar. "Something for Commander Teague," said Holmes in a normal tone.

"Thank you, sir," said Teague, as the girl pulled a tall cider for him, already knowing exactly what he would request. "This has made me all rattled, and that's for sure." As he took a long draw from the glass, I had a chance to examine him. Middle-aged, soft-looking, no wedding ring. A career man in a backwater post. "We would have called you in, sir, I'm sure of it," said the commander. "What with someone of your reputation living amongst us now, so close, we would have been fools not to. Old Mr. Emerson would expect it."

"Mr. Emerson?" questioned Holmes, still irritated at the interruption of our other business, but becoming intrigued by this matter as well. "And he would be – "

"He is the grandfather of the murdered man," said Teague. "Ebersole Emerson, of Manchester."

"Ah," replied Holmes, "the celebrated and self-made industrialist."

"That's right, sir," said Teague. "It is his grandson, Lieutenant Andrew Warren, who has died not half-an-hour ago in his bed in the guard houses, and not a mark on him."

"You said 'murder'," I interrupted. "Was it poison?"

"Well, to be honest, I don't know. I wasn't there when he died, although two of the other lieutenants currently on station were. I was summoned in just after, being in command, you see. From how it was described to me, I would have thought it might be some type of seizure, except that Warren was able to gasp out 'murder' to his two mates before he went.

"The duty roster is rather light, today being Saturday you understand, and it's never very demanding there at the worst of times. There are never many of us assigned here anymore, even during the season. As I mentioned, I am in charge, and as soon as I heard, I put my second to watch the two men who were with

140

Warren when he died, and set out as fast as I could to find the constable."

I could see that Holmes was about to ask another question, but the door opened, interrupting him. It was Anderson, the constable for that area. He was a large man with a strong touch of Scandinavia somewhere in his background. I had met him several times before, while visiting Holmes on other occasions.

He seemed as pleased as Teague had been at finding Holmes in the inn. A quick recap of what Teague had told us was enough to get him moving. He led us outside and down the narrow lane, away from the green and onto the small road that wound south toward the sea. His wagon was already hitched and waiting, and we climbed aboard and set forth. Personally I was glad to be pulled by a horse, and not conveyed by another automobile.

The way was not far, but there would have been enough time to talk. However, Holmes pointedly did not ask any further questions, preferring to wait until we reached the scene of the murder so that he could form his own impressions, instead of those that were filtered through the eyes of Commander Teague. Seeing that Holmes did not want to overhear Anderson asking anything either, the constable instead talked to me.

"I've been reading your stories to my boy," he said. "He's five now, so he doesn't understand it all, but he's bright, and he follows most of it."

We passed wide grassy fields on the left, and sloping up toward stands of trees on the right. Both fields were filled with sheep that paused in their grazing to watch us, with one or two trotting curiously toward the fences for a few steps before stopping to watch us pass.

"After one of the stories," continued Anderson, "I asked him if he wanted to be a detective like Mr. Holmes. Do you know what he said, doctor?" he asked enthusiastically. I smiled politely and said that I did not. "He said that he wanted to be a 'p'liceman' like his da." Anderson beamed with pride.

I murmured that he was fortunate indeed, and wondered privately how many other professions the boy might choose between now and when he reached his majority.

Within a few minutes, the land on either side of the road opened, and I could see the abrupt edge of the horizon that indicated the cliffs were rising before us. The road aimed toward a lower spot, where a cluster of buildings had been constructed. I knew that even here, the land did not open directly onto the beach. Rather, the cliff line dipped, and was simply lower than what was on either side. This was Birling Gap, where the Coast Guard cottages were located, as well as some other newer homes stretching up the hill to the west.

"The road here used to go all the way down to the beach, long ago," said Anderson, nodding ahead. "As the cliffs have fallen away over the years, the gap there that sloped gently down to the sea and gave the old smuggler's wagons access to it in dark of night has cracked away and been lost. I fear that eventually the cliffs will keep falling, a bit at a time, until they take the whole village." I thought of Holmes's earlier comments regarding the little church and graveyard with sadness.

At Birling Gap, the road upon which we traveled turned sharply east, back toward Eastbourne. Holmes's villa was less than a mile in that direction, but that was not where we were going. Our destination was that grim set of buildings on our immediate left as we faced the sea, perched back from the cliff top, where the Coast Guard kept a few men stationed. According to what Teague had told us, there weren't many men there right now, but I was unsure whether this was a seasonal choice, or simply because the place was slowly being abandoned. I didn't see any men in uniform standing outside, although there were certainly clusters here and there of civilians, residents of the nearby cottages, no doubt, pointing and whispering. Some, having spotted our wagon, began to gesture in our direction. Was it because of the arrival of the constable, I wondered, or perhaps at the unexpected appearance of the famed and celebrated local personality, that retired consulting detective down from London only a couple of years earlier, and still not here long enough to be considered a true resident?

We stopped in front of one of the central buildings, a two-storied affair that did not seem to be too unpleasant, compared to some military-type residences where I have been quartered. We climbed to the ground, and I struggled as I lifted my heavy travel case. "You can leave that in the wagon, doctor," said Anderson, but I simply shook my head.

Teague led us inside and upstairs to the room of the dead man, Warren. It was a dark and windowless room, reached by a single door from the hall. The hallway itself had a window, which allowed a small amount of light into what was little more than a cell. Warren was laid out on his bed, his limbs contorted and wound in the twisted sheets. He was in his uniform. There was only a strong lantern lighting the room, which was very close indeed. In addition to Holmes and myself, Anderson, and Teague, the room also contained two uniformed men sitting upright on chairs just inside the door, and another small and grim-looking fellow, also in uniform, standing over them. From the way that he was addressed by Teague, he was obviously the second-in-command left in charge.

"You didn't have to keep them in here with the body, Fellows!" he cried.

"You did not specify, sir," said Fellows with grim authority. "I thought that facing the victim might force the guilty party to confess."

Teague turned away, muttering, "Idiot," under his breath. Then, as an afterthought, he turned back to his second. "Did it work?" he asked.

"No, sir," replied Fellows. "The only one that said anything was Lester, here, who begged that we might shut Warren's eyes." Fellows glanced at the man on the right, apparently Lester, as if he had admitted his guilt then and there by such an action. Lester was slumped in his chair, his hand to his face, shielding his view of the unfortunate on the bed. "I knew better," continued Fellows, "than to tamper with the body, sir."

143

"Quite right, quite right," said Teague, turning back to Holmes, who was already leaning over the bed. He was muttering to himself, patting the man's clothing, examining his hands, and finally leaning in to smell the dead man's mouth.

"Fresh uniform," said Holmes. "He had not slept in it. He had arisen and prepared for the day. He is freshly shaved, as confirmed by the used razor, and also the ewer and bowl of soapy water on the table there. Rough going by lantern light."

We looked toward the wall where the plain table stood. It held the shaving implements, as well as a tall mirror, the previously mentioned lantern, and a few other objects of interest. Holmes moved in the direction of the table, saying as he went, "Watson, would you mind examining the body?"

I bent to my task as Holmes made his inspection of the table. Anderson did not say a word, having completely given the matter over to Holmes. The four guardsmen clustered along their wall, with Fellows giving frequent glances to the two seated men, as if one or both were about to bolt.

I examined the victim, who looked back at me with the filmy gaze of the dead. "Shutting his eyes now," I said softly, doing so. I saw no evidence of rigor, although I would not have expected it to have manifested so quickly, unless Warren had been diabetic. His hands were smooth, with no roughening indicating any laborious activities. Finally, I copied Holmes's actions and smelled the man's mouth. Then I arose and joined Holmes at the table.

He was kneeling, so that his eyes were at a level with items on the table top. Besides those that were related to shaving, there was a fairly new and open bottle of peach brandy with its top lying beside it, some plain brown wrapping paper, wrinkled and torn, and a single glass with dregs of liquid within it, presumably a portion of the brandy.

"Pray," said Holmes, "take special care not to touch the bottle or the glass."

I nodded, and then leaned over carefully and sniffed first the glass, and then the open bottle top.

"Cyanide," I said softly, so that only Holmes could hear me. "The same odor still lingers on his lips."

"Quite," he said. Straightening himself, he pivoted and took a couple of steps across the small room, placing himself in front of the seated guardsmen.

"I understand that Lieutenant Warren said the word 'murder' during his final struggles. Is that correct?"

Both of the seated men nodded. "Did he say anything else? Anything at all?"

The fellow on the left shook his head, while the man Lester said, "He seemed to be in too much pain to say much of anything."

"Show them," said Fellows, abruptly. Both seated men looked blankly at him. The one on the left revealed, upon slightly turning his head, a set of finger-spaced scratches, still raw, down the right side of his face.

"Show them, Lester," said Fellows again. "Show them your coat."

Lester rolled his eyes in disgust. Then he plucked out the coat in question and revealed that there was a missing button, the loose threads still prominently attached and quite obvious.

Fellows took a step toward us and held out his hand. Resting on it was a matching button. "This rolled out of Warren's right hand after he died," he said with little-disguised triumph. Clearly, he thought that he had the evidence that solved the case.

Lester snorted in disgust. "When we heard him having his attack, we ran in to see what was the matter with him. Gates and I leaned over the bunk, trying to hold him steady. He must have grabbed the button then as he grasped at me."

"No doubt," said Holmes, reaching to take it from Fellows. "Is that when Lieutenant Warren scratched your face as well, Lieutenant Gates?"

Gates, the man on our left, involuntarily moved his hand toward his face. "Don't touch it," I said. "We don't want that to get infected. I will clean it momentarily."

Gates nodded, and answered Holmes. "Yes, sir. He was bent backwards, almost double at one point, with his teeth clenched in

145

agony. His hand got loose and swiped at my face. I didn't even know it had happened until later, when things settled down."

"There is evidence of the tissue scratched from your face under the nails of his left hand. You stood on that side," he said, pointing to the side of the bed corresponding with the victim's left hand. Gates nodded. Turning back to Fellows, Holmes said, "Why did you assume the button to be of significance? Wouldn't the scratches have also been an indication of possible guilt, according to your way of thinking?"

Fellows was at a loss, finally saying something about a detective story that he had once read as a boy, wherein a button found in the dead man's hand had been of the greatest significance. Holmes turned away from him in disgust. To me, he said quietly, "I do not have time for this, Watson. We must wrap this thing up and return our attention to more important matters."

"A murder is also important, Holmes," I murmured.

"In this case we can only avenge a death. In the other we can perhaps prevent one." Then, to the larger group, he asked, "Who is the woman that Warren has been seeing?"

There was silence for just a moment, and then Teague said, "Why, that would be Miss Collins, from one of the cottages up the hill. But how did you know about her?"

Holmes waved an impatient hand. "I must speak with her. These are not exactly appropriate surroundings, although I suppose that we could . . . ." He seemed to lose himself in his own thoughts for a moment, before returning. "No," he said. "I had thought that it might be of some benefit to question her here, in the presence of the victim, but perhaps it would be better to do so at her own home. Do you think that she is there now?"

"She should be," said Teague, glancing inexplicably toward Lester of the missing button. Lester did not notice, as his gaze was directed toward the floor.

"Then let us be off," said Holmes. Then, to Teague and Anderson he said, "Get these men out of here, and lock this room up tight. Make sure that no one touches anything in here. And Anderson, in that group of villagers standing around outside, is there someone that you trust?"

"Yes, sir," replied the constable.

"Excellent. Put him in a chair in front of this door. I want no one to enter it until we get back."

"Right away," said Anderson, hurrying out of the room.

By the time we had moved to the hallway, and Teague had locked the door, Anderson was back with a gnarled man, old before his time, a former soldier from the look of him. "Brown, here, will do," said Anderson. Holmes nodded and quietly gave the man his instructions before putting him in a chair before the door. The man crossed his arms, planted his feet firmly on the weathered floorboards, and looked as if the Devil himself would not get by.

I requested some medical supplies, and quickly treated the scratches on Gates's face. While I did so, Holmes took possession of the room key from Teague and slipped it into his pocket. Holmes, Anderson, Teague, and I then exited the building and started walking west toward a line of cottages stretching up to the end of a lane that terminated at the top of the hill. I shifted my heavy travel bag from side to side as we ascended.

Teague chatted at Holmes as we walked, pointing out this and that as we went, and toward the last house at the top, known as "The Haven." It had a corner tower and a slate roof, and had recently been taken by the Bellamys, a local family that owned all the boats and bathing cots there in Birling Gap. "The daughter, Maud, is quite a beauty," said Teague. "She's going to be the cause of trouble around here someday, mark my words."

"Is she relevant to today's affair?" snapped Holmes shortly. "Does this Miss Bellamy have any association with the dead man or the other lieutenants?"

"No," replied Teague, in a more subdued voice. "No, I don't suppose she does. It is Miss Collins that we go to see. Although I can tell you that, in my experience, if two beauties such as Miss Bellamy and Miss Collins are living in such a small village as this over too long a time, there will be fireworks, and that's for sure!"

"Tell me of this Miss Collins," said Holmes, turning away from Teague and toward Anderson, who gathered his thoughts for a moment. We were nearing our destination, and as the man needed more time to answer, he stopped in the lane, really little more than a rutted path. We turned to face him.

"She is an American girl, probably not more than twenty years old. She and her father leased one of the houses back in the early summer. They only have a local woman that they hired for cooking and housekeeping. They don't have visitors, and there has been idle speculation as to why they would shut themselves up in this little corner of the world.

"Of course, a girl like her is bound to attract some attention. She's a dainty thing, with fine blonde hair and blue eyes. Some of the ladies here do not care for her. The landlord at the Tiger, for one, told me that his wife believes the Collins girl is going to cause some strife, but perhaps I am just being unfair and repeating gossip."

At this point, Teague interrupted. "In any case, it was not long after she and her father arrived that she took up with Lieutenant Lester, whom you just met. We've had a difficult time keeping his mind on his duties, and he used to make any excuse that he could make to slip away and see his Edith. That is, Miss Collins.

"Then, inexplicably, a couple of weeks ago, she turned her attentions to the dead man, Lieutenant Warren, Lester's cousin."

"What?" exclaimed Holmes. "There is a family connection between the two of them?"

"That's right," said Teague. "First cousins."

"I thought that he seemed rather more shaken about the death than Gates," I said.

"So is Lester also a grandson of the industrialist, Emerson?"

"That I would not know," said Teague. "I try not to delve too closely into any of the lads' backgrounds."

He was finished speaking, and Holmes did not ask any further questions. We turned and resumed walking until we reached a plain-looking house about halfway up the slope. The grounds were tidy without being immaculate. Somehow, the place did not seem to have any personality, having gained nothing from its residents.

Anderson knocked on the door, with no response. He tried again, with more force, and in a few minutes the door was thrown open by a short, solid man, his face red with anger.

"What is it?" he asked in an abrasive American accent. "We don't want any!"

"I am Constable Anderson," said the man patiently. "There has been a murder at the guard houses, and we need to speak to you and your daughter about it."

"A murder?" cried the man. "Well, it has nothing to do with us!" He began to shut the door, but the constable's large boot had edged in to block the way.

"Police business," Anderson said in a flat tone, pushing the door steadily open. He took a step forward and said, after he was inside, "May we come in?"

The man, presumably Mr. Collins and the father of the girl in question, gave up with sullen acceptance and allowed us to pass. We found ourselves in a plainly furnished front room, with a large window looking out and down the hill, toward the small cluster of buildings. One could easily see the groups of people still standing and discussing amongst themselves. There would have been no way to spend any time in this room and not see that something was happening there.

Mr. Collins walked ahead of us, and then turned and planted his feet. The light from the window showed a network of fine lines across his choleric face, a visage that was marked with foul passions and ill tempers.

On a chair near the window was a girl, as opposite from her father as could be in every way, the late-morning sunshine reflecting from her blonde hair. With the light behind her, she appeared angelic. However, when she stood and took a step toward us, there was something wrong in some subtle way, almost too insignificant to be noticed. Perhaps it was just a smile behind her eyes, even as her face showed horror as she asked in a throaty whisper, "There has been a murder?"

No one immediately answered as the girl resumed her seat. Anderson remained standing near the front door, while the rest of us found chairs. Then, Holmes faced her and began to speak.

"That is correct, Miss Collins. Lieutenant Warren of the guards was poisoned this morning, and is dead. We understand that you and he had been seeing something of each other in recent weeks."

"No!" she said. "Not Andrew!"

"Now, wait a minute," said her father, standing near his daughter. "What are you trying to do? We barely knew any of those people."

"Nevertheless," said Holmes, "this is a very small community, and it is known that your daughter had been associated with the dead man. We would not be doing our duty if we did not at least ask her a question or two." Turning back to face the girl, he said, "Clearly, this has upset you." He reached into his pocket, fishing out a silver case. "Would you care for a cigarette?"

Mr. Collins bellowed, and Anderson muttered something about the inappropriateness of offering something like that to a delicate lady. Teague simply looked scandalized. Holmes raised his eyebrows in innocence and returned the case to his pocket.

"My apologies. I have often found the use of tobacco to be relaxing, and thought that Miss Collins might benefit from it as well." Turning back to her, he said, "Is there any information whatsoever that you can provide for us that might help to clear up this matter?"

"No," she said, softly. "Nothing at all. Andrew, that is to say, Lieutenant Warren and I were simply acquaintances, that's all. I enjoyed talking with him, and sometimes walking along the shingle at the base of the steps. He had traveled some in his youth, and was full of such interesting stories. It is so lonely here, ever since father chose to come to this place. I was just – " She stopped, dropping her head with a small sob.

We were all silent for a moment, embarrassed and not sure what to say. Then Holmes reached into another pocket and pulled out his small memorandum book, a gift from a grateful former

150

client. It was small, only three inches tall, and about two inches wide. The book consisted of a mirrored metal case, enclosing minute sheets of notepaper inside, and it had been useful to Holmes on at least two occasions, not for making notes, but for signaling by turning the mirrored surface this way and that into the sun. I myself had fond memories of that memorandum book, as once it had helped to save our lives.

Holmes fished the stub of a pencil out of his pocket, opened the book, and wrote quickly for a moment or two on one of the tiny pages. Then he closed the book and rested its metal surface on one knee as he spoke to Miss Collins, who had raised her head in curiosity in the meantime, to see what Holmes was doing.

"I have prepared a statement, just a sentence really, indicating that you know nothing of this matter. Would you care to read and sign it?"

She nodded, and he handed her the case. She opened it, and read aloud, repeating what Holmes had essentially just said. " 'I, Edith Collins, know nothing about the murder of Lieutenant Andrew Warren.' "

"Here now," said her father. "Why do you want her to sign that, anyway? My daughter isn't signing anything." He began to reach for the notebook, but Holmes was quicker, retrieving it from her hand.

"Oh well," he said, taking it back. I noticed that he held the shiny case by the edges, and did not return it to his pocket. "It is not necessary, and perhaps you are right, sir. I apologize if I have overstepped my welcome."

"Quite right, you have," muttered Collins.

Holmes rose abruptly. "Gentlemen, our business is elsewhere, then. Thank you both for your time."

I could tell that both Anderson and Teague were surprised that we had made the effort to climb the hill and take the time to see the lady, only to leave almost immediately. Anderson, having worked with Holmes on a few occasions in the past, probably had an inkling that Holmes was working toward some goal. I, who knew Holmes much better, was certain of it, and besides that, I was fairly sure that he must have managed to accomplish it.

Before I knew it, we were back outside and on the lane, walking down toward the low area that was Birling Gap. Anderson and Teague were out in front of us, speaking about the murder, and more specifically, about how someone like Miss Collins could not help but to be a motivation for a passionate crime. Holmes and I fell back, and then stopped altogether. I set my travel bag on the ground by my feet. Anderson and Teague noticed our absence and turned, but Holmes waved them on, and they continued their walk down the hill. I nodded toward Holmes's hand, which still carefully held the metallic memorandum book by its edges.

"Did you get what you needed?" I asked.

"I believe so," he said. "I want just a moment to examine this when we return to the guard houses." He held it up, turning it this way and that in the light. "It is likely that our first arrow hit the bulls-eye. If it had not, we might have found it necessary to repeat the same subterfuge with Miss Maud Bellamy.

"I would like to finish this distraction up quickly and get back to our real business. I'm taking something of a short-cut through this murder, although perhaps a leap would be a better metaphor, as we are so close to the cliffs. But if it works out, we can quickly put this distraction behind us."

He glanced back toward the house, and his eyes narrowed. Following his gaze, I saw Miss Collins, standing framed in the large window, watching us intently. Holmes glanced toward his memorandum book, still held prominently by the edges. Then he seemed to relax, saying, "That may have been an unfortunate mistake, but it cannot be helped now." Then, mysteriously he added, "Perhaps it will even provoke her into doing something to our advantage. Now, let us rejoin our companions."

Back at the guard houses, we were met by Hipkins, who was standing outside waiting for us. He handed Holmes a note, and said something to him softly in that odd voice of his. Holmes nodded and thanked him. "Do you want me to take your bag on to Mr. Holmes's farm?" asked Hipkins, reaching for the portmanteau in my hand. I shook my head, saying that I would keep it with me. Hipkins touched a finger to his forehead, and turned to go.

Holmes followed him for a moment, giving him some whispered instructions. Hipkins nodded and continued on his way.

Holmes then returned and faced me, while Anderson and Teague waited by the door to the building. "Hipkins followed Chetwood when he left the inn," said Holmes. "The man hung about until he saw us depart with Anderson, and then went back inside. He wrote a note and asked that the innkeeper make sure that it was delivered to me. He then went back to his hiding place off the Eastbourne road, which I located yesterday. Hipkins saw no sign of any associates along the way, or of the boy. He returned to the inn, managed to convince them that he was working for me, and retrieved the note for personal delivery, as you saw.

"According to his message, Chetwood realized that the interruption of the ransom exchange was not my fault, and he has rescheduled for tonight, with certain conditions."

"And those would be . . . ."

"Later, Watson. Let us proceed with this business while it is still fresh."

Holmes walked to the building, where he asked Anderson and Teague to continue to wait. Then he led me back inside and upstairs to the dead man's room. Dismissing the man, Brown, guarding the room, after ascertaining that there had been no attempts by anyone to enter, Holmes pulled the key from his pocket and unlocked the door. We went in, and Holmes motioned toward the table.

The lantern was still lit, but otherwise the room was very dark, as it had been during our first visit. However, this worked to Holmes's advantage.

"Lean over and look at the brandy glass with the light behind it."

I did so, and saw that there were several finger marks on it, obviously from a man's hand, based upon their size. "Do you see anything significant?" Holmes asked.

I pointed to a place on the glass without touching it. "This mark in front is the thumb, and the other prints, four of them, closer together on the opposite side of the glass, are clearly the fingers."

"And?" prodded my friend.

"There is only one set. He must have only picked it up once, when he took it up to drink the brandy, and set it back down again."

"What else can you determine?"

"It was his left hand that lifted it, based on the angle and direction of the marks." I added.

"The victim is left-handed," said Holmes. "It is obvious from an examination of his muscular development."

"That is the hand that he used to scratch Gates's face," I said. "It was the hand that had some of Gates's tissue under the nails."

"That is of no significance," said Holmes. "The man was in his death throes. If he had been mysteriously attacked and strangled, for instance, and then found to have tissue under his nails, it would have been damning for the suspect that was found with such corresponding marks on his face. But we believe that this man was poisoned. The scratches mean nothing. What is of significance," Holmes said, "is that the dead man's left thumb, the thumb that held the glass, has a scar across the large pad, as shown in the finger mark on the glass."

I bent to look at the glass again, and saw that indeed the evidence of the scar was there. "What of it?" I asked. "We are going on the assumption that the brandy in the glass is poisoned, since we can smell the bitter almond scent of cyanide wafting up from the dregs. We have smelled it from the bottle, and from Warren's own mouth. We can also assume that he poured the drink for himself, probably just after he finished his morning toilet and got into his uniform, as he was preparing to leave and start his day."

"Correct," said my friend. "Now look at the brandy bottle with the light behind it as well."

I bent again, and with a bit more difficulty, saw a similar-sized set of male finger marks on it, some from a left hand and some from a right. This time I was careful to note that on the left-hand thumb there was indeed a scar across the thumb pad.

"Again, I do not see the significance," I said. "Obviously, Warren used his right hand to hold the brandy bottle as he took off the cap with the left. Setting the cap down, he shifted the bottle to his left hand, his dominant hand, and then poured some of the brandy into the glass on the table. He left his finger marks as he did so, and then set down the brandy bottle to pick up the glass, again with his left hand. Holmes, what does this accomplish, other than to confirm that the man poured the poisoned brandy for himself? The question is, who put the poison *in* the brandy?"

"Look at the bottle once more. And look *past* the victim's finger marks this time."

I peered at the bottle with the oily marks illuminated by the lamp behind them. At first I was ready to admit defeat. And then, suddenly, I saw it. It was as if I were a child again, lying on a hillside looking at clouds with my brother. He would point at one and tell me that it looked like a horse or a dragon or some such shape. I would look and look, seeing nothing, and then suddenly it would lock into shape, as it did this time.

"Exactly," said Holmes, seeing my enlightened expression. He brought around the memorandum book, and, still holding it by the edges, positioned it beside the brandy bottle.

"The other finger marks – "

"The ones partially underneath those of the victim?" he said.

"Yes. Warren's marks overlay a set of smaller ones, superimposed on top of them."

"Because the smaller fingers held the bottle at some time *before* the victim."

"And the finger marks on your notebook case there – "

"Indeed. They match exactly. You will notice the three slight grooves or wrinkles, running parallel on the pad of the right index fingers as seen on the polished memorandum case cover when she held it to read what I had written."

I nodded "These three parallel marks are also on the brandy bottle."

"As I said, it was a long shot. I had seen these finger marks during my initial examination, and read from them that a woman, based on their size, had initially handled the bottle. Mind you, the marks belonging to Warren and the woman are the only ones on the otherwise clean bottle. I already knew from an examination of Warren's hand that the thumb mark with the scar on the larger set of marks belonged to him, placed there when he poured his final, fatal, drink, which took place sometime *after* the smaller marks were applied.

"One can also make a small leap, when considering the paper there on the table that was no doubt wrapped around the brandy bottle. Perhaps it was a gift? If so, then obviously the victim had not touched the bottle until *after* he unwrapped it. *Quod erat demonstrandum*, the person who *had* wrapped it was the last person to touch the bottle before giving it to the victim. And is it not reasonable to assume that this was the same person who poisoned the brandy?

"Having decided a woman was the poisoner, we then learned that a specific woman was involved with the victim. As you recall, we do not have a lot of time to waste trying to break down her story. I therefore devised a quick and crude stratagem to get the girl's finger marks."

He thought for a moment, and then said, "I know that you are aware of the theory that every man, woman, and child has unique markings on their fingers, and that efforts are being made to devise some way to classify them through various points of congruence.

I nodded, and he continued. "Before my departure from London, I had worked some on the problem, and I later passed on my findings to the Yard. Just a few years ago, they started making use of this finger mark classification system, but we certainly did not have the time to go through the whole process today, especially when this short-cut has essentially told us what we wanted to know. Why bother to collect and record the lady's finger patterns to match established classifications, when the three parallel lines on that one fingertip tell us all that we need to know?"

He glanced toward the dead man. "And here we are."

"But what is her motive?" I said. "Was her honor violated in some way? Was it revenge?"

"I cannot say for sure, but I have one or two ideas that I intend to explore. I suspect that she was simply running out of time."

Holmes turned toward the door, but stopped when I asked, "Do you think that her father could be involved in some way? I've rarely met someone who resembles a more likely criminal."

Holmes shook his head and laughed, that peculiar silent laugh of his. "I have already done some research on Mr. Collins. I make it my business to keep track of any new neighbors that arrive in this little community. He was the sole witness in the Grantham Trials earlier this year, in Chicago. He bravely testified, despite numerous threats against both himself and his daughter, and as a result, nearly two dozen evil men were convicted, with seven terminating their journeys at the end of ropes. Afterwards, it was certain that he would be safer elsewhere, and he made his way to this sleepy little corner of the world, where he and his daughter have tried to live quietly ever since. Unfortunately, his daughter has rashly ruined his plans."

Holmes led me out into the empty hallway, where he relocked the door. Downstairs, Holmes asked Teague for the private use of a telephone, and he was led into one of the adjacent houses. He was back in ten minutes or so, informing us that he had arranged for one of his agents in London to verify some information. He did not expand on what that information might be. In the meantime, all that we could do was to wait.

Teague made a cup of tea for me, but Holmes refused the offer. Instead, he paced back and forth, sometimes stepping outside to smoke his pipe. As we passed the hour mark after Holmes's telephone call, the enthused conversation that had been going on between Anderson and Teague seemed to reach a lull.

Teague had been explaining that for the last few weeks, it had only been the five guards who were occupying the post, which was never considered important, even at the best of times. Holmes roused himself to ask whether it was planned for the men to depart from the station completely. "Why, yes, Mr. Holmes," said Teague. "We are entering a political climate where manning of this post is considered unnecessary, and we are closing it down for now. This, however, has happened often in the past, and will again. Soon, purse-strings will loosen, and someone else will be back here, staying until such time as the politicians once more become parsimonious."

Both Anderson and Teague resumed speculating on which of the two men, Lester or Gates, seemed the most likely to have poisoned Warren's brandy, with Lester being the obvious candidate. It was generally assumed that in any case, it must be due to some tangled connection to Miss Collins, and the competition for her affections. Teague idly pronounced that perhaps it was Fellows who had poisoned the brandy, but he had no real reason for this assertion, as it turned out. It was just wishful thinking.

After sitting in silence for a while, we were suddenly roused by the sound of Fellows's voice, calling to Holmes, who had stepped outside. A man was on the telephone, reporting to Holmes from London. We heard Holmes acknowledge the information, as he went to speak to his agent.

Knowing that Holmes did not want us listening over his shoulder, I encouraged my two companions to wait with me. It did not take long before Holmes came in and told us the summary of his conversation.

"The dead man, Lieutenant Warren," he began, "was the sole heir of his grandfather, Ebersole Emerson. The next in line is the dead man's first cousin and fellow guard, Lieutenant Lester."

"I knew it!" cried Teague, rising to his feet. "I knew that he was the killer!"

Anderson shook his head. "If so, how could he have been so stupid? Surely there would have been a more discreet way to go about it, and to avoid being so immediately and closely connected with the crime. He could have done it somewhere else, at some other time – any other time! Is this Lester an impulsive or stupid man, commander?"

Teague shook his head. "No. No, he is not. But you can be sure that it was because of that girl's involvement. After all, just a few weeks ago, she threw him over for his cousin, Warren. Perhaps Lester was jealous. A man bent on murder does not think clearly." Turning from Anderson, he said, "Do you not agree, Mr. Holmes? That Lester killed him because of the girl?"

Holmes, lost for a moment in thoughts of his own, and having no interest in the ongoing speculations of Anderson and Teague, raised his eyes and said, "What? Lester the murderer? No, not directly, at least. Tell me, Commander, how did these two cousins come to be assigned here together like this? Isn't that somewhat odd?"

"Warren's assignment was purely through the influence of his grandfather, or so I understand. He wanted him to put in several years of service of some type, in order to build his character, so to speak. He probably arranged things so that both cousins would serve together. It's not unusual, when someone of position and influence takes an interest and throws his weight around."

Holmes nodded, and then looked sharply at the door, which had been suddenly thrown open with great violence. Standing there was Mr. Collins, the American. Behind him, looking flustered, was Fellows. "Where is my daughter?" the older man thundered.

We looked at him in shock, but with no answer. He repeated his question, adding, "She left almost as soon as you did, heading down the hill. I couldn't stop her. I've never been able to stop her. She said something about speaking to young Lester. When I finally decided to come find her, I met a man who said that she had gone off toward East Dean with the scoundrel, riding in the back of a wagon-for-hire."

"What?" said Teague. "Lester has gone?" He turned to look toward Holmes.

159

My friend simply smiled. "She has been provoked, after all," he said cryptically.

"I knew we should have guarded them," muttered Anderson.

"He has well over an hour's head start on us," said Teague. "I guess that answers the question. Lester *was* the murderer."

"There is more to this matter than you know," said Holmes.

"I don't care about any of that," bellowed Collins. "I want my daughter brought back now!" He turned toward Holmes. "You're the famous detective. Find her!"

Holmes made no move to spring upon the girl's trail, simply saying, "She will be back here shortly, I assure you."

That did not satisfy Collins, who turned to Anderson.

"You then. You're the police. Rescue her from that murderer!"

"At once," said Anderson, standing up and moving toward the door. "I will telephone immediately and have every direction watched. If you will come with me, then, Mr. Collins?" He led the fuming man outside, and shut the door behind him. Holmes resumed his contemplations, and did not appear overly concerned.

Anderson returned in a few minutes without Collins, but accompanied by another man, a stranger, who stood by the doorway. Anderson informed us that he had sent Collins home to await word, and that he had arranged things so that a watch would soon be in place for Lieutenant Lester and Miss Collins, in whatever direction they might happen to go. "But I hope that they don't go across the open country," he added. "There are paths every which way out there. But if they reach another town or village after leaving from Eastbourne, they will be spotted."

The man who had returned with Anderson was old, short, and suspicious. Anderson called him forward from where he waited by the door, stating, "This is Goins. Lester hired him to drive them both to Eastbourne in his wagon."

"Oh, yes?" said Holmes, with only mild interest. "And did you deliver them there successfully, Mr. Goins?"

Goins mumbled something that was totally incomprehensible to me, but seemed to make sense to both

Anderson and Holmes. The gist of the man's statement, after it had been translated, was that he had deposited both Lester and Miss Collins at the Eastbourne station, and the last he had seen of either of them was when they went inside. Each had been carrying a small bag. Goins was thanked and dismissed.

At that moment, Anderson was called back to the adjacent building to receive another telephone call. He quickly returned, beaming. "They've got them! Caught two stations up the line, they were, standing on the platform, arguing, and calling attention to themselves." He shook his head. "It seemed someone had recognized them and brought them to the notice of a constable on watch."

"Yes," interrupted Holmes, "that someone would have been my agent, Hipkins. I asked him to keep an eye on Miss Collins, should she choose to do anything interesting, such as arrange to meet with one of our suspects, or to depart the local area. I told him that if she left with someone, he was to stay on their track, and then to turn them over to the police as soon as it was feasible."

Anderson gave Holmes a strange look, a mixture of admiration and vexation. I had seen that same look on the faces of many a Yarder for more than two decades now. "I was told," continued Anderson, "Lieutenant Lester had changed his mind about leaving with the girl. He had just purchased two tickets *back* to Eastbourne when he was caught, and was telling the girl that she had to come along with him, although she was very much in disagreement with that idea. Now why would he decide to come back?"

"Perhaps he had learned the truth and knew that it was the right thing to do," said Holmes. His statement made sense to me, but I could tell that the other two men were puzzled. "Let me explain.

"I approached the scene as I have done at so many others before, with no preconceived notions in my mind." He then continued to lay out his reasoning for Anderson and Teague, telling them of his observations that a woman had first handled the poisoned brandy bottle, why he wished to obtain samples of

161

Miss Collins's finger marks, once he learned that she was the girl most likely involved, and how he had determined that she had held the poisoned brandy bottle at some time before the victim, making it probable that she was the killer.

"While this is only a theory, I believe she felt that she could marry one of the lieutenants, thus becoming the wife of the heir to a fortune. It was probably several weeks ago, when she switched her attentions from one cousin to another, that she probably learned that her first interest, Lieutenant Lester, was not as interesting as Lieutenant Warren, since the latter was actually first in line to inherit his grandfather's fortune. No doubt she discovered this fact from conversations with one or the other of them, or from both. She threw over Lester for Warren, as her prospects in this place must have seemed very remote indeed. With the discovery of a couple of heirs to a vast fortune right under her nose, and the opportunity to marry one and escape this dreary life with her father, she was surely and overwhelmingly tempted.

"I had learned from my source in London, as related to me here by telephone, that Warren was the primary heir. For some reason, Edith Collins decided to kill Warren and make Lester the heir. Perhaps she thought that she had a better chance with Lester, and wanted him placed in the more advantageous position. She may not have originally intended to murder Warren so soon, but was possibly provoked into acting quickly, as she had learned that the station was being closed and the two men would soon be transferred beyond her grasp.

"I doubt if she had any true plan, but rather she was clumsily reacting to situations as they presented themselves. I've seen this type of situation before, as has Watson. A rash action is taken, with no thought as to the consequences. Sometimes, even with a clever murderer, the effort to control events leads to additional murders, each easier for the killer than the one before. In this instance, the girl could think of no better plan after her foolish impulse of poisoning the brandy and giving it to Warren than to convince the other heir to flee with her.

"After we all left the Collins's house, I stopped to show Watson the memorandum case with her finger marks. I then looked back to discover that Miss Collins had seen me doing so from her window. Although I'm certain that she could not know *why* this was of interest to me, she probably *did* remember holding the case, and she perceived that I suspected her involvement and guilt.

"She is young and unsophisticated and not very clever, and is not cut from the same cloth as a hardened murderer. Therefore, she reacted without thought, as would be expected, and came down the hill to convince young Lester to flee with her. I do not think that he was actually involved in the murder. He could have arranged for the death of his cousin any number of ways at other times, rather than relying on whatever scheme the Collins girl could devise. I believe that shortly up the line, he realized the entire truth about what she had done, or else she had already told him something about it before they left, and he comprehended the full consequences of escaping with her. He then immediately purchased tickets to come back here and face the music, and was in the process of forcing her to join him, when both were apprehended."

And such proved to be the case. When they both arrived back at the house where we waited, they were brought before us, Lester standing upright, and Miss Collins spitting and struggling like a trapped cat. Her father was kept outside by a suddenly and surprisingly able Fellows.

Lester confirmed Holmes's solution of the matter. "You must understand that neither Andrew nor myself," he said, glancing coldly toward Miss Collins, "were completely attached to the lady. However, she was pleasant enough company, while we were stationed here, and it was certainly interesting to meet an American girl. I enjoyed our little flirtations, but when she took up with Andrew a few weeks ago, I did not find myself suffering from any serious disagreements about it."

"You lie!" cried the girl. "You said you loved me!"

"A summer romance," said the young man offhandedly. I had thought he might have been of better character, after learning

163

how he had already chosen to return to the village just before his capture. Now, I felt that I understood his nature more clearly. How sad that this girl had allowed herself to commit murder in order to make this young man the heir and subsequently – she foolishly hoped – her chosen husband.

After we had departed the Collins's house, the lady had realized that she had fallen under suspicion, although she did not know how or why, exactly as Holmes had theorized. She had decided to convince Lester to flee with her before it was too late, and to marry him once they were away.

"If she meant nothing to you," said Holmes, "then why were you convinced to leave with her so easily? Surely you must have understood that such an action would draw attention toward you as the guilty party."

Lester fumbled at that point, and Miss Collins burst in. "Because he knew that he had been hinting to me that he would be better off with his cousin dead. He didn't know yet for sure that I had done it right then, but he was afraid that I might tell someone some of the things that he had said to me, and that would get him in deep. He finally agreed when I said that we should run away together. It was only a little later, when he made me admit everything to him on the train, that he realized that just because he had wished for Andrew to be dead and had put the idea in my head, it didn't make him guilty. He said he had come to know that running away with me was foolish, and that we must go back. He dragged me off the train. I ran out of the station, but he caught me and brought me back. I went easily enough, as I didn't want to attract any attention, and I thought that I could still talk him around to leaving. He bought the return tickets, and that's the spot where we were caught."

"She is correct," said Lester, pulling himself together. "Simply mentioning that my life would be eased considerably with Andrew's *departure*, so to speak, does not make me guilty. I cannot be blamed just because someone else foolishly chose to act upon that statement without my knowledge or consent."

"Ah," said Holmes, "the tired defense of Henry the Young King after the murder of Thomas Becket. 'Will no one rid me of this turbulent priest?' I fancy your grandfather will not be sympathetic to your position, Lieutenant Lester."

"Alas, I fear that you are correct."

Lester's situation resolved itself as expected. In spite of the fact that no actual or direct instruction could be established from young Lester to the girl regarding the murder of his cousin, the wealthy grandfather, Ebersole Emerson, quickly disinherited Lester, instead favoring his fortune on a great-niece of excellent character who subsequently used the money to assist the poor with great success.

Later, after the Collins girl was officially in custody and Lester held for further questioning, Holmes and I departed. Anderson had seemed rather ill-tempered after the girl's arrest, as if it pained him that a young woman would commit such a crime. He had offered the use of his wagon to drive us to Holmes's villa, but Holmes insisted that we would rather walk. I must have given some sign of dismay, for Holmes himself took my heavy travel bag and carried it. "After all," he said, as we watched Anderson's wagon, along with the prisoner and Lester disappear over the distant hill, "it is my fault that you are bearing such a heavy burden."

"That statement," I replied, "could apply to more of our adventures together than I care to count."

He laughed, and started up the hill along the cliff tops behind the guard houses, choosing to walk that way, rather than along the road below.

The views were incredible, though we both stayed well back from the edge, where every now and then a long crack ran parallel to the cliff-line, indicating where the next collapse would likely occur. There were also numerous pits and holes in the ground as we walked, some hidden by the thick grasses that grew along our way. Occasionally I would see a grouping of dark snail shells, some as big as my thumb joint, clustered here and there around these holes. These allowed the rainwater to run down into the ground, and on into pockets and voids behind the cliff face. As each of these tiny chambers in the ground beneath us grew with each rainfall and winter freeze, the cliffs were further weakened. I saw that Holmes was correct and that, over time, the edge of the country at this point would keep receding, and long past the span of our lives, the entire shape of the coast would become unrecognizable. However, this knowledge could not take away from the beauty of the place that afternoon. The sun, the color of the sky, the birds wheeling in the air, were all nearly indescribable. And then I saw the travel case swinging at the end of Holmes's arm, and I felt a chill. The matter of the kidnapped child quickly put my postcard reverie in perspective.

We were climbing slowly toward one of the higher cliffs, which rose to the south of Holmes's farm, directly between it and the sea. Once I turned and looked back toward Birling Gap behind us. The locals were still standing and talking in groups of various sizes. There was no one at the Collins house, halfway up the far hill.

"I feel sorry for the man," I said. "They came all this way in order to hide, and to protect his daughter, and then she destroyed everything during a moment of stupidity."

"Quite," said Holmes. "Perhaps, if her path had never crossed that of Warren and Lester, her life, and theirs, and even that of Mr. Collins, would have had far different outcomes." He had been looking with me back toward the village. Resuming his walk to the top of the tall cliff, he said, "Hopefully the fact that our path is now converging with that of the kidnappers will provide an outcome for them that they did not anticipate."

We walked silently for a moment, and then I asked about the new arrangements for the delivery of the ransom.

"The exchange is set for tonight," Holmes said, shifting my bag from his right to his left hand. We had reached the top of the cliff, and he stopped, but he did not set the bag down. He looked at the sea, and then down the hill, across the scrub, toward his farm in the distance and across the road. "I sometimes think that I should drag a bench up to this spot, so that I might come up and contemplate life's mysteries in solitude."

"You would be too obvious up here," I said. "Constable Anderson would find you and try to involve you in every petty crime in the district. If you do not make yourself visible up here, then he will have to go to the villa whenever he wants your help, and there attempt to pass Mrs. Hudson, who will never let him know whether you are actually at home or off on one of Mycroft's quests."

"Ah, Mrs. Hudson. My own Cerberus."

"Holmes!"

"Hmm? Perhaps that is too harsh. I do not know what I would do without her."

"Speaking of doing," I said, reminding him of my earlier question about the new arrangements, "what is the plan for tonight?"

"I am to deliver the money to a house north of the road to Eastbourne. From the directions given in the note, it is the very same house that I had previously determined to be Chetwood's current den. I suspect that after he gets the money, he has arrangements in place to immediately flee to the Continent, trusting that even though he has been seen, we will not know who he is or how to trace him. Oh, the arrogance of the stupid criminal. One would hope that, somewhere in the midst of his escape plans, he intends to release the boy, or at least tell me how to find him.

"When the time comes tonight," Holmes continued, "I am to bring the money alone. Your presence here is unexpected, and you were specifically mentioned in the latest letter from Chetwood. He insists that you remain seated in the front parlor of the villa over there during the time of the exchange, in front of a window with a lit lamp beside you. I don't know if it is so that I'll know that you are exposed and can therefore be threatened while I carry out the delivery of the money, thus keeping me in line, or if the kidnappers simply want to make sure that I don't have the use of my good right arm."

I appreciated this compliment, but bristled at the idea that Holmes was required to deliver the money alone, and I said so. "It is surely a trap," I concluded.

"A valid argument, Watson," he said. "But do not forget that we know Chetwood's identity, and that we already knew about the house where the exchange is to take place. I have other

167

assets in place on the chessboard, and this change of plan does not spoil anything."

I knew that one of the assets was Hipkins, but I did not know who else might be involved. Constable Anderson had given no sign that he was privy to anything about the kidnapping, which was in accordance with the instructions originally sent to the Earl, forbidding police involvement.

Holmes took one last look toward the sea, and then with a deep breath, he set off down the hill, leading to right or left as necessary through the undergrowth. We soon reached the road, and crossed to the drive leading toward the house, nestled nearly invisible back in the trees.

We made do for ourselves for the next several hours, discussing old times and Holmes's current activities. Mrs. Hudson had left more than ample supplies in her kitchen, and we had a late luncheon, although I must admit that mine was considerably more substantial than Holmes's. Soon after, I was not surprised to find myself falling asleep into a pleasant afternoon nap. When I awoke, it was clearly getting on toward evening, and Holmes was moving about in another part of the building.

He came in a few minutes later, wearing a rough, worn, and familiar-looking suit. While I tried unsuccessfully to place where I had seen something like it before, he crossed the room, positioning a lamp underneath the large window facing the road. Turning toward me, he said, "I will be leaving soon, Watson. Get what you need to pass an hour or two comfortably here in this chair by the window. Might I suggest some of that tobacco in the tin on that table? It was a recent gift from a vicar in Berwick-upon-Tweed, after I located a particularly bonny emerald that had been secreted two hundred years ago in a hidden cavity in his mantel."

He left the room, and then returned once more, stopping near my chair and leaning down to retrieve my portmanteau, where it had been sitting since our arrival several hours before. "My thanks for bringing this," he said. "When the Earl needed someone to go around to his bank and collect the quarter-of-a-million pounds for transport to Sussex, I could think of no better man."

I grumbled a response, and said, "I wonder how people would have reacted today if they had known I was carrying such a sum with me as we traipsed back and forth across the countryside."

"You might have even turned poor Miss Collins's head, had she but realized the nature of your burden."

I admonished him that such a statement was in poor taste. "Perhaps you are right. In any event, I shall attempt to take care of your case, and to bring it back to you in as good a condition as I have received it."

I laughed, thinking of the many strange places the poor bag had already visited during the course of my adventures with Sherlock Holmes. But my attention was called back as he gave me one final instruction.

"Stay here in the chair until I return if at all possible," he said. "In case someone is truly watching the house. I will finish my arrangements and slip out the back. Hipkins is waiting with the Rover in the barn, and he will drive me from there. I should be back with news soon, and I trust that it will all be good."

And with that, he left the room. I heard him in the rear of the house, and then he walked through and out the back without any further communication. In a few minutes, I heard the low rumble of the automobile as it pulled out of the barn, and then past the front of the house and out to the road. It turned toward the east, and was gone.

I could see nothing from the window except my own reflection. It was unnerving indeed to think that I might be watched at this very minute. Perhaps an assassin was lining up the sights of a rifle, or an air gun perhaps, on my silhouette in the window. How could Holmes have asked me to make such a target of myself, considering the number of enemies that both of us had accumulated over the years?

But no, I said, calming myself. I trusted my instincts, and I felt nothing of the well-honed and long-earned sensation that one has when he is being watched. Sitting there in the comfortable chair, I felt nothing. I was certain that, in spite of the instructions to keep me out of the action and to deprive Holmes of my assistance, no one was out in the darkness that night.

Nearly two hours later to the minute, I heard an automobile pull into the yard in front of the house. It stopped, and then there was the sound of a single door opening and closing. Footsteps crossed the gravels, and the front door flew open. Standing there, with an evil look upon his lean and sallow face, was Hipkins.

I stood up, the book on my lap falling to the floor. "What is the meaning of this?" I cried. "Where is Holmes?"

"Do be careful with that volume, Watson," said the voice of Holmes from Hipkins's mouth. "It is nearly a hundred years old, and I paid a pretty penny and even greater effort to track it down." I realized why Holmes's old suit had looked familiar before he left. He had clothed himself in nearly the same clothing that I had seen earlier that day upon Hipkins, although I could not fathom why. He stepped to a mirror, and began to rearrange his face back from Hipkins to Holmes. "That book came from the basement of a shop in Charing Cross Road, and I nearly broke an ankle fleeing up the uneven steps to lead the owner's nephew, who just happened to be Phelps, the Bickleigh murderer, into my trap."

"I trust," said I, as I bent to pick up the book on the floor, "that you can explain everything. But that can wait. The boy?"

"Safe in his father's house," said Holmes, pulling wadding from his mouth that had changed the shape of his face, making his cheekbones more pronounced and adding gaunt shadows underneath. "Most of my time has been spent at the manor, explaining the sequence of events to the Earl. The rescue itself was almost immediate."

He excused himself, and returned in a few minutes, attired in his own clothing and a dressing gown, and wiping the last of the sallow coloring from his face. While he had stepped out, I retrieved my bag from by the door, where Holmes had dropped it when he entered. It was back to its normal condition – that is to say, not filled with a quarter of a million pounds.

Holmes settled into his chair and thanked me for the brandy that I had poured and placed by it. "So Hipkins was involved?" I said.

"I am afraid so," said Holmes, "up to his eyes. I am very disappointed in him, but it seems that his greed, or perhaps simply his loyalty to his stepbrother, outweighed any feelings he might have had for staying on the right side of the law."

"His stepbrother? Chetwood, you mean?"

Holmes nodded. "After I traced Chetwood and learned who he was, I set my agents to finding out details of his background. One thing that was repeated from several sources was his close association with his stepbrother, one Alfred Hipkins. Imagine my surprise at this unexpected connection, as Hipkins had been acting for me for several years now. He was never an Irregular, you understand, as he was recruited more recently by Shinwell Johnson, and I had always found that I could trust him. He had certain skills that sometimes came in handy. You may have noticed his odd voice?"

I nodded, and Holmes continued. "The result of being too close to an explosion a few years ago, when he was trying his hand at safebreaking. He had no difficulty reaching the location of the safe, but he was not so skillful with his use of explosives. It was thought that the experience, for which he was never implicated or arrested, had been enough to scare him onto the straight and narrow.

"At first, the relationship that I discovered between Hipkins and Chetwood was nothing but a curious fact. However, when I asked the Earl for a list of current and former employees at his estate, thinking that the ease in which the boy was taken right under their noses might be explained by the familiarity possessed by a former staffer, I was amazed to see that Hipkins had worked for a time in the Earl's stable, back in the mid-'90's. He had been let go then after being implicated in a theft, although he had vociferously maintained his innocence. Here, then, was a link, although its exact shape and connection would have to be explored. However, I now knew that Chetwood, who was definitely involved in the kidnapping by his action of mailing the ransom letter, had a close stepbrother who had worked on the estate where the child was taken, and also had reason to be angry with the Earl.

"I set some further inquiries in motion in London regarding Hipkins as well, and learned that he had been out of town since approximately the time of the kidnapping. He had not been seen in this area, but he could have been here, possibly acting as the boy's captor, and keeping himself out of sight.

"I arranged for a message to be passed to him, wherever he might be, by one of his trusted associates in London who did not realize my true purpose. I urgently requested his aid on a matter in Sussex. This might not seem unusual to him, as he has helped me numerous times before, especially since my retirement, and of course he knew that I lived here now. Certainly it would be an odd position in which to find himself if he was already here, involved in the kidnapping. In any case, he could not easily refuse to help me. And within a few hours, he presented himself here to offer his services.

"My agent here confirmed that Hipkins did not arrive by train, and further determined that the Rover driven by him was rented in Eastbourne two days before my message was sent asking for his assistance."

"Who is your agent?" I asked. "Siger?"

"Of course," said Holmes, without elaboration. I nodded. This is not the place to explain or discuss the assistance provided to Holmes by young Siger during those early years of the new century, but suffice it to say that Holmes would have been greatly hobbled as he carried out various tasks for his brother Mycroft throughout that time had he been deprived of the aid provided by his young apprentice.*

"So Hipkins arrived on the scene, then?"

* Editor's Note: For more information about the true identity of Holmes's apprentice, Siger, see "The Adventure of the Other Brother" in *The Papers of Sherlock Holmes,* Vol. II (2013).

"Correct. He officially presented himself to me, and we discussed the proposed arrangements for delivering the money to the kidnapper at the Tiger Inn. I did not let on that I knew the kidnapper's identity, and I did not mention Hipkins's connection to Chetwood. And I did not tell him that you were the man who would be bringing the money down from London. He could honestly perceive, from his position on the inside, that I was not involving the police, and was seemingly attempting to faithfully adhere to the kidnapper's demands.

"It must have shocked him to see that you were the man who arrived this morning in Eastbourne with the money. But upon reflection, he would understand that you were the obvious choice. My only worry was that he would knock you on the head and take the bag during that short drive from the station to St. Mary the Virgin. However, he was being watched during that time, and he would not have escaped."

"I suppose that you did not tell me because you felt that I would have shown to him in some way that I was aware of his involvement," I said, having experienced this same type of controlled ignorance many times before. "It would have been nice, however, to know going in that I faced the possibility of having my head knocked."

"Ah, but I did not truly think anything of the sort would happen. They had no reason to believe that the ransom would not be paid, allowing the two villains to slip away into wealthy anonymity – or at least they planned for that. If Hipkins had stolen the money from you directly, then his association with *that* crime would be undeniable, and he would be an identified fugitive. Besides, neither Hipkins nor Chetwood has ever shown any indications of truly violent actions in their past."

"A quarter of a million pounds can make a man alter his behavior fairly quickly. But do go on with your story."

Holmes took a sip of brandy. "As you know, the exchange this morning was interrupted by Teague, and then by our subsequent involvement in the murder investigation. As Chetwood fled the inn, I nodded that Hipkins should follow him. Actually, I wanted Chetwood to know the truth, that the meeting

173

was interrupted for an unexpected and legitimate reason, and that we had not reneged on our agreement to meet at a neutral location and deliver the money. Later, Hipkins lied to me and reported back that Chetwood had waited and written the note to revise the details of our next meeting. In fact, as Siger let me know later, Hipkins and Chetwood had a close discussion and wrote the note together. It was never left for me at the Tiger Inn, as Hipkins said. Rather, it was simply brought by him to me at the guard houses."

"Where Hipkins then offered to take my bag with the money in it and deliver it here."

"Well, he might not have hit you on the head for it an hour or so earlier, but you can't blame him for trying to get it another way," said Holmes, laughing.

"And your disguise? What did that accomplish?"

"It was something spur of the moment. By then I knew that Siger was waiting there at the house, and I wanted to rattle Chetwood. When I left you here by the window, I completed my transformation into Hipkins. Then I went out to the barn in the darkness. Hipkins paid little attention to me, so I was able to approach him from behind and quickly render him unconscious with chloroform. After binding him and tossing him in the back of the Rover, I drove to Chetwood's house.

"I parked and went to the door. Chetwood answered my knock, no doubt expecting to find Sherlock Holmes standing there with the money. Instead, he discovered Hipkins, back in the shadows, urgently explaining in Hipkins's odd voice that the plan had gone wrong, and that we needed to move the boy as soon as possible.

"With a curse, Chetwood flew past me and around to the back of the house. I followed as he led me into a distant copse of trees, and on through onto a narrow trail down toward a marshy hollow. On the far side of that was another stand of trees, and at its verge was an old building, not much more than a roofed pen, used at some point in the past by a sheep farmer, but now obviously abandoned.

"Chetwood forced his way inside through the nearly collapsed doorway and pulled aside a stack of lumber to reveal the Earl's son behind it, tied and gagged against the back wall, and watching us with large terrified eyes. I later determined that he had not suffered any damage, but it was certainly not clear to me at that moment. As Chetwood leaned toward the boy, I stepped up with my chloroform bottle and pad, making good use of it for the second time tonight. Then I gave two blasts on my cab whistle, which is a sound rarely heard in these parts, I can assure you, and Siger seemed to form out of the very shadows. We freed the boy, bound Chetwood with the same ropes taken from the lad, and got them both back to the house and the car. The two men were left with an astonished Constable Anderson, along with a quick explanation and a promise for more soon, and the boy was returned to his father."

"All in all, a good night's work," I said.

"It is not over yet, I fear," said Holmes, as the sound of a wagon drawing up outside became louder. "I believe that will be Anderson, asking for the promised elaboration upon the capture of the two men that are now in his custody."

And so it was. Holmes spent the next hour or so sociably explaining to Anderson the full nature of the events of the last few days. At first, Anderson was quietly irate that such a matter had not initially been brought to his attention, but he eventually realized that his involvement would have been noticed, and might have led to more danger for the boy.

Finally, Anderson rose to depart, and the house returned to silence as Holmes and I resumed our seats, with one more brandy poured for each of us. We did not speak for some time.

Then, Holmes said to me, "What you said before. About feeling sorry for Mr. Collins, moving here from America to hide from his enemies and protect his daughter, only to see his plan come apart because of her stupidity."

I could see that he was exploring his thoughts as he went, and allowed him to find his way. After another silent moment, he continued. "Is there a pattern to it all, Watson? Does one person cross another's path for a reason? Was Lieutenant Warren destined to die here because of the awkward machinations of an American girl, who was only in this location at this time because of her father's activities? If we could fly over London, like the bees resting in the hives out there, and perceive the paths and wanderings of all the habitants below us, what strange intersections would we see, where each encounter pushes a person off in one direction or another along a dark and unknown path?"

I took a sip of brandy. "Living down here so close to the sea has inflamed your philosophical side," I said. "What is it that brings on these pensive thoughts?"

"Perhaps it is being involved more and more with Mycroft's work," he answered. "For years, Mycroft has been a voice crying in the wilderness, warning of the possibility, nay, even the likely inevitability, of a European war, the likes of which have not been seen before. My involvement in these cases has brought me to an awareness that I have not previously had of his perceptiveness."

"You and I have both been involved in certain matters before this, wherein the possibility of a European conflict has been identified and diverted. You were not completely unaware of this type of thing before your supposed retirement a couple of years ago."

"I was aware, but it did not affect me on a daily basis. Down amongst the trees, taking on this or that case, I did not fly above and see the forest. The bigger picture, you understand. Perhaps I should have assisted Mycroft sooner, or more often, as he kept insisting. As I did during those three years when I was presumed to be dead."

"You have done a great deal of good with those cases 'down amongst the trees' over the years," I said. "You have helped many people."

"But could I have helped more, perhaps, on a greater scale?" He shifted in his seat. "Do you know how a bee leads the members of the hive to a discovery of food?"

"No, I suppose that I never considered it."

"When a likely find is made, say flowers at that critical peak of bloom, with the nectar at its most tempting, the explorer bee returns to the hive and performs a dance of sorts, simply loaded with coded information that will give the direction and distance from the hive to the treasure. I have seen this for myself."

"I fail to understand – "

"Do you recall the hornets that you observed this morning on the path leading down toward the inn?"

"Yes."

"I am afraid that some day, one of those hornets will cross paths with one of my bees. Perhaps it will be part of the plan, or instead it could just be a puff of breeze that makes one or the other go left instead of right, up instead of down. On that day the hornet might not be interested in finding a food source that has been discovered. Instead, he may find it a more useful service to lead his own troops to where my bee's home hive is located. He will return to his own place, and do a dance of death letting them know exactly where to go. Man is not the only creature that goes to war, Watson."

"So you fear that the hornet tribe might attack and destroy your hive?" I said.

"Exactly. And the more that I perform tasks for Mycroft, the more aware I am that at some time in the future, almost certainly, a hornet, by plan or chance is going to find or be given a reason to lead his attackers against our peaceful domestic hives. I am troubled, Watson, because I do not know which seemingly random encounter, which piece of shared information, which riot or insult or even assassination of some unknown pawn will be the spark that touches off the powder keg that all our tangled treaties have wrapped around us, to mix a metaphor. Is it any wonder, then, that I ponder whether there is a plan for us all, or if we simply function in a kind of mindless chaos?"

I had never heard my friend sound as worried or resigned as on this night, and I did not know quite what to say. "All of this possibly random entanglement that you perceive around us is not a bad thing," I finally offered. "I have said it many times before: if I had not encountered you following my return to England after Maiwand, I would likely have ended up broken or dead, like so many of the other poor injured soldiers that washed up in the cesspool of the capital. That random encounter certainly turned out to be a good thing, branching out from there in many ways."

Holmes smiled. "Perhaps you are right, Watson. I've become maudlin in my old age."

I shook my head in mock dismay. "Old at fifty-one. How should that make me feel, then, a full year and a half older than you are?"

"Indeed." He stood then, and walked over to the side of the room, where a desk was piled with papers. "I was looking through some old documents from my trunk the other night. Would it surprise you, Watson, to learn that our meeting at Barts was not the first time that our paths had crossed?"

"Not at all," I said. "Over the years I've become aware of several instances when we met unknowingly before that New Year's Day in 1881. London, after all, is not that big a city. Especially in the late 1870's."

Holmes found the sheet that he was looking for and tossed it to me. "Do you remember anything about that?" he asked.

I glanced at the writing. Although faded, it was obviously Holmes's distinctive fist. The date at the top was 19 November, 1879. I scanned the contents of the document, and then a flash of memory washed over me.

"I recall this," I said. "I was on leave from Netley, and I had come up to London for a few days, and had gone to see the race-walking competition in Islington."

"A wobble, they called it," interrupted Holmes.

"Exactly. Those poor fools would walk for a week round and round a track for very poor rewards indeed. One of the men had taken ill, and I was called into the tent where he was resting to examine him."

"And he later died, as you might recall," said Holmes. "From strychnine poisoning."

I nodded. "It initially seemed to be a saline deficiency, and I recommended rest and that he be pulled from the race. Later, his symptoms worsened, and he passed away. I made my report at the time to the policeman in charge, and returned the next day to Netley. I never heard what happened after that."

"The important part, as far as you are concerned, is that you were allowed to return to Netley to complete your training to become a military surgeon, thus making it possible for you to be in Afghanistan, where circumstances caused an injury that forced your return to London, where you met me, and – having tied up your fortunes with mine for so many years – it seemed the logical conclusion that you would be called down here today when I needed your assistance once again, leading us to have this conversation here tonight. More brandy?"

"Certainly, but what about this matter has brought it to your attention now? Obviously you were involved, as this document is a report or diary entry about the case. Perhaps if I read it again more closely – "

"Do not bother. I shall summarize for you. When the competitive walker was taken ill during the *wobble* and you were summoned, there was no indication that he was truly dying. It was only after your visit that it was ascertained that he had been poisoned with a massive overdose of strychnine. The police sergeant in charge of the case, realizing that you had spent some time alone with the patient before his condition became worse, theorized that *you* might have given him the fatal strychnine yourself for some unknown reason during your examination. After all, who would suspect a doctor? The victim was initially only somewhat ill before you examined him. After you were with him, alone, I might add, he became worse and died."

"But . . . but I had no idea of any of this!" I cried, feeling a defensive panic for an event that had happened and then been settled over a quarter-century earlier. "It was ridiculous to think that I might have murdered the man."

"Obviously, but the sergeant did not know anything about you. To him, you were just another young man in his late twenties. You might have had your own hidden association with the dead man, and finding yourself with the means, determined to kill him. You and I have seen something similar in the past. Do you recall the unexpected encounter with Dr. Mells of Templecombe? Or more recently, the sinister plan of Dr. Knox and the Waringstown Tincture?

179

"It was only after the police sergeant consulted me during the course of his investigation, visiting my rooms in Montague Street, that I was able to nudge him toward the correct solution. You never even knew that you had been under suspicion."

"That is true. I simply went back to Netley and resumed my studies."

"But this is my point," said Holmes. "If the sergeant had not questioned me, then things might have taken a different turn. At that time I was preparing to leave the country for many months, to join the Sassanoff Company in their American tour. What if I had already been gone? The sergeant might have arrested you on suspicion, just to be on the safe side.*

"Most likely your innocence would have been proven, but even so, the simple fact that you were involved could have been enough to be a blot upon your record. Your entire future might have been altered. Might it have been better? Who knows? You could be living in a fine house, winding up an honored career while looking out over your heirs. Or you could have started a decline then and there that ended your story far sooner than it should have.

* Editor's Note: The events of the "wobble" contest and the murder that took place there in November 1879 are obviously those that are recounted in *Wobble to Death* (1970), presented to the public by Peter Lovesey. This is the first published of eight excellent books (and one short story, along with several television episodes from the early 1980's) featuring Sergeant Cribb, the unnamed policeman to whom Holmes refers. Interestingly, *Wobble to Death* does not mention Cribb's consultation with Holmes at all, nor the fact that Watson, who simply appears as an unnamed doctor examining the dying man, was ever under any suspicion.

"So tell me, Watson, was it part of the plan that the police sergeant consulted me, thus freeing you from his suspicions early in the process, or was it random? Are we all simply specks suspended in solution, attracting or repelling one another in some Brownian Motion of humanity until the end?"

This was too deep for me, so late at night with one too many brandies inside me. I tried to divert the subject. "Why were you looking at these papers from your trunk?" I asked.

"Ah," Holmes replied with a smile. "Perhaps it truly was part of the plan that the former police sergeant, and subsequently a respected inspector, sent me a letter a day or so ago, requesting my assistance on a new matter. In a fit of nostalgia, I pulled out the old papers to review various instances of my previous aid to him over the years, and when I saw the details of this case from 1879, including your name and profession as one of the suspects, I realized just how our paths had crossed before. The story suggested itself to me as we were discussing the random versus predetermined nature of existence. Is your wife expecting you back soon?" he asked abruptly.

"Why, no. I told her that I might be here for several days, possibly until the next weekend. Why?"

"The inspector is now retired and settled in the west of England, specifically in Chudleigh Knighton, not so very far from that place that you called *Coombe Tracey* a few years ago in one of your publications."

He reached for an additional document from the mound teetering on the desk and handed it to me. "It relates to this," he said. I glanced down. It appeared to be a monograph of a dozen or so worn pages, entitled, *Some Instances of Sacrifice and Subsequent Hauntings in the Middle Ages in Order to Obfuscate Information Regarding Treasure.*

"He seems to have come across an interesting little case down there," said Holmes, "and if you are so inclined, we will leave for there in the morning. I think that you will find it to be an excellent addition to your chronicles."

And his assessment of the situation turned out to be true, although I did not know why then. Over one more brandy,

Holmes told me a few more details, and I agreed that it certainly sounded interesting indeed. When he had revealed all that he was willing to for the moment, I left him there, smoking his pipe, and ascended the stairs to get some rest for the morrow.

The Gower Street Murder

Part I: A Chance Encounter

The sky that morning was as bright a blue as one could hope
for, reflecting the crisp bite to the late September air. I remarked
on the day's beauty as I dismissed my cab, and the driver agreed
with me. I had thought that I would walk back to Baker Street
upon the completion of my errand. However, my appointment
took quite a bit longer than expected, and by the time I exited the
austere and imposing residence, a line of dark clouds had hove in
from the south, along with a brisk damp breeze promising rain.

Still, I stubbornly decided that I would walk at least part of
the way before the weather overtook me, and I set off on foot,
crossing Constitution Hill before entering the tree-shaded
protection of Green Park, already unnaturally dark but
temporarily protected from the rising wind at my back.

Traversing the wide pathways, I glanced at the occasional
man or woman who passed me, each facing straight ahead or
looking fixedly at the ground before them, intent on their own
personal thoughts. Several times as I crossed the Park, I patted
my breast in order to reassure myself, although I had no reason to
believe that the official missive tucked into my pocket had
managed to work its way loose.

It had been to take delivery of this document that I had
journeyed to the Palace that day, representing my friend, Mr.
Sherlock Holmes, in a matter that has no relation to the present
narrative, and must remain unrecorded until such time as a future
Prime Minister deems it prudent. Holmes had felt that it would
be better if the final loose ends of the affair were tied up without
his participation, and considering the harsh words and vile
epithets that had been hurled toward him the night before by the
broken and beaten nobleman, Lord D------, in Holmes's sitting
room, I tended to agree. Therefore, I had made the excursion and

subsequently taken possession of this *second* handwritten confirmatory confession, which – like the first that had been signed the night before by his co-conspirator – would never see the light of day, provided that Holmes's conditions were followed to the letter.

I had no fear that anyone would try to take the document from me, as it was in everyone's best interest, at least for the immediate future, that it be placed into Holmes's safekeeping as soon as possible. And yet, I was beginning to rethink my desire to walk part of the way home, not because I feared that the document would be taken. Rather, I suspected that it might be damaged by the rapidly approaching rain.

As I reached Piccadilly, I looked in both directions for a hansom, but surprisingly there were none to be seen just then on that busy street. Quickening my pace, I crossed and turned toward the east.

I had passed by Brick Street and White Horse Street when the rising wind from the south increased. As I moved past Cambridge House, a young man appeared in my path, pulling the Out gate closed behind him. He was facing away from me, and did not see my approach, forcing me to shift my stride to avoid a collision. It was then that the first of the rain began.

I reached Half Moon Street, and quickly turned left and ducked into the most accommodating doorway, No. 4, in order to shelter myself while I attempted to open my umbrella. I was not the only person to have this idea, as suddenly the young man who had been departing Cambridge House also dashed into my doorway, instantly placing me on my guard. Our eyes met, and we nodded at one another, with my expression rather more wary than his. He must have followed me.

"Dr. Watson?" he said softly.

As I acknowledged the fact, the wind gusted, pushing several larger drops of rain with it. My new companion, on the uphill side of the doorway, was more exposed than I, and appeared to catch the brunt of the spray. I noticed that he did not have an umbrella. At this time, after knowing Sherlock Holmes for so many years, I could not help but also observe that he appeared to be a clerk in his mid-thirties, right-handed and accustomed to writing often, as shown by his worn sleeve. He was a wiry fellow, about five feet and nine inches, and not much more than twelve stone. His clothing was modest but well-kept, and he looked like half a million other similar fellows that might be seen but not necessarily observed on any day of the week around the Capital. There was nothing unusual about him, save for the mourning band on one sleeve.

He noticed my glances up and down his figure, and he formed a faint smile. He quickly looked at the rain, now falling steadily onto the street, and returned his gaze to meet my own. I started to look away, having been discovered studying him, but the sudden smile lighting his face stopped me.

"You don't recognize me, do you, doctor?" he asked.

"I'm afraid not," I admitted, with wariness rather than any sudden relaxation. Working with Holmes has provided a great deal of excitement over the years, as well as numerous rewards, but unfortunately, it has also caused a number of people, including family members of criminals exposed and brought to justice along the way, to have a certain amount of antipathy towards us.

"I'm Wiggins," he said. "Peter Wiggins. Of the Irregulars."

A flash of recognition passed over me, as I associated this neatly dressed man with the ragged boy from so many years ago. He was the first of many of Holmes's lieutenants, the leaders of his Baker Street Irregulars, who had carried the name "Wiggins."

"Of course," I replied, finally lowering my guard, and holding out my hand, which he shook heartily. "I must admit that I did not recognize you, Wiggins." I turned my head toward the street, where the rain already seemed to be tapering into a steady soaking drizzle. "How have you been? It's been so many years since I last saw you . . . . "

"Nearly twenty, doctor," he agreed. "Then I moved on and my brother took over my duties with the Irregulars. I have been quite happy with my life since then, thanks to the assistance given to me by Mr. Holmes so long ago. I work for a man in King's Bench Walk, near the Temple."

"You're quite a distance away from there to be caught without your umbrella on a day such as this," I said.

"Oh, no sir, I'm not working right now," he declared. He gestured toward the mourning band. "I'm making some final arrangements for the funeral later today. Will you and Mr. Holmes be stopping by? We would all appreciate it so very much."

I confess that I was completely puzzled by his question. Holmes had made no mention of anything of this sort, and I did not have the faintest idea to what Wiggins was referring. I think that I must have shown my confusion, for Wiggins continued, "My mother, sir. She passed away last Thursday."

"I'm so sorry to hear it," I murmured.

"Thank you," Wiggins replied, quietly. "I believe that she was quite ready. She had been ill for several years now, and my sister had been living with her."

I nodded, still trying to catch up, and he continued, "Her last years were quite comfortable, certainly more so than they might have been, had not Mr. Holmes done so much for both her and our whole family."

"Really," I said, unsure of my ground, "I am afraid that I was not aware . . . ."

He smiled knowingly. "I see that Mr. Holmes has not told you the story. I'm not surprised. Well, it's not my place, if he has chosen not to reveal it after all this time, and I must be getting on. However, you are certainly invited to my mother's home, where we will all be gathering early this afternoon, before the funeral this evening. I know that my sister was to send a card to you both, and it will provide you with the address, although I'm certain that Mr. Holmes still recalls it." He glanced out at the street, where the rain was already drawing to a close. "I must dash, but I hope to see you this afternoon!"

And with that, he was gone. While he returned to Piccadilly, I refolded my barely used umbrella, and continued up Half Moon Street to Curzon Street. Turning right, I worked my way into Berkeley Square, and managed to hire a hansom in front of General de Merville's corner home, the site of Holmes's disastrous interview with the general's daughter, just weeks earlier.

The streets were fairly clear at that time of morning, and it wasn't long until I was back in Baker Street. Entering the front door, I let Mrs. Hudson know that I had returned, and hung up my hat and coat. As I climbed the stairs, I could see from the window upon the landing that the day was already clearing again, returning to the bright blue skies that had initially greeted me when I started upon my errand.

As I stepped into the sitting room, I found Holmes reclining in his chair, pondering an unlit pipe. Crossing to the hearth, I removed the document that I had carried to and from the Palace and placed it into his hand.

"Any difficulties?" he asked, barely glancing at it. He had written most of it himself the night before, along with its twin, before forcing the first grudging signature from one of the guilty parties. Today's additional signature had simply been sewing up the final stitch of the complicated tapestry that had taken Holmes two full days to complete.

"Not at all," I replied, turning toward the sideboard. It had been a difficult morning. Holmes responded to my unspoken question by indicating that he did not wish to join me in my early restorative. "And the document's final resting place?"

"With Brother Mycroft, I think," he replied. "Then it will be someone else's problem."

"So all is well," I breathed. "I did not like the idea that you might wish to keep it here, or that you would have me keep it with *my* papers."

"Indeed," Holmes responded. "The political mind that would create such a convoluted scheme as this would not hesitate to burgle these rooms someday, or even the vaults of Cox and Company, should he ever reconsider his confession and come to believe that a vigilant government has stopped keeping track of him and these papers."

Turning toward him, I wanted to ask about the steps that he had taken over the past couple of days, leading from a cryptic reference about a cormorant in the Agony Column, followed by the desperate dash to the Kent lighthouse on a hastily hired Special. But I could see that his thoughts were already on some other matter as he tossed the document carelessly onto the small octagonal table by his chair. I settled into my seat across from him, and sighed as I stretched my feet toward the fire.

"How far did you walk before the rains overtook you?" he asked.

I glanced down at my damp cuffs. "Elementary," I said. "You heard the hansom arrive, but you see that my clothing is wet from the earlier rain."

He nodded and began to scrape inside his pipe. "As you say."

"The deluge, though arriving and departing quickly, caught me in Half Moon Street. And can you deduce with whom I shared a doorway while waiting for the rain to pass?"

He dramatically touched the stem of the pipe to his forehead and closed his eyes. Then, with a smile, he opened them and said, "A Wiggins, of course. But I must confess that I do not know precisely which one."

I snorted, amazed as usual, and totally at a loss to explain how he had reached his conclusion.

I did not need to ask him to confirm his supposition, as he continued, "Upon sitting down, your eyes began to look quickly from here to there, searching for something. You glanced significantly at the mantel, where my correspondence is usually affixed by a jack knife. After several seconds, you looked away, but you continued to glance about, indicating that what you were seeking was some sort of communication that you would have expected to arrive while you were gone, and what you sought was not there.

"Immediately thereafter, you spotted the black-bordered envelope which stands here upon my side table, propped against my morning coffee cup. You then showed a satisfied expression, as if your conclusions had been verified. That led me to understand that you somehow expected that such a letter would be here.

188

"Since it arrived while you were out this morning, neither of us could have known about it beforehand. Therefore, you had somehow learned of it while you were out on your errand. Knowing as I do that it came from the Wiggins family, and realizing that you could not have learned about it from any other source, since I have ascertained that there was no mention of the lady's death in the morning newspapers, I concluded with near certainty that you had spoken with a member of the family. Since, as far as I know, the only Wiggins's that you have ever met have been members at various times of the Irregulars, the only question that remains is to determine which one it was?"

"Peter," I replied. "From 1881."

"Ah, yes. Wiggins the First. From several years before 1881 as well, however," Holmes explained. "He was my lieutenant for a while, before you had occasion to first encounter him during the Jefferson Hope matter."

"There have certainly been a passel of them over the years," I replied.

"Indeed. Even I sometimes have trouble keeping track of all of them."

I took a sip of my brandy. "How did you meet them?" I asked. "The Wiggins family? When we first met, back in '81, you already had your system of Irregulars firmly in place. At what point did the Wiggins clan become the official and perpetual leaders of the group?"

"My dear Watson, that is a story. And as I hear Mrs. Hudson climbing the stairs with our lunch, which I asked her to prepare early today, perhaps I can relate it before we depart for the Wiggins home to pay our respects."

Part II: The Gower Street Murder

I did not question that he would assume I was going with him, since in fact I had planned to, once I learned about it. I agreed that an early lunch would suit me, and rose to open the door for the long-suffering landlady.

She had provided us with some cold beef left from the night before, and bread for making sandwiches. I thanked her, while Holmes nodded in a distracted way and began to prepare something small for himself. I could see that he was recalling the details of his story. In a moment, he began.

"You may recall," he eventually related, "that when I left Oxford and came up to London following the events relating to the matter of 'The Gloria Scott,' I lived for several years in Montague Street, immediately beside the British Museum."

I nodded. "I lived in Bloomsbury for a time myself, while finishing at the University of London and before joining the army," I reminded him. "South of Great Russell Street, in Southampton Street.* Number 6 it was."

"Quite," Holmes said. "I have no doubt that our paths crossed many times without even knowing it."

"Exactly," I said, warming to memories of my younger days. "For instance, on that occasion when you and I visited the Alpha Inn a few days after Christmas back in '87, I meant to tell you about one of the earlier times that I had been there with Stamford. We had left Barts that evening, only to discover – "

* Editor's Note: Several locations mentioned by Watson in this particular narrative now go under different names in modern London. For instance, Southampton *Street*, located south of Great Russell Street, the British Museum, and Montague Street in Bloomsbury, is now known as Southampton *Place*.

"As I was saying," Holmes said, with no rancor while interrupting my reminiscences, "I was living in Montague Street, in a house leased by the widow of one of my father's cousins, a Mrs. Holmes. If I ever knew her first or maiden name, it is completely lost to me now. The lease was initially in her family name, before she renewed it with the Bedford people as Mrs. Holmes. Mycroft had first resided there, when he came up to London after Oxford, and it was to that same house that I went after leaving old Trevor's place in Norfolk in the summer of 1874.

"Over the next few years, while making Montague Street my base of operations, I set about learning my craft. I studied some at Cambridge during this time, but also spent a great deal of my energy in London, finding clients when I could, intruding into police investigations as much as I was able and allowed, and making the acquaintances of various lesser underworld figures, learning whatever skills from them that they were willing to teach. The rest of my time I spent in the British Museum, directly across the street from my meager lodgings in No. 24.

"As I recall, it was in the fall of 1877, when I had established enough of a practice that I could afford my rent, and an occasional bit of bread and cheese besides, when I first made use of the Irregulars. You understand, they didn't have a title then. It was only when you and I moved into these quarters, and you were being introduced to my little methods, that I made some joke or other about utilizing the 'Baker Street division of the detective police force.' Over time, we began to refer to them by the noble *sobriquet* which they now use to identify themselves.

"In those early days, I would simply hire one of them here and there, as needed, and as I could afford it, to watch a house or visit an address to see if a fact could be observed or verified or extracted when I did not have the time to go there myself. Soon the two or three lads that I had initially hired told others, and it became known that a man on Montague Street was doing detective work, and paying real money for assistance.

191

"And so I began to be pestered quite seriously by the lads, all wanting to participate in something or other in order to earn a coin. I could not step out of No. 24 to go to the Museum or the Alpha 'round the corner without being stopped in the street with questions about 'where are you going?' and 'do you need any help?' And I can assure you that my landlady, the grim Mrs. Holmes of distant relation and dubious memory, was not nearly as tolerant of these fellows as our dear Mrs. Hudson has come to be.

"It was at this point that I turned to young Wiggins to organize these Irregulars, as they came to be known in later years. Already, I had found that he was more intelligent than his fellows, and that often I could entrust him with the complicated tasks that I would not choose to delegate to his comrades. I could usually explain in much greater detail what it was that I was looking for in any given matter, and he would grasp the object of the exercise and go forth with my complete confidence, usually returning with exactly what I needed to complete, or at least further, my case.

"I spoke to Wiggins about better organizing the group, so that he would be the leader, and more importantly, the principle person with whom I would have dealings, so that Montague Street would not be choked with street lads, waiting to catch a glimpse of me whenever I stepped out, rather like a school of South American *piranha* fish, hoping that some sluggish agrarian beast might wander into their river realm to be picked clean."

I laughed at Holmes's simile, picturing exactly what kind of agrarian beast that he would turn out to be, and reached for the makings of another sandwich. "So that was how you met the first Wiggins," I said. "But that in itself does not explain the family's fierce loyalty to you, or the fact that other Wiggins's over the years have taken Peter's place as the leaders of the group. Obviously, there must be more to the story."

"Obviously," said Holmes dryly, pushing back his plate with its half-eaten sandwich. "And it all relates to how Peter's widowed mother was saved from the gallows."

With that statement, he stood up. "Perhaps I am being overly dramatic. It was but the work of a day or so, and the gratitude of *famlias Wiggins* over the years has been far too exaggerated for the small effort that I made."

He stopped for a moment to gather his thoughts, and then moved to the fireplace, where he reached for a pipe. As he began to pack it with shag, he glanced at the clock and pronounced, "We have a little time before we must depart. You will accompany me, of course? Your name, after all, is also on the note."

"Certainly," I said, taking a bite of the second sandwich. "I had planned on it. Pray continue your tale."

Holmes sank into his chair, his back to one of the tall windows looking out onto Baker Street. I, having twisted myself around at the dining table to watch his progress across the room, turned back to face my plate while the story continued behind me.

"It was in August of 1879, just a few months before I would sail to America for a year with the Sassanoff Company, when Wiggins came to see me. I had no investigation taking place at that time, so I was mildly surprised that he would make such a dramatic appearance.

"He seemed quite agitated, very unlike his usual confident young self. I had only managed to get him seated in my small front room on the first floor, overlooking the street, when he bounded up and began to pace, telling me that there was no time to talk, and that I needed to accompany him immediately, because his mother had just been arrested for murder.

"I must confess that up to that time, I had not really given the idea of Wiggins having a mother very much thought. Although I was not quite twenty-six years old at the time, I was still rather insular in my thinking, and had not devoted much concern to how any of the troops in my unofficial force made their way when they were not working for me. I had observed that Wiggins seemed to be better dressed and fed than the others, but I suppose I had ascribed that to the fact that his greater

193

intelligence had simply found a way to live a more prosperous existence.

"I attempted to calm the boy. I again directed him to a seat and began to question him in an organized manner. He explained that he lived with his mother and brothers on the first floor of a small house on George Street, north of Euston.

"I know the place," I said. "I took Wiggins home in a cab once, years ago. Going north on Gower Street, we crossed Euston into George Street*, and it was in a small, drab house on the left side of the street.

Holmes nodded. "Wiggins's father had been dead for several years at that time, and his mother had found work as the cook and housekeeper in the home of an old widower several blocks away to the south. The fellow seemed to have no family, and had been quite accommodating regarding Mrs. Wiggins's need to only work during the daylight hours, in order to be home at night with her family.

"As I began to frame more questions, Wiggins sprang to his feet, having none of it. 'You can ask me on the way!' he cried. "I am sure the inspector is still there. Hurry, Mr. Holmes!'

"He fairly dragged me down the steps and into the street. Although he had indicated that I could question him as we went to the scene of the murder, it was obvious that I would not be able to do so, as he kept running ahead, and then stopping to make sure that I was following, rather as if he were a small dog on a long leash, out for a stroll with his master.
"We did not have far to go at all. Not long after starting north on Montague Street, we turned left into Montague Place, passing behind the Museum and so into Gower Street, where Wiggins dashed unheeding into the foot traffic there before veering right. I followed more carefully, until we had almost reached Keppel Street. There, on the eastern side of Gower Street, and almost at

---

* Editor's Note: *George Street*, the location of the Wiggins home, is now known as *North Gower Street.*

194

the corner, was our destination, as shown by the solid and unbreachable presence of a constable standing in front of the door.

"Perhaps you know those houses in that area, Watson. There is a certain sameness to that block, on the southeast corner of Gower and Keppel, all with their grim dark brick and lack of ornamentation. I had passed that way a number of times, but like so many buildings, they were simply part of the background, to be ignored as one goes from here to there."

I had my doubts whether anything was ever part of the background to be ignored for my friend Sherlock Holmes, but I held my tongue, lest I interrupt the flow of his narrative. Pushing back my plate and dropping my napkin, I made my way toward my chair.

"In those days," Holmes continued, "the London constabulary did not know me quite as well as they do now, and in any case, the individuals that did recognize me had no great affection for me. However, I was able to convince the constable that it would be advantageous for me to speak to the inspector in charge of the case, should he still be on the premises. After a long moment of ponderous consideration, the constable turned and went inside. There was a moderate crowd gathered outside the door of the house, as you will have seen at the presence of any London murder, and it spread beyond the width of the building in question, and past the houses on either side as well, all the way to Keppel Street on the north, one house away.

"With the temporary departure of the constable, the crowd behind me surged a step or two closer, pushing Wiggins and myself onto the small square stoop, only three or four inches higher than the adjacent pavement, and surrounded by sturdy iron bars over the area below. When the constable reappeared, he looked suspiciously at us, and glared at the restive assemblage pressing behind us. Then, he stepped aside to let the two of us in before planting himself firmly again, ready to defend the castle at all costs.

"I did not know whom or what to expect. Stepping inside, Wiggins and I followed the sound of voices upstairs, where, on

195

the first floor, we found a small group of three men congregated in the back bedroom, two standing by the window in discussion while looking out over the mews behind the house, as the other was leaning over a still figure on the bed.

" 'Ah, Mr. Holmes," said a voice that I recognized. In some ways I felt fortunate, as I had worked with this man on quite a few previous occasions. However, I also knew that he was still resistant at times to my contributions to a case, and a part of me had hoped that I might find a different inspector in charge with whom I had had no previous dealings.

"The inspector, as you may have determined, was our old friend Lestrade. By that time, he and I had known each other at least five years. We had met not long after I first set up lodgings in Montague Street, but when these events were taking place he was only then starting to realize that I looked upon what I did as a profession, and not as a dilettante seeking distraction from some other less interesting portion of my life. And, as a matter of fact, I had been quite useful to him in the past, so I do not believe that he truly resented my appearance that day in Gower Street.

"As Lestrade spoke to me, his voice was neutral, but then he perceived that Wiggins stood behind me, unable to look away from the grim figure lying on the bed near the window. 'I told you to be gone, boy,' he began, before realization crossed his face, as he understood that I had been brought there by Wiggins.

" 'I see,' he continued gravely. 'The boy has asked you to save his mother from a charge of murder.'

" 'She didn't murder anyone!' cried Wiggins, moving from behind me and up to Lestrade, who was forced to take an awkward step back. The man who was leaning over the bed, obviously a left-handed police surgeon, Crimean veteran, and inveterate low-level laudanum addict, snickered to himself, and continued to make a cursory examination of the dead man. The third man, a stolid constable, made no comment whatsoever.

" 'Hear now,' said Lestrade, righting himself and placing a not unkind hand on the boy's shoulder. 'I'm afraid we can't change what's obvious. I'll be happy to discuss this with you,

Mr. Holmes,' he said, turning toward me, 'but the boy must wait downstairs.'

"Wiggins started to protest, but with a glance and a wink from me he was given to understand that I would represent his interests in the matter, even in his absence. With a truculent expression on his face aimed toward Lestrade, he turned to go.

"After his departure, which was signaled by suspiciously heavy steps going down the stairs, I pushed the door partly shut, but not all the way closed. If I knew my Wiggins, he would be listening through the crack in the moment or two that it would take him to silently return up the stairs. Turning back toward Lestrade, I asked him to summarize the events that had led to the arrest of the boy's mother.

" 'The dead man,' he said, gesturing toward the figure on the bed, 'was a reclusive fellow named Silas Raines. Comfortably well off, and not in the best of health. No close family, no demands on his time away from this house.'

" 'And you have ascertained this how?'

" 'Some we learned from questioning the neighbors, and other information we gleaned from Mrs. Wiggins herself. Before she knew that she was under suspicion.'

" 'How was the body discovered?' I asked.

" 'By Mrs. Wiggins. Her story is that it was her duty to arrive here every morning, clean the house as necessary, and prepare the daily meals. She is a widow who lives not far away, up near Euston Station, with her children. The one that brought you, Peter, is the oldest. She indicated that Mr. Raines had no objection to her leaving in mid-afternoons, when she had completed the evening meals, which he would then eat later as the mood struck him.'

"At the bedside, the physician stood and backed away without comment. I took his place, taking several moments to examine the dead man. He had obviously had a weak heart, and the froth at his lips, combined with the sour unnatural odor emanating from his open mouth, made the cause of death all too obvious. The remains of a meal, spread out on both the bedside

197

table and spilled across the man's sheets, further confirmed the conclusion.

"I looked at the doctor and said, 'Poison? A fast-acting alkaloid, perhaps?'

"The man nodded. His predilection for the soothing joys of the poppy did not diminish his medical abilities. 'Probably in the pudding, no doubt,' he replied, indicating the bowl and its half-eaten contents that had dropped onto the bedclothes beside the body, the remains of its contents smeared down the man's nightshirt.

" 'It seems obvious,' said Lestrade, 'that he was in the process of finishing his meal when the poison took effect. He was in poor health to begin with, so it would have been easy for him to be carried off."

" 'The process was accelerated,' interrupted the surgeon.

" 'Perhaps,' continued Lestrade, 'if he had not been elderly and alone, he might have been able to seek help as the symptoms overtook him. Instead, he died alone. I wonder if he realized who killed him.'

"The surgeon nodded. 'At his age, and in his condition, it would have been quick.'

"I must say, Watson, that I was not convinced the poison had been in the pudding. Perhaps it was in a portion of the meal that had been consumed before he started the pudding, and it took longer to take effect than the surgeon estimated. 'Was it usual for him to eat his dinner in bed?' I asked.

" 'According to Mrs. Wiggins, it was,' replied Lestrade. "She would arrive in the mornings, straighten up the house as needed, and usually retrieve the dinner dishes from the night before from this room. Mr. Raines did not like to eat breakfast, but he would eat a small luncheon in the dining room downstairs, looking out onto Gower Street, and then spend the rest of the day researching a book that he was writing. Something about the Lost Tribes or some such drivel. He had an arrangement with the British Library whereby they would send materials to him as needed, relieving him of the necessity of leaving the house.'

198

" 'And you say that he was comfortably well off, in order to be able to maintain such an arrangement?'

" 'It isn't confirmed yet, but the neighbors who knew him – and none of them knew him very well – indicated that he had made a fortune as a young man, traveling in the Canadian provinces, before returning to London ten or twelve years ago. His health was irretrievably shattered, and he was able to use his accumulated resources to set himself up here, writing his book. Often on warm evenings he would take a turn in the mews behind the house, which are shared commonly with the other houses on this side of the street. He was quite voluble in explaining where he had come from, and what he was currently doing.'

"I gestured toward the remains of the food. 'Will that be analyzed for poison?'

" 'Certainly,' replied Lestrade. 'Although knowing what type of poison it is won't change the fact that he was murdered.'

" 'Nevertheless,' I said, 'I wonder if I might take a sample as well, to perform my own analysis. As you know, I am a student of crime, and every lesson, no matter how small, is valuable to me.'

" 'Of course,' Lestrade agreed tolerantly. 'As long as you share your results with me,' he added. I removed a few of the small glass vials from my coat that I invariably carry with me, even in those early days, and began to retrieve samples of the food.

" 'What do you need that for?' asked the doctor as I placed the top on the vial containing the pudding, and began to take some of the scraps of meat from the plate on the bedside table. 'The poison is in the pudding.'

" 'Hypothesized, but not confirmed,' I replied. I was curious about the remains of the unusual sauce that seemed to be on top of the last of the meat. It was a dark color, and laced with a half-dozen small specks that appeared to be fragments of some type of seed. I made sure to leave an equal amount for the doctor, should he choose to examine it. Finally, for the sake of completeness rather than because I believed that it might be revealing, I placed three of the neglected peas into a vial of their own as well.

"Standing, I said, 'And Mrs. Wiggins found the body this morning, when she came up to retrieve the dishes?'

" 'That is what she says,' replied Lestrade. 'Her story is that she thought Mr. Raines had suffered from a fit during his evening meal. His contorted limbs, as well as the expression on his face and the matter expelled from his mouth, might seem to suggest such a thing. She ran to the neighbor's house for help, and they in turn summoned Constable Henry here.'

" 'And what was her demeanor when you arrived?' I asked the constable.

"He pondered for a moment, and then said, 'She were upset,' he finally said, gruffly.

" 'Unusually so?'

" 'No,' he replied. 'About what you might expect, I suppose. She were crying a bit.'

" 'A very natural reaction,' I said. Turning back to Lestrade, I said, 'So far, there is nothing that points to Mrs. Wiggins as the culprit behind this crime. What is there about any of this to make you specifically think that she is the murderer?'

"Lestrade appeared to become exasperated. 'Mr. Holmes, she was the cook, the food was poisoned, and she is the only other person that the man ever had in his house. According to the neighbors, it was no secret that Mrs. Wiggins had set her cap for Mr. Raines. The neighbors that we spoke to said that it was fairly obvious. In all likelihood, Raines had given her to understand that such a marital alliance was not going to happen, and she killed him because if it in a fit of female rage.'

"I thought that I heard a low growl through the cracked door, and spoke quickly to cover it. 'But why kill him then, Lestrade? That seems a little drastic, don't you think? If she *did* hope to marry him, that would be the way that she could gain access to his money. By killing him, she not only loses any future chance to win him over, but she also loses her comfortable position as well.'

" 'A woman spurned, and all that,' Lestrade replied with a rueful smile. 'They don't think rationally, they simply act. If you'd seen the same thing as this as often as I had, Mr. Holmes, you would have recognized it immediately for the situation that it is. And after all, poison *is* a woman's favored method.' Then his smiled broadened, as if I'd fallen into a trap. "There is one other piece of evidence.'

"I simply waited, until after a long awkward moment he reached into the pocket of his coat and withdrew his leather wallet. Opening it, he pulled out a scrap of paper, originally a quarto-sized sheet that was torn along one edge. He handed it to me, and I observed that it was a very cheap paper, with fibers still obviously visible in the texture. Written on it with a dull wide-leaded pencil were the words *Mrs. Wiggins did it.*

"I looked at it for another moment, attempting to determine any other fact of importance. There were one or two that I docketed away for further consideration before handing it back to Lestrade.

" 'Exactly where did you find it?' I asked.

" 'It was lying beside him on the bed, tucked down in the sheets where Mrs. Wiggins wouldn't have noticed it when she discovered him.' He folded it, and replaced it within his wallet. 'I think that you must agree, Mr. Holmes, that this fact, combined with the opportunity and possible motive, indicates that there really is no question about who murdered Mr. Raines.'

"I wanted to argue with him. I wanted to question why a supposedly rejected and irrational woman would take the time and trouble to find and use an alkaloid poison, rather than some other less subtle but more immediately satisfying emotional method, such as clubbing him with a poker or pushing him down the stairs. And as far as his assertion that poison was a woman's weapon, I had already investigated a number of cases in which poison was used by men as well as women. Besides all that, there was one fact that Lestrade was ignoring. However, all I said was, 'It still does not hang together,' to which Lestrade simply replied with a smug smile, similar to the many others that I had seen from him on a number of occasions, and would see again over the years.

"Without asking permission, I stepped to the bed and made a thorough examination of the bedclothes. Then, I extended my search to the floor underneath, and finished with the top and interior of the small bedside table. What I was looking for, what should have been there, was not. And Lestrade had missed it.

"I glanced around the room. 'Have you examined his private papers?'

" 'I have,' he said, misunderstanding me. He pulled a folded sheaf of papers out of his pocket. 'These were on the dead man's desk downstairs, in his study. They are a representative sample of his handwriting. And before you can point it out to me, Mr. Holmes,' he added, 'even I can see that these examples of his fist do not exactly match that which is on the note identifying Mrs. Wiggins as the murderer. However, the man was dying, and it cannot be expected that he would exhibit perfect penmanship under those circumstances.'

"I glanced at the papers, and saw that he was right: The writing did not match. I had to agree with him that under the circumstances that was not unusual. However, that was not why I had asked about his papers.

" 'Does the man have an heir?' I asked.

" 'Not that we could determine, although we have not made a complete examination of his personal effects. All of that type of material appears to be in his study downstairs,' said Lestrade. 'If you would care to follow me.'

"I perceived a faint scrambling sound outside the bedroom door, as if someone had been caught surprised by our intention to leave the room and was quickly creeping down the stairs. Lestrade did not seem to hear it, and when he pulled the door open, the landing outside the bedroom was empty. He led me downstairs, leaving the doctor and the constable with the unfortunate deceased.

"We found Wiggins innocently leaning against the front door frame. Lestrade looked at him and said, in a rather sour tone, 'Could you hear everything all right?' Then he turned toward the back of the house, leading us behind the stairs and into a small study, piled with papers and teetering stacks of books. The room was dim, and had a musty smell to it. Heavy drapes were closed behind the desk, and I stepped around the inspector and pulled them open. It appeared that Mr. Raines had preferred to do his work in near darkness. The disturbed dust set us all to coughing, including Wiggins, who had followed us and was standing in the doorway to the hall.

"I sat down behind the desk and began quickly sorting through the papers. Lestrade watched for a moment, and then, seemingly becoming impatient, said, 'Let me know if you find something useful.' Then he turned and departed the room.

"Taking advantage of the opportunity, I quickly said to Wiggins, 'Do not become angry because I ask, but did your mother truly have any hopes of marrying Mr. Raines? Be honest now. Remember that I need the truth.'

"He seemed reluctant to answer for a moment, and then said, 'She might have. She talked several times about what a nice man he was, and so easy to take care of. But there's no way a man like that would want to take on a family like ours, now is there?'

"I nodded, and thought how perceptive the young man was. I could see just from examining the various piles of handwritten papers on the desk that this fellow had been lost to his own interests, and the idea of tearing himself from that world and becoming a father to a brood of Wiggins chicks would have horrified him. He would not have traded his work to become the husband of his housekeeper. Wiggins had unknowingly confirmed a fragment of Lestrade's theory, as had my own small observations.

"I examined the rest of the victim's papers, finding very little of relevance. He had a bank book for the Oxford Street branch of his bank, showing a substantial sum indeed, but no other meaningful financial documents, if one did not count those relating to the usual household accounts, the baker, the butcher, and so on.

"I did find one small packet of old letters, resting on top of a pile of documents in one of the drawers and tied with a blue ribbon. The ribbon had recently been retied, as evidenced by the new knot in an unmarked section. The letters were all short, never more than a page or two each, and addressed to Raines. Dated from nearly thirty years before, they were written by a barely educated girl named Abigail Tremblay, replying to letters from Raines, and answering his romantic questions in the affirmative.

"While I was reading through the letters and the other material, Wiggins sat quietly in a chair on the other side of the desk. At one point I was aware of the sounds of men entering the house through the front door and going upstairs, only to return a few minutes later, moving much more slowly and carefully. The body was being removed. Soon after, Lestrade returned to the study.

" 'Did you find anything? A will, perhaps?' He glanced at the boy, who scowled back in return. 'Anything that mentions the housekeeper?'

"I shook my head, and held up the packet of letters. 'There is nothing romantically inclined here whatsoever, except for these ill-written and awkward love letters from the last generation, addressed to our Mr. Raines when he was younger and living in Canada. However, they are mere flirtations and promises to wait for him, and there is no conclusion to the unfinished tale of whether he ever went back and found his princess.'

"Lestrade snorted, and indicated that if there was nothing else, he was going to lock up the house and leave it under the care of a constable. As he shepherded us toward the front door, he suddenly stopped and laid a hand on Wiggins's shoulder. 'I am sorry about your mother, lad,' he said. 'I would change things if I could.'

"I could see that Wiggins was tempted to toss his shoulder and throw the hand from him, but instead he bore it, though it must have burned him to do so, and said, 'You're wrong. She didn't murder anyone. You'll see.'

"Lestrade simply shook his head sorrowfully and led us out onto the pavement. The crowds had thinned following the removal of the corpse, but there were still a number of busybodies, standing in clumps and clusters, whispering their ignorant theories to one another and pointing toward us. I distinctly recall one of them pointing a sausage-like finger directly at me and whispering to his neighbor, 'I think that skinny one there did it.'

"After Lestrade departed with a reminder to let him know if I discovered anything of relevance, Wiggins and I spent the next hour or so knocking up the different neighbors in that part of the street, all of whom shared the common mews with the deceased's house. None seemed to question either my right to ask questions, or the fact that I was being accompanied by a young street Arab, even one that was better dressed and behaved than most that roamed the area.

"Each neighbor essentially provided the same information. Raines had been a relatively quiet – but not unfriendly – man who had moved into that street nearly fifteen years before. He had employed a series of housekeepers over the years, with Mrs. Wiggins being the one with the longest tenure. The neighbors knew her from occasional conversations in passing. I asked each neighbor about a possible romantic association between her and Raines, although I was reluctant to do so, as Wiggins was always by my side during these interviews. However, in each case, the neighbors, who did not realize that my companion was the accused woman's son, had no hesitation in answering the questions. They all agreed that there had never been any sign of either romance or impropriety between the employer and Mrs. Wiggins. However, the fact that the poor woman had been arrested seemed to incline them to quickly accept the notion that something must have been going on that had remained undetected.

"Only one neighbor was able to offer any additional information. Mr. Howett, who lived in the corner house situated between the victim's residence and Keppel Street, had noticed that Raines had an occasional visitor during recent weeks. 'I often step out my back door in the evening, especially this time of year, to have a smoke. Don't like to do it in the house, you know. The smell gets in the draperies.'

" 'Starting about a month ago, I noticed on three or four occasions that Raines, who would often take a turn about the mews of a summer evening, was at the back gate, letting in a fellow. They would then sit on that bench over there, where the mews opens into Keppel Street, and talk for fifteen or twenty minutes. Then Raines would let him back out and shut the gate before going inside.

" 'Sometimes I would still be standing here when Raines would return to his own door, and we would speak. But he never elaborated on who his visitor was, and the young man never joined him in the house that I knew of.'

"Answering my next question, Howett said, 'No, no signs of any arguments between them. They would simply talk. Mr. Raines was never in a bad mood after his visitor left, but never in a particularly good one, either.'

"Upon further questioning, Howett said, 'Did I mention that he was a young man? I meant to. I guess that he was. Looked to be in his late twenties, or possibly a little older. Strongly built, dark hair, common clothing. That's really all that I could say about him. I never heard them speak, they kept their voices low. I don't know if they knew that I was out here, but more likely they just didn't want to disturb the peace of the evening or be heard from the street behind them, over the wall."

"Howett confirmed that these visits would always take place near twilight, long after Mrs. Wiggins had departed for the day. And that information about Raines's mysterious visitor, received from his one observant neighbor, was the last data that I received at the Gower Street location.

"The constable keeping the house told me where Mrs. Wiggins was being held, and Wiggins and I set off at a brisk pace. In those days, shekels weren't as plentiful as they are now, and hiring a hansom was a luxury that was not really a consideration.

"Mrs. Wiggins was still being held at the Bow Street station, where I managed to convince Wiggins that he would not be able to accompany me while I questioned his mother. Leaving him in a hard and uncomfortable chair, I was led back to a room where I could meet with the prisoner.

"She was a small woman, careworn and upset, and she had not yet been placed into prisoner's clothing. She knew who I was, and immediately thanked me for the opportunities that I had given to her son, and also for taking an interest in her own problem. I knew that we would not have long to talk, and brushed aside her thanks, anxious to discuss more relevant matters.

" 'The police,' I began, 'believe that you killed Mr. Raines because you wished to marry him and he rejected the idea.'

"I expected an emotional denial, but instead she gave a reasoned nod. 'I know it,' she said. 'And I must admit that the idea had passed through my mind once or twice. And why not? I certainly didn't love the man, but he was kind in his own way, and seemed to be quite well off for someone so alone. I'm a mother, Mr. Holmes, with a great number of mouths to feed. I can't be there for them all the time, and I know that as they get older, they will try to run wild. And they might not all be as lucky as Peter, finding work with you as he has.'

" 'But I realized a long time ago that a man like Mr. Raines would not be a good father to my children. He was so wrapped up with that book he thought that he was writing, and I knew that I was much better off staying on as his housekeeper, instead of taking a chance that it would all be ruined if I chased him to make him a husband.'

" 'You state that he *thought* he was writing a book. Do you mean that he was actually doing something else?'

" 'No,' she said. 'He really believed that he was working on something important. But he'd been at it since I went to work for him, and he never made any progress that I could tell. He would have books sent from the Library, and he'd start in on them as if he had received candy at Christmas. He would make notes, and talk to himself, and send for more books, often the same ones that he had borrowed only a few weeks before. But I never, in all the time that I was there, actually saw him make a start on writing a single thing.'

"This fit with my own observations of the scattered and unorganized notes on the man's desk. I wondered if he would have ever reached the point where he considered his researches complete, and felt that he was ready to begin his opus, or if he would have happily played with his notes for the rest of his life, moving them from old pile to new pile, without accomplishing anything. As it turned out, no doubt to Mr. Raines's most sincere surprise, it was the latter.

" 'If I may change the subject,' I uttered, 'It is obvious to both the police and to me that the man was poisoned by way of last night's dinner, although we may have some minor disagreements as to specific details. The man had no visitors in his house that we can discover, and you were his cook. How do you explain the fact that the poison was most likely introduced into his food?'

" 'I cannot,' she said. 'Yesterday was no different than a thousand other days. I cooked his noon meal, and he ate it as usual in the dining room. Then, it being a Wednesday, I went marketing in the early afternoon, before returning to prepare the evening meal. It was a piece of beef, peas, and a little pudding. Mr. Raines liked things simple, and he was never any trouble. After the food was cooked, I set it on a plate, told Mr. Raines that it was ready, and departed like I did every day.'

" 'I didn't know that anything was amiss until I returned this morning. I entered the house and went upstairs to retrieve the dinner dishes and make up the bedroom. I believed that Mr. Raines was already in his study, as he usually was at that time of the morning. Many was the time that I did not see him until his luncheon was ready. At that point, I would summon him from his work to the dining room. Then, while he ate, he would often like me to stay with him while he chattered about the progress that he thought he was making on his book. After the meal was over, he would return to the study, and I to the kitchen.'

208

"I thought for a moment, and then something that she had said prompted a question. 'You said that Mr. Raines liked his food simple.'

" 'Oh yes. He was never interested in anything fancy, which worked out well, since I only know how to prepare good, plain food.'

" 'And yet,' I said, 'I noticed that there was some form of sauce on the remains of the beef.'

"She appeared to be genuinely puzzled. 'Sauce?' she asked. 'Not from me, there wasn't. I never made a thing like that, the whole time that I was there. Just the beef."

" 'And you never purchased or prepared anything like that?' I asked.

" 'Never," she stated, emphatically.

"She did not realize that she had provided me with a thin thread. A few other questions gave me to understand that she had nothing else useful to offer. 'It's not my own reputation that I'm worried about,' she said. 'I know that nothing improper ever happened between myself and Mr. Raines. But I need to get back to caring for my boys. Please help me.'

"I assured her that I would do everything possible, both to earn her freedom and restore any stain on her reputation. And then I left her there as she stood to watch me go. The last glimpse that I had of her was when she was being warded deeper into the building by a grim matron.

"Outside, I offered Wiggins the chance to carry on with his own activities, but he made it quite clear that his path was with mine. And mine was to Barts, where I wanted to carry out my own analysis of the food samples from Mr. Raines's last meal. For it takes no great feat of deduction to realize that I had concluded there was something about the sauce that seemed questionable. I disagreed with Lestrade when he asserted that it did not matter what type of poison it was. And in this case, it seemed that discovering whether the poison was actually in the pudding or the sauce might be an important factor in catching the true murderer. I had no doubt that the police would determine as easily as I would wherein the poison had been hidden, but I had

209

no confidence that they would be able to do so anytime quickly, or be able to do anything with the fact once it was established.

"In those days, as you know, I had that curious arrangement with Barts wherein I was able to come and go as I wished, making use of the laboratories as needed, and attending those lectures which I thought might be useful to advancing my unusual education. All of this was due to the gratitude of a certain Mr. Blevins, whom you may recall, after the slight service for him which resulted in his son's fortunate and timely escape to America.

"Finding the laboratory free, I was able to begin my analysis immediately. It is one of my foibles that I tend to lose track of time when involved in a chemical question, and therefore it was approaching mid-afternoon when I had settled to my own satisfaction the issues at hand. I glanced up to find that Wiggins had fallen asleep on the floor, his back against one of the walls. I was fearful that I would require another trip to interview the boy's mother, but fortunately he knew the answer to my question, having accompanied her on several occasions when she did the marketing for Mr. Raines.

"I had expected that we would have to travel a fair distance, but I should have realized that Mrs. Wiggins would do her marketing close to home. We found the shop in question in a busy portion of the Tottenham Court Road. After receiving Wiggins's assurance that he would remain outside, unseen, I went in. Fortunately, it was quite crowded, and I was allowed to wait my turn for several minutes, while other customers before me took care of their business and I made a number of observations.

"By the time the way was clear for me, I had learned all that I needed, and could have departed. However, in order to see things through completely, I stepped to the counter and engaged a certain fellow in conversation, asking his advice and pretending an interest in his answers. After doing so, I was glad indeed, because I saw behind the counter, an additional item that helped me to seal the guilty person's fate.

"Departing the shop with my purchases, I considered throwing some of it away as unwanted, especially as I now had the evidence that I needed. However, I realized that I would have to spend some time considering what I had learned, and would be best served doing so in my own rooms in Montague Street. Wiggins and I returned there, and I gave the unwanted purchase to the landlady, asking her to prepare it for our early dinner. Then we went upstairs, where Wiggins entertained himself with the particularly gruesome and graphic illustrations in one of my anatomy texts, while I sat by the window, smoking, and trying to think of the best way to trap the killer.

"For I knew now who he was, and I could theorize why he had committed the murder, but there were still a great number of gaps in the narrative. And I was not sure how to snare him into an admission of guilt that would subsequently free Mrs. Wiggins.

"An hour or so later, I knew what I had to do. I realized that poor Mrs. Wiggins might have to spend a night behind bars.

"I had written the necessary note and given it to Wiggins, along with his instructions, when the landlady brought up the item that I had purchased, now cooked in her plain way. I could see that Wiggins wished to be gone, but I knew that, in his urgency to aid his imprisoned mother, he might not eat at any time in the foreseeable future. I insisted that he put off his errand for a few minutes and consume the food. As I had no appetite at that point, I did not join him. After Wiggins finished, surprising himself with how hungry he had turned out to be, I sent him on his way. I was quite anxious to see if my deductions were correct. In any case, I had to speak to Lestrade as soon as possible, and I realized that if I could not, my plan would fall apart."

With that, Holmes turned his head toward the clock, and then stood abruptly. "And I see that the time has slipped away from me," he said. "We must prepare for departure."

"You should have been a storyteller," I said with a laugh, as Holmes walked toward his room, shedding his dressing gown as he went. "You knew just where to stop to increase your audience's dramatic interest."

"The next chapter," he called, "will be told in a cab, heading toward the Wiggins's home."

"Shall I summon a hansom?"

"It has already been arranged," he replied cryptically.

Part III: The Inspector Joins Us

We stepped outside to find a four-wheeler waiting by the curb. Inside, to my great surprise, was our old friend, Inspector Lestrade.

"Didn't expect to see me, did you, doctor?" he asked with a grin. Then his mirth faded as he seemed to recall our destination. He was dressed in black, and it took no great deductive feat to realize that he, too, was going to the Wiggins's home. My only question was why? I had never noticed any great feeling between Lestrade and any of the Wiggins clan that had been around Baker Street, one way or another, for over twenty years.

We took our seats, and the cab moved away at a stately pace. No instructions were given to the driver as to our destination, and I therefore concluded that Lestrade had already indicated our route before we had joined him. Looking at both my friends in their dark clothing made me wish that I had been able to return home and change as well.

We turned from Baker Street into Marylebone Road, heading east. The streets were quite crowded, thronging with a warm London afternoon multitude, and our progress was slow. I glanced away from the teeming humanity in the streets toward Holmes, who smiled and seemed to read my thoughts.

"I believe that we have a few minutes before reaching our landing place. During that time, Lestrade, you may be willing to add a fresh perspective. I have been recounting for Watson the events of Mrs. Wiggins's arrest, so long ago."

"Twenty-three years ago," said Lestrade. "I was thinking of it myself, earlier today."

"We had reached the point," said Holmes, "where I had approached you and asked if would throw in with my scheme."

Lestrade shook his head. "I didn't know you so well, then, Mr. Holmes," he said. "Doctor, what he wanted seemed ludicrous at best."

"And that was – ?" I prodded.

"To set a trap for the real murderer." He adjusted himself in his seat, turning slightly to face me.

"And who was the murderer?" I asked.

"All in good time, Watson," interrupted Holmes. "He needs to be sewn into the pattern of the story, one stitch at a time. I had to do the same thing then. And I needed to convince Lestrade that I had identified the true killer."

"I didn't want to believe you," added Lestrade. "When young Wiggins brought me your note, Mr. Holmes, I must admit that I was not inclined whatsoever to meet you back at the victim's house. But even then," he said, "you had already been of some help to me in the past."

"Once or twice," murmured Holmes.

Lestrade nodded with a smile. "Once or twice. I owed you some consideration, at the very least. So off I went. When I arrived, doctor, I was led by Mr. Holmes straight through the house and out into the mews, where we sat on a bench, and he explained his theory."

"The same bench," said Holmes, "where Raines had reportedly met with his evening visitor."

"First," continued Lestrade, "Mr. Holmes told me of the results of his research, earlier that day at Barts. Would you believe that the poison was from a lowly cocklebur?"

"Pardon me?" I said. "A cocklebur? Are you referring to the Xanthium plant?"

"Very good, Watson," said Holmes. "Native to North America, and invasive in many other regions as well."

"As I recall from the time I spent in San Francisco, the cocklebur produces symptoms of weakness, vomiting, rapid heart rate with a weak pulse, breathing difficulties, and eventually death."

213

"Correct," said Holmes. "The entire plant is poisonous, but the seeds are the most toxic part. The particular species of seeds in this instance were quite small, not much different from a fennel seed, and would not have seemed completely out of place in a sauce, especially if the victim were trying something new and unusual, or possibly sampling a reminder of his youth in Canada, and did not know that the sauce was not supposed to have that type of seed in it."

"I take it, then, that the seeds were the poisonous substance present in the unexplained meat sauce, and not in the pudding, as was hypothesized by the police surgeon."

"I fear that you have been around me for too long, my friend. I cannot surprise you any longer. It was indeed the small seed that I had observed in the sauce, of which I took half and left the rest for the police to analyze. My research confirmed that it was a small example of the cocklebur seed."

"I would like to mention," said Lestrade, "that the surgeon also confirmed that the seed was a cocklebur, although it did take him another day or so, by which point the murderer was already in custody."

"So," I said, "a North American seed, and Raines had spent his youth in North America. There was a connection?"

"Quite," said Holmes. "After I had identified the poison, and its probable location of origin, I devised at least seven separate theories which might explain how it ended up in Raines's last meal, always going on the assumption that Mrs. Wiggins was innocent of the crime. As you recall, she had professed to have no knowledge of the sauce, and I went forward from that point. I did not find any indication of the sauce elsewhere in the house. There was not a jar of it in the pantry. In fact, there was not a jar of that type anywhere in the house, or, I might add, in the rubbish. And there was one other clue at the scene that seemed to point to where the sauce might have originated."

"And I missed it," said Lestrade with a rueful grin. With a nod from Holmes, he continued. "I was so interested in the note found by the body, stating that 'Mrs. Wiggins did it', that I neglected to notice that there was no pencil in the bedroom that Raines could have used in order to write the note." He shrugged. "It didn't occur to me that if Raines had been forced to arise and find a pencil in order to write the note, he could have sought help as well. It isn't reasonable to suppose that, upon discovering there was no pencil in the room in which he was expiring, he would go downstairs to find a pencil, write a note naming his killer, leave the pencil where he found it, and then return upstairs – carrying the note – and crawl back into bed to die alone."

"And not only that," said Holmes. "I recognized that the broad soft-leaded strokes comprising the message were unique, and were usually found associated with certain kinds of pencils that are only used in a few professions, one of which was that of butcher. You will have noticed, Watson, butchers using that type of pencil to write on the paper that wraps cuts of meat at the time of purchase. This, coupled with the fact that an unusual sauce was found with the remains of the meat, indicated that I should visit the butcher used by Mrs. Wiggins when shopping for Mr. Raines.

"Upon locating the shop with Wiggins's assistance, I had stood behind several customers while waiting for them to be served. It gave me a chance to observe all of the employees, and particularly the butcher's assistant. He was a young man, in his early thirties, with a marked Canadian accent. Thus, another tie to Raines's past. When it was my turn to receive assistance, I made an excuse to discuss cuts of meat with the man in question before making my purchase, which was the very same piece of beef that I took home and had served to young Wiggins."

"You neglected to mention that you had specifically purchased meat," I said. "Perhaps if that bit of information had been revealed too early, your story might have been less of an interesting tale, possibly too tinged with romanticism, and more like the Fifth Proposition of Euclid."

"I bow to your knowledge and experience as a writer," said Holmes, "without confirming or denying anything. But to continue with my story . . . .

"As I started to leave the shop, I saw for sale, on a shelf behind the counter, several small jars of a reddish sauce. Asking what it was, I was informed by the Canadian gentleman that it was a recipe that he had brought with him from across the sea when he came to England a few months earlier. The preparation was to be placed on meat, providing a New World alternative to horseradish. His employer had allowed him to mix it up in batches and sell it in the shop to their more adventurous patrons. I myself bought a jar, and later found that it matched the color and consistency of the sauce on Raines's plate. But without the cocklebur seeds, I might add.

"Although it seemed certain that this was the man that I was looking for, what was not certain was the exact motive for killing Raines. Possibly it was a revenge killing, for some long-ago crime committed by Raines against the young Canadian's people. Perhaps there was some other motive that I was not even considering. However, in my opinion, the greatest probability was that he had a personal relation to Raines, and it was upon that basis that I decided to proceed."

We were passing Park Crescent, and I knew that in just a few minutes we would arrive at our destination, assuming that the Wiggins family still lived in the same home as before. I quickly reviewed Holmes's reasoning, and could see that, although he had made a few leaps, it generally held together.

"But," I asked, "where was your proof? How could you find a way to connect him to the crime? The meat sauce and the butcher's pencil led you to him, certainly, but those facts alone would not be conclusive. He could simply claim that the pencil might have come from anywhere, and that Mrs. Wiggins had bought the sauce from him at the butcher shop, and added the poisonous seeds to it herself at some later date."

"Yes, that was a problem," said Holmes. "And that was why friend Lestrade was asked, that evening in the mews, to take a leap of faith and go along with my plan."

Lestrade shook his head. "Mr. Holmes had never led me astray, but it was asking a lot at the time, and I was not so senior or secure in my position myself then, either. It was something of a professional risk, but he had convinced me."

I turned my head, indicating that he should continue. After a silent moment, and with a glance toward Holmes to see if he wished to take over, Lestrade spoke.

"As we sat on the bench, and I heard the results of Mr. Holmes's investigations, my first inclination was to make excuses. We've all known each other far too long for me to pretend otherwise now. I had missed the clue about the pencil, but I didn't want to give up my suspicions of Mrs. Wiggins. Then there was the writing on the note in Raines's bed, which matched that on the butcher's wrapping paper Mr. Holmes had obtained earlier in the day. Then the evidence of the sauce and the seeds, tied to the Canadian at the butcher shop, was compelling. But when the list of facts concluded with Mr. Holmes telling me the man's name, which he had inveigled out of him during their conversation, I could no longer deny that he was likely on the right track."

"Ah," I said. "The confirmatory fact."

"The confirmatory fact," said Holmes.

"This Canadian?" I asked. "Would it be revealing too much at this point in your story to now ask his name? Was it perhaps Raines, the same as that of the dead man?"

"Now the fellow is stitched into the pattern, Watson," said Holmes. "You see the way that this path is leading. Should I ever attempt to write up any of my investigations, as you have so often urged me, I will need to do better at hiding the clues. But," he added, "in spite of the fact that the Canadian man did indeed turn out to be Silas Raines's illegitimate son, his name was actually Martin Tremblay, the same last name as that of the girl, Abigail Tremblay, who had sent the small packet of letters that I had found in Raines's study."

"Too many connections to ignore," interrupted Lestrade.

"At the conclusion of our conversation in the shop," continued Holmes, "after I had obtained opinions about cuts of meat and his sauce recipe, I inquired after his name, with many thanks and a promise that I would be back in the future." He

217

smiled as he recalled it, that dangerous smile that has boded ill for so many over the years. "I'm sure he believed at the time that I would be returning as a customer."

"The meat sauce and even the pencil might have been explained away, or blamed on Mrs. Wiggins," said Lestrade. "By itself, the fact that Tremblay was living and working so near to Raines was not damning, since he had ties to the old man, and had in fact visited him in what was observed to be a friendly way. But the poisoned sauce and the old connections together became too significant to ignore."

I nodded. "It all becomes clearer now. The son, abandoned by his father at some early age, tracks him down in England and travels here with murder in his heart, either due to motives of revenge, or perhaps intending to claim an inheritance. But you did not know any of this for sure at that time. You did not know that Raines was the man's father. All you knew was that the sauce with the poisonous seeds had come from the butcher shop, where it had likely been prepared by Tremblay."

"But I was proceeding from the assumption that Mrs. Wiggins was innocent," said Holmes. "Therefore, someone else had to be guilty. Tremblay had been seen visiting Raines on a regular basis, and the poisonous seeds found in his sauce were from North America. Of the various theories that I had constructed, the family relationship seemed most likely, and it was enough to be going on with. And it was also enough to enlist the participation of our friend here."

"First," said Lestrade, "The fact that the man's unusual name, Tremblay, was mentioned prominently in the package of letters was quite convincing. I cabled the Canadian authorities and queried them regarding this butcher's assistant. And then – "

He stopped and looked down at his hands, shaking his head. "I still don't believe that you talked me into it. We just did not do things like that in those days."

"You always were the best of the Yarders," said Holmes quietly. Lestrade looked up quickly. He gazed intently at Holmes, and then swallowed. "Thank you, Mr. Holmes," he said after a moment. Then, clearing his throat, he said more clearly, "Thank you very much for that. It means a lot."

We did not speak for a moment, each lost in our thoughts. Finally, as the cab rattled across Tottenham Court Road, I was moved to state, "Gentlemen? How *did* you catch him?"

Holmes straightened in his seat and said, "I'm afraid Watson, that the explanation must wait a little longer, as we are rapidly approaching our destination, and have still more history than journey left. Perhaps, Lestrade, you would care to join us afterwards, as we raise a glass to Mrs. Wiggins, and recount the trapping of Martin Tremblay in the Keppel Street Mews?"

Part IV: We Pay Our Respects

Lestrade readily agreed to Holmes's proposal, and we spoke no more of the matter then. However, my thoughts continued to dwell on that long-ago case, when these two men had worked together to prove Mrs. Wiggins's innocence. I doubt whether Holmes could have imagined that saving the woman would have led to so many years of devoted service by the various members of the Wiggins family. It had probably been no more than another problem to him, as so many others had been throughout his career. And yet, even as that thought passed across my mind, I remembered all the times that his great heart, which he labored to hide behind that cold and logical veneer, had been moved to action when someone in trouble had needed his help.

The cab swayed as we turned out of the bustle and energy of Euston Road and north into the relative quiet of George Street*. It was only a moment until we stopped before a narrow brick building on our left. As we alighted, Holmes dismissed the cab, tossing a coin to the driver.

---

* Editor's Note: Again, this is now known as *North Gower Street.*

"Many thanks, Mr. Holmes," said the driver, a bluff fellow named Giles who would have died on the gallows in '97 for a murder he didn't commit, if not for the timely intervention of Holmes, who had produced a plaster-of-Paris cast of a *third* left footprint, found at the scene of the brutal crime.

There were several men standing near the door of the house, smoking in grim silence. As we approached, I recognized all of them as Wiggins's that I had known over the years. There was Michael, now a shopkeeper, and young Henry, who had been instrumental in the successful resolution of the incident at Colwyn Bay, and some of the others. I nodded to Warren, now recently returned from the Navy.

There were a half-dozen of them all told, and I knew that they were not all Peter Wiggins's brothers. Rather, there were some cousins of the first and second order mixed in, and to a man, they all pulled themselves a little taller and straighter as Holmes approached them. Holmes nodded as we passed amongst them to reach the door. One said, respectfully, "Mr. Holmes," and reached by him to turn the doorknob.

We stepped inside the dark interior and removed our hats, which we hung on pegs. Removing and hanging our coats as well, we started up the stairs. I was aware that the men who had been loitering outside were following us in.

As we turned at the first floor landing, I could see the large front room overlooking the street. The shades were drawn, and the room was in shadow. Underneath the windows was a coffin, supported by a bier. A number of people were sitting in the dark places around the perimeter of the room.

I identified some of the other faces seated around us. There was Joseph Wiggins, who had led the lads during the search for Mordecai Smith's boat along the Thames back in '88. And there was Sally Peake, *nee* Wiggins, who had been of such vital assistance during the affair of the kidnapped costermonger's daughter. She had been so fearless on that cold night, when she took it upon herself to disobey Holmes's instructions and cut the tarred rope around the frightened child instead of just locating her, while the killers argued with increasing ferocity in the adjacent room. It was hard to believe that this girl, who had shielded the kidnapped child when the shooting began, was the same person, a woman now, singing softly to the tiny baby held in her arms.

There had been the low buzz of conversation as we came in, but it stopped, replaced by the sound of every man and woman in the room rising to their feet to acknowledge the presence of Sherlock Holmes.

Holmes seemed unaware of the great respect directed toward him. He glanced around the darkened room until his eyes rested on Peter Wiggins, my companion this morning in the doorway in Half Moon Street.

Peter took a step forward, saying, "Thank you for coming, Mr. Holmes. I know that your being here would have meant a lot to my mother." He looked toward Lestrade and me as well. "Thank you."

We nodded, and Peter led us to the coffin, where we stood for a moment in silent contemplation. Mrs. Wiggins had been a tiny woman, even before the age-related wasting illness that had eventually claimed her. Her white hair was combed neatly, straight back from her forehead, and her gnarled and veined hands, reflecting a lifetime of hard work, were folded peacefully.

"If you hadn't saved her that day," said Peter, "her life would have turned out much differently. It would have for all of us."

"That's right," said one of the shadowy figures behind us gruffly. Whoever had spoken cleared his throat, but spoke no more. I believed that it was Albert Wiggins, formerly one of Holmes's bravest irregulars, and now a constable on the Surrey Side.

"She never forgot what you did for us," said Peter. "We always toast you at Christmas, Mr. Holmes."

"She was innocent," replied Holmes simply. "I would have done the same for anyone."

"But it was more than that," said Peter, taking a step forward, closer to the coffin, so that he might face Holmes directly. "After you obtained her release, and discovered the real

221

murderer, you found her new employment at Cambridge House. And I cannot even begin to tell you what opportunities you have provided for me, and my brothers and sisters, and my cousins as well. You gave us an income, and more importantly, a purpose, and respect, and when we outgrew our usefulness as Irregulars, you found us professions. Truly, and speaking for my mother in her presence here today, as well as all the rest of us, we thank you."

Behind us, Simon Wiggins, formerly trained by Holmes in the art of pickpocketing, and now a newly ordained minister, said softly, "Amen."

Another voice, one that I did not recognize, muttered, "Hear, hear!" and several others repeated it. I was moved to notice that one of those voices belonged to Lestrade.

Holmes lowered his head for a moment, and then raised it to face Peter Wiggins. And then he turned to the others as well. I wondered what he would say. It had only been a couple of years before that Holmes had been deeply moved after receiving praise from Lestrade, following the masterful recovery of the stolen Borgia Pearl. "We're not jealous of you at Scotland Yard," Lestrade had said then. "No, sir, we are very proud of you, and if you come down tomorrow, there's not a man, from the oldest inspector to the youngest constable, who wouldn't be glad to shake you by the hand."

Holmes had awkwardly thanked him that day, and had then abruptly changed the subject, dismissing Lestrade by requesting that I search his files for a case that had already been completed. Lestrade had understood Holmes's difficulty, and had left with no hard feelings.

And now Holmes was facing a room full of men and women who thought the world of him, in the presence of their departed mother. Would he say something abrupt or awkward? If he did, it would not surprise or offend these people who had known him for so long in so many different circumstances, and it would not diminish their feelings for him in the least.

But Holmes simply said, "Thank you," in a quiet and sincere voice. And, after laying a hand on Peter Wiggins's shoulder, he said, "I am very sorry for your loss." Then, nodding to several of the standing figures around him, he turned to go.

The occupants of the room remained standing as we made our way back to the head of the stairs, and so on down. After retrieving our coats, we found ourselves in the street, and I wondered to myself why we had dismissed our cab, if our intention was to leave so soon after our arrival. My unspoken question was soon answered.

"We are not too far from the Alpha Inn, at the Museum," said Holmes. "Shall we stroll down that way and have some refreshments, and finish telling the rest of our tale?"

Lestrade and I agreed immediately. Some of the Wiggins men had followed us downstairs and had resumed their places by the doorway. Peter was standing with us nearer the edge of the sidewalk, and he nodded as well, realizing that Holmes's invitation had also included him. He turned and spoke to his brothers and cousins for a moment, informing them that he would be back in an hour or so, before the funeral, and then joined us as we began walking to the south.

As we waited to cross Euston Road and on into Gower Street, Holmes told Peter the subject of our earlier discussions, as he and Lestrade had related to me the events of his mother's arrest, years earlier. "We had reached the point in the narrative where I was convincing Lestrade to help trap Martin Tremblay. My plan was to use his greed, plus the surprise of learning that someone knew about his connection to Raines, to trick him into revealing what had happened."

"You make it sound so simple," muttered Lestrade.

"It was," interjected Wiggins. "You see, doctor, Mr. Holmes simply made Tremblay believe that Silas Raines had another son who was set to inherit, possibly ruining all of Tremblay's plans."

"And this other son was . . . ?"

"Why, it was Mr. Holmes, of course."

Part V: The Trap

We walked for several blocks down Gower Street, with Holmes setting a pace that did not encourage conversation. After a very few minutes, we crossed Keppel Street, and he abruptly pulled up in front of the second house on the left, south of the intersection.

"There it is, Watson," he said. "That is the house where Silas Raines was killed."

It was a plain-looking place, with dark-colored bricks and a door set in the right side of the building, under a simple fan light. It was three stories tall, and there was an area-way leading down beneath the walk. The stoop was only a few inches high, and I could almost see Holmes and young Wiggins as they approached it, those many years ago, identifying themselves to the constable before being admitted, where Lestrade waited inside with the body.

"There is not much to see here," said Holmes. "Even if we intruded upon the current residents and made an examination of the interior, I do not believe that it would add anything to your understanding of the matter. However, let us walk around to the next block, behind this one, and I will point out one or two places of interest in the mews."

We went down Keppel Street, along the side of the buildings. In the distance in front of us, I could hear an atonal ringing sound, almost musical, and the voices of children at play. About halfway to the next street, the house ended at an opening into the Mews. There was nothing unusual about it at all.

A little way in front of us, we could see a number of children running up and down the walk, banging the lampposts with sticks. Each rang with a unique tone, and the faster the children ran, the more musical the glissando of tones became.

It was a pleasant sound, encountering the laughter of children on that quiet back street. And then I glanced at Wiggins, who had a look of sadness on his face. I realized that his childhood had been quite different from the one shared by these well-dressed and carefree children. Although he had experienced many unique adventures as a child, before growing into an adult with a secure job, it could not have been an easy life. Again, I understood how grateful the entire Wiggins family was toward Holmes, and for the opportunities that he had provided for so many of them.

Holmes stepped to the entrance to the mews*, and the children, eyeing us with suspicion, retreated to the far end of the block, although they did not leave entirely. Turning into the mews, he glanced around before waving me over as well. "There, Watson," he said. "Do you see that bench?"

I moved to his side. It was a low marble affair, quite stained, and unusually wide from side to side. It would have been able to comfortably seat three or even four people, instead of the usual two-person bench of similar construction. It was placed very near the wall that we had just passed, along Keppel Street.

I indicated that I had spotted the bench, and Holmes said, "And over there, the back of the row of houses? That second door, the red one at the top of the steep steps? That was Raines's house."

He shifted back and brushed his hands. "Now you know where the trap was laid. The rest of the story will make more sense now. On to the Alpha Inn. Faces to the south, then, and quick march!"

Passing through the Mews, we turned left into Montague Place, quickly reaching Russell Square. I realized that we were entering Montague Street. Holmes was feeling sentimental today, although he would never admit it as such, and was revisiting several old points of interest along our way.

* Editor's Note: These mews are now a portion of *Malet Street* and specifically the *Malet Street Gardens*.

It was only a moment before we reached the white front of No. 24, where he had lived when he first came up to London after deciding to pursue his vocation as a Consulting Detective.

I wondered if he would pause there for a moment, or decide to keep walking around the corner to the Alpha Inn. The decision was taken away from him, however, when Lestrade, who happened to be in the lead at that moment, stopped and looked up at the first-floor window, directly over the door.

"It has been a long time," he said, nodding his head toward the building. "Whatever happened to that landlady that was your distant relation?" he asked. "She did not like me."

Holmes shook his head. "I do not know. She was only a Holmes by marriage to some cousin of my father's, and after I moved out in early '81, I lost track of her whereabouts. Several years later, when Watson and I were called here to investigate a murder in my old rooms, there was a new owner who knew nothing about her."

"Gregson's case," said Lestrade. "He never visited here in the old days as often as I did."

"Only a few times," said Holmes. "Inspector Plummer was often here, but he retired soon after I moved away. I liked to think that he had put in a good word for me down at the Yard before he departed."

"He did," said Lestrade. "It made things easier for the rest of us when we started to make use of your abilities more and more often. He paved the way for us at the Yard to consult with you."

"Gentlemen," said Wiggins softly, "we appear to be attracting attention."

I followed his gaze to the Museum which loomed behind us. There were a number of people gathered in one of the tall windows, pointing excitedly toward our party, and more specifically at Holmes. In his unique fore-and-aft and Inverness, which he insisted on wearing both in the city and the country, he had become quite recognizable.

With a final glance up at the window over the door to No. 24, Holmes said, "Let us be off, then. We'll join together to tell

Watson how we removed Mrs. Wiggins from under the shadow of suspicion."

Entering Great Russell Street, I glanced over toward the gardens in Bloomsbury Square. I could not see through them, but I knew that Southampton Street was on the other side. I had lived there at No. 6 for a short time in 1878, earning some small fees as a new doctor before deciding to leave England and explore the world. I knew that Holmes and I had frequented this neighborhood at the same time in the late seventies, and was certain that we must have encountered each other before Stamford introduced us in the lab at Barts on New Year's Day in '81, following my return to London after Maiwand. However, for the life of me, I could not recall a single instance when I had taken notice of him.

Reaching the corner entrance of the Alpha, Wiggins held the door while we preceded him inside. It was quiet this time of day, which suited our moods, and there were very few patrons. Holmes walked unerringly down the narrow path between the bar on the left and the tables under the windows on the right, reaching a small table just past the bar at the back. Fortunately, it was empty, and he began to divest himself of his hat and coat.

I noticed that he had intentionally passed several other empty tables, aiming for this one. With sudden perception, I said, "Was this your favorite table in the old days?"

Holmes smiled. "It was. Although I was never a social creature, even in my youth – or perhaps especially in my youth – I did have a certain set of cronies that I would meet on random occasions. And this is where we would sit."

"I remember you!" I cried. "It was winter, and I had come in with some of my friends. This was our favorite table as well, and you and some others had already occupied it. My friends and I sat nearby instead, over there by the window, but I recall that you looked up and noticed my obvious disappointment. You raised a glass of beer to me!"

Holmes nodded. "I recollect that incident. Your dismay when seeing that table was occupied was palpable. I considered offering to move, but my companions, which you may not recall, were too far gone at that time to suggest it. I hope that the evening was not spoiled for you."

"I must admit that I don't remember anything else from that night," I said with a smile, seating myself in a chair.

Holmes motioned to the man behind the bar, holding up four fingers. In a moment, the fellow was placing a glass of beer before each of us. "The beer is excellent here," said Holmes.

"As good as their geese?" asked Lestrade softly. I looked at him with surprise, and he was smiling in my direction. "I read *The Strand*, doctor," he said. "back when you were still publishing the stories. I remember that you stopped here while following along after that jewel thief, nearly fifteen years back." He shook his head. "And I also remember that you let him go because it was Christmas."

"Enough of that," interrupted Holmes. "We are here to conclude the post-mortem examination of the matter of Silas Raines, and *not* to rehash the matter of the Blue Carbuncle."

"Agreed," I said. "Tell me then of this trap, and how it relates to the mews behind Raines's house."

Lestrade seemed ready to take up the tale. "First I wired to America for details regarding our Mr. Tremblay. They didn't arrive in time to provide us with any additional facts before his arrest, but we did receive enough information later that helped us know that he was the right man, which we already knew by that time anyway. It was no secret where he came from that Raines was his father. His mother never married, waiting for Raines to come back for her. She lived in her father's house until she died young, and then the old man, her father, had brought Tremblay up the rest of the way. Cruel he was, too, it sounded like.

"In the meantime, I went around and talked to my superior, explaining Mr. Holmes's plan. I also made sure that Mrs. Wiggins was comfortable, and was not treated as a regular prisoner, since it was likely that we would have her there until late that night, after the trap was sprung.

"In the meantime, Mr. Holmes had holed up in Raines's house for over an hour, forging documents after Raines's handwriting."

"Even at that age, I had the gift," murmured Holmes with a smile.

"Lord help us all," Lestrade muttered. Wiggins laughed.

"I required something to show to Tremblay when I approached him that evening – something that would shake him loose from his confidence that his plan was working. I needed a document indicating that Raines had two sons, and that – unknown to Tremblay – I was the second."

"Our plans were in place by early evening," said Lestrade. "It was then that Mr. Holmes waited outside the butcher's shop as it closed for the night."

"I stayed well back," said Holmes, "as Tremblay and the butcher came out together. The butcher locked the door, and Tremblay said good night and started south down Tottenham Court Road. I followed discreetly behind him.

"By this time we had ascertained that he lived not too far away. I let him get almost to his lodgings before I increased my pace and approached him, calling his name.

"He turned, and for a moment I could see him try to place me. Then he recognized me, although he still appeared puzzled, wondering why someone from the butcher's shop earlier that afternoon would now be at his place of residence.

" 'Yes?' he asked good-naturedly, 'Was the cut of meat to your satisfaction? I'm afraid the shop is closed, but I'll be happy to speak with you tomorrow.'

" 'I'm not here about the meat', I said. 'That was an excuse to get a look at you. We have something else to discuss, which will benefit us both.'

" 'And that would be?'

" 'Perhaps I should introduce myself. My name is Thomas Raines.'

"He made no connection for a moment, and then I could see that the last name meant something to him. 'Raines?' he said.

" 'That's right,' I said. 'You knew my father. I am Silas Raines's son. And your half-brother as well.'

"That rocked him back right away, and with a shake of his head he backed up against the steps leading to the door. Finally, he muttered, 'Not possible. It's not possible.'

" 'Ah, but it is,' I said, pressing forward. 'Come over here, away from the street, and I'll show you.'

"He followed me to the side of the building. There was still light enough to see the document that I pulled from my pocket, the very one that I had forged not an hour earlier. He read it quickly, and then again, more slowly this time. At times his lips moved as he mouthed the words. I knew the parts that were causing him the greatest consternation. I had written them to do so.

"Essentially, the document, supposedly written by Silas Raines, stated that he had *two* sons, one by Abigail Tremblay in Canada years before, and me, Thomas Raines, from a short marriage after he had arrived in England. Thomas's fictional mother had died soon after giving birth, and Silas had placed me in the care of trusted friends, since he was in no position to raise me himself. However, he did not want to neglect either of his sons, and had written this statement in order to record his acknowledgement of both of us.

" 'He left this with me several months ago. You'll notice,' I added, as he finished re-reading it for a third time, 'that we have to claim the inheritance together, and vouch for one another, or neither one gets anything. I think that he meant to introduce us to one another before he died so suddenly last night. He had told me about you, obviously, and how you found him after coming over from Canada. I'm guessing that he hadn't managed to get around to telling *you* about *me*.'

"I reached out and took the forged sheet back, replacing it in my pocket. He shook his head, trying to get his thoughts in order. Then, he said, 'That paper won't be enough,' he said. 'I have the letter that he wrote to my mother in Canada, after she let him know that I had been born. That will be enough to prove that I'm his son and heir. He acknowledges it, and I know that there is not a will. What other proof do you have?'

" 'How do you know there isn't a will?' I asked.

"He shook his head and asked, 'Where is your proof?'

"I pulled the second forged sheet out of my pocket. 'Here,' I said. 'I'm afraid that it's rather like a treasure map.'

"He grabbed it, and I let him take a good look at it. 'It won't do you any good to take it from me and use it by yourself without me,' I said. 'We both have to be present to inherit. It says so in the letter. And there *is* a will, as you can see from that drawing, which tells where to find it. I think that he was trying to be clever, but it isn't too hard to see that he buried it by the bench in the mews.'

"He looked at the sheet, a crude hand-drawn map that made clear in the simplest terms possible that the 'treasure' was indeed buried under a paving stone by the bench in the mews, the same bench where Raines and Tremblay had met on several occasions. Tremblay stared without speaking for the longest time, and then nodded once, and again. Finally, he said, 'What do you suggest?'

" 'Simply that we go and get it,' I replied. 'We may have to hold on to the will for a while, until things calm down, before we can use it. I was in Gower Street today and heard that they had arrested our father's housekeeper for poisoning him. But the crowd outside the house said the poison was in the meat sauce. What with you working for a nearby butcher and all – you can see the connection, I'm sure – that made me curious, and I thought that I'd step around and get a closer look at you.'

" 'The housekeeper killed him,' he asserted. 'Everyone in the shop today was saying so. I heard that the old man wrote a note accusing her before he died.'"

" 'I didn't hear anything about them finding any note,' I said, thinking to make him a little uncertain about the success of his plan. 'All I know is we'll have to time things right to make sure the police are happy with the person that they have arrested, but not so late as to let the estate get away from us. Now, are you with me? Shall we go?'

"He looked over his shoulder uncertainly, as if he wanted to go into his lodgings and shut the door, pretending that I had never accosted him. But I was there now, and he did not know what I might do if he let me get away. I had hinted that I knew of

231

his complicity in the murder, and in spite of the conditions of the forged letter, saying that we had to inherit together or not at all, I might be able to throw him over if it could be proven that *he* had been the killer. He really had no choice but to come with me.

"We walked the few blocks back to Gower Street, as the sun dropped behind the buildings, and the streets fell into shadow. We went past Raines's house, and I noted with satisfaction that there were no lights showing inside, and no sign of a constable keeping watch."

"We had removed him," said Lestrade, "and also warned Howett and the other neighbors to keep inside and to themselves, no matter what they heard outside in the next few hours."

Holmes continued, "Turning down Keppel Street, Tremblay said, 'Perhaps we should wait until it's later.'

" 'No,' I replied. 'It would be more suspicious if we came back and were caught out digging in the middle of the night. Right now, people are inside and distracted. The map shows right where it is. We'll just get in and out, and then we'll discuss what happens next over a pint.' Then, I added, 'Surely you can see the sense in that, brother.'

"That startled him, but he nodded, and we turned into the mews. He walked straight to the bench. 'When did you first come over from Canada?' I asked, in a voice a little louder than the situation called for. Tremblay, obviously very nervous by this point, hissed for me to be quiet, and turned on me as if he were going to strike me. It was then that Lestrade, wearing a very suitable set of old clothes, walked up out of the darkness.

" Tremblay nearly jumped back in surprise. 'Who is this?' he whispered.

" 'My friend, Geoffrey,' I replied. 'He doesn't know what's going on exactly, but I wanted him to know that I was here, and to get a good look at you, just in case. I'm sure that you understand. Have you seen him, Geoff?' I asked. Lestrade nodded, but did not speak. 'Good. Go on to the pub then, and we'll meet up later.' "

Lestrade interrupted. "I walked away and out of the mews, and then kept on going slowly, whistling as I went. But as soon as I was out of their hearing, I ran around through the next street, and so on until I was able to sneak back into Keppel Street, where I took up my position with the others, right outside the wall, just alongside the bench where Mr. Holmes and Tremblay were standing inside. When I got back, the two of them were having some kind of argument."

"A very quiet argument, indeed," said Holmes. "I had repeated my question concerning when Tremblay had first come over from Canada. He turned it over in his mind for a moment and did not see any harm in answering. 'Three months ago,' he finally whispered. 'In the spring.'

"He then turned back to the bench, and in two steps was kneeling beside it, scrabbling his fingers in the dirt around the paving stone that had been identified on the map. In just a moment, he had found the small iron box, which I had placed there myself just before starting off to follow him from the butcher shop to his residence.

"He stood up with it, and tried to open it, but it was locked. He shook it in anger, and we could hear something inside, presumably the will. I had known that it would be locked. When I had chosen it from among several similar boxes in Raines's house for just this purpose, I had made sure that it was sturdy, and that it would keep him out until I was ready to let him in. As he groaned in frustration, I gained his attention and held up a key. 'This,' I said, 'was with the map and the letter.'

"He made to reach for it, but I yanked it back. 'First,' I said, 'another question.' He neither agreed nor disagreed, but simply stood there, clutching the box, and beginning to give off the smallest hints of panic. His plan, which must have seemed to have started so well for him, was falling apart, and he was quite off balance. Another son of Silas Raines, who knew so quickly of his connection to the dead man, was not supposed to have appeared.

" 'Earlier you said that you knew there wasn't a will. What made you think so?'

"He frowned, and then said, 'What?'

" 'You said there wasn't a will. How do you know?'

233

"Because I looked for it, and didn't find it," he said, his stress becoming a little more obvious and pronounced with each passing minute.

" 'When?' I asked. 'When did you look for it? On some night when the old man was asleep in the house? He told me that he always visited with you out here, at this bench, and that you didn't go inside.'

" 'That's right,' snarled Tremblay. 'He wouldn't even invite me in. Oh, he would talk in the mews 'til the sun went down, but I wasn't fit to soil his castle.'

" 'And did he tell you there wasn't a will? Because if he did, then he must have lied, since we just found his treasure box where he said it would be.'

" 'He never said a word about a will, one way or another. I thought, however, from the things he said to me after the first time I met with him, that he wasn't going to give me anything.'

" 'So if he didn't tell you there was no will, how did you know that there wasn't one? When did you look for it?' I asked.

" 'At night.'

" 'When he was asleep?'

" 'No, last night.'

" 'Last night, after he died?'

"That stopped him, as he realized what he was about to admit, and I thought that I had overplayed my hand. To distract him, I handed him the key to the box. With a lurch, he grabbed it and turned toward the dim lights coming from Howett's windows.

"He twisted the key, and with a wrench had the box lid open. He reached in and drew out the false will that I had created, duplicating Raines's handwriting and phrasing as well as I could in the short amount of time that I'd had.

"He dropped the iron box with a clatter, by then seemingly oblivious to the need to stay quiet. He was nearly panting as he unfolded the document, and then turned it this way and that as he tried to read it. In a moment he gave a little cry. I knew what he had just read.

" 'What is it?' I asked. 'Here, let me see.' I made as if to move toward him, but he pivoted and took a step back. There was a new look of madness in his eyes.

" 'It doesn't mention me,' he said. 'It doesn't mention me at all. It simply refers to his *only son*, Thomas Raines. You inherit everything.'

" 'Here, let me see,' I repeated to him.

" 'It was supposed to be *me*,' he said softly. 'It was *my* mother that died of a broken heart, waiting for him to come back. It was *me* that was raised fatherless by that evil old man, while over here *he* was starting a *real* family.' He took a step toward me.

" 'So you poisoned him?' I asked.

" 'All that stands between me and the old man's money,' he replied, 'is this will and that piece of paper in your pocket naming both of us as his heirs.' He took another step, and I fell back to match it. "If I get rid of those, all that will be left will be my letter that he sent to my mother, telling the truth!"

" 'Did you poison him?' I cried.

" 'Yes, damn you, I poisoned him!' He was reaching for me, and I backed toward the gate to the street. 'And when I came in last night to leave the note and take away the jar, he was still alive. He was looking at me when he died, and I cursed him to hell when he drew his last breath. He knew it as he went. I could see that he did.' I stopped retreating, and he closed the distance toward me.

" 'And then I spent all night looking for the will, so very carefully, so that no one would realize that I had ever been there, but I couldn't find it! I thought that there was no will, but I had to make sure before I told anyone about my letter! Sometimes I would go back upstairs and look at him there. I wanted to spit upon him, but I couldn't leave any indication that anyone had been there. Then I looked some more for the will. And all along he'd buried it out here, naming you as the heir!'

"It was then that his hands touched my throat. Before he could squeeze, however, before he could exert any kind of force or pressure at all, a hellish shriek shattered the quiet night. It seemed to echo off the walls of the mews and the backs of the houses, and there was no way to tell where exactly it originated. Even I, who had expected it, was momentarily struck with a kind of paralysis and terror. Tremblay jerked as if he had been shot, stood upright, and would have bolted if Lestrade and his men, who had been hiding behind the wall right outside the gate, had not boiled around us at that instant and taken him into custody."

"We had heard everything," said Lestrade. "His entire confession. He fought like a madman, and it took six big men to bring him down. He nearly bit off Carter's thumb in the process."

"And the scream?" I asked. "The one that stopped Tremblay for just a crucial second?"

"That was me, doctor," said Wiggins. "A talent that – sadly – gets little demand these days in King's Bench Walk."

"The confession was as clear as could be wished for," said Lestrade. "He broke down later that night and told the whole thing. He had been raised by his grandfather, a sinister old man who had whipped him often simply because he was his father's son. Eventually, as we confirmed from information in the cables received from Canada, he had beaten his grandfather to death. Thus, the provinces had become too hot for him, and he fled to England, intending to find his lost father along the way. Even then, he had devised his basic revenge, as he had brought the poisonous seeds with him. Once here, he located Raines, obtained employment nearby, and began to observe and make more detailed plans."

"After living here for some little time, he had finally approached the old man," Holmes continued, "and identified himself as his son, but he was not as warmly received as he had hoped. This only confirmed in his mind the designs that he had made for his father, and he bided his time, waiting to determine the best circumstances in which to carry them out, and also whom he could frame for the crime.

"Finally, he felt that he could wait no longer, and he met with his father for what seemed like just another usual visit in the mews. Tremblay, knowing that Mrs. Wiggins had bought meat that morning at the butcher's, brought along the poisoned sauce, and suggested that his father try it, indicating that it might remind him of the old days in Canada. As we know, Raines *did* try the sauce, that very night. Tremblay made his way into the house, picking the lock without leaving any evidence that I could detect, using skills that he had acquired during his younger days in Canada.

"By the next morning, Tremblay had not found any will, and was convinced that none existed. He retrieved the poisoned jar and left the accusatory note in Raines's bedclothes, stupidly forgetting to leave the pencil with which it was written. Then he made his way out of the house before Mrs. Wiggins's usual arrival time. He went to work as if it were simply another day, intending to bide his time for several weeks, certainly until after Mrs. Wiggins's guilt was firmly established, and then he would make his claim as Raines's heir, using the old letter that acknowledged him as Raines's son as his only proof."

"As you may be sure, we released Mrs. Wiggins later that night," said Lestrade. "Tremblay's plan was full of holes, but it was the best that he could come up with."

"And even if the true villain had eventually been unmasked," said Wiggins, "my mother would have had to suffer untold horrors before the truth was discovered, if it ever was." He turned toward Holmes, holding up his nearly empty glass. "A toast to you, Mr. Holmes." Lestrade and I raised our glasses as well.

The tale having been told, we looked at one another. There did not seem to be anything left to say. The fine beer was gone, and we all stood and prepared to depart.

"I'm sure it would not inconvenience Mrs. Hudson too much if you were to all join me for dinner," said Holmes as we walked along the bar toward the door.

"I truly appreciate the offer, but I must return for my mother's service," said Wiggins. "The minister will be arriving soon. But she would have wanted me to spend this time with you, of that I'm certain."

"I must be getting home as well," said Lestrade. "The missus will be expecting me."

237

"I, too, should be getting back," I agreed. "My wife returns from her visit tonight."

We stepped outside into the twilight, only to be confronted by a tall man, wearing evening clothes, and weaving slightly from side to side as if in the grip of strong drink. In his right hand was an Italian dagger, the blade long and thin.

"You've ruined me, Holmes!" growled Lord D------, looking much worse than he had this morning at the Palace, when he had grudgingly affixed his name to the second confession that I had carried there. "It has all come crashing down! I'm a ruined man! You must make amends!"

Lestrade and I separated ourselves slightly on either side of Holmes, as the three of us tensed to make whatever defense was necessary against the raving criminal. However, before we could make any sort of move whatsoever, a piercing scream shattered the early evening around us. It echoed far to the Museum walls, and back again onto the pub behind us. It was everywhere at once, and terrifying. Lord D------ jerked back to see who or what had made such an ungodly noise. Before he could determine its source, however, Wiggins stepped quickly past us, grabbing the enraged peer's knife arm, and deftly using the man's weight against him, throwing him over and onto the pavement. Holmes stepped forward, stomped a foot onto Lord D------'s arm, and with the other foot kicked away the knife into the street.

As Lestrade blew on his police whistle, bringing constables running from all directions, Wiggins cleared his throat and grinned. "Just like you taught me, Mr. Holmes?"

"Exactly like that, Wiggins," replied Holmes.

"And did he teach you to scream like that?" I asked, astounded that a human throat could make such a noise. Wiggins simply tried to look humble, and then laughed.

Later, after Wiggins had said his goodbyes and started back toward his mother's home, Lestrade stood with us for a moment while Lord D------ was loaded into a growler by two burly constables. "He'll be out by tomorrow," Lestrade said with disgust.

238

"Nevertheless," said Holmes, "he is a broken man. Look at him. He won't find the fortitude to try anything like this again."

Lestrade nodded to both of us, climbed in the four-wheeler, and departed.

"Well, Watson," said Holmes. "Are you up for a walk?"

We were quiet as we wound our way gradually west, over to Wigmore Street before turning toward Queen Anne Street. Finally, pausing before No. 9, we stopped. The lights were on inside, and I suspected that my wife was already home from her travels.

"Would you care to come in?" I asked, but I knew that Holmes would decline.

"Another time, perhaps." The gaslight threw shadows across his face, hiding his eyes underneath his fore-and-aft cap. "Give Mrs. Watson my regards."

"I shall."

"And do stop by in a day or so. I've received an interesting letter from a man in Exeter with a rather unique problem. He is the verger at St. David's Church. The current building was completed only two years ago, but there are reports of a hooded figure from Anglo-Saxon times rising from the crypts of the former church, threatening the nearby residents, especially the children. It sounds . . . intriguing."

With that, he turned and walked away towards Baker Street. I stood on the pavement for another moment until he vanished from sight, and then turned and went inside.

Chronology Notes

For those Chronologists who are interested in such things – and I am very much in that camp, having spent over twenty years compiling a *Whole Art of Detection* of the lives of Holmes and Watson, consisting of a massive Chronology that includes events from the Canon as well as any information from countless other sources that relate true and correct versions of cases involving Our Heroes – these are the dates (some approximate) when the narratives contained in this volume took place:

- "The Mystery at Kerrett's Rood" – April 7-8, 1883 *and* early to late September 1878
- "The Curious Incident of the Goat-Cart Man" – September 27, 1890
- "The Matter of Boz's Last Letter" – Early to mid-June 1897
- "The Tangled Skein at Birling Gap" – September 23, 1905
- "The Gower Street Murder" – Late September 1902 *and* August 21, 1879

David Marcum began his study of the lives of Sherlock Holmes and Dr. Watson as a boy in 1975 when, while trading with a friend to obtain Hardy Boys books, he received an abridged copy of *The Adventures of Sherlock Holmes*, thrown in as a last-minute and little-welcomed addition to the trade. Soon after, he saw *A Study in Terror* on television and began to search out other Holmes stories, both Canon and pastiche. He borrowed far ahead on his allowance and bought a copy of the Doubleday edition of *The Complete Sherlock Holmes* and started to discover the rest of the Canon that night. His parents gave him Baring-Gould's *Sherlock Holmes of Baker Street* for Christmas and his fate was sealed.

Since that time, he has been reading and collecting literally thousands of Holmes's cases in the form of short stories, novels, movies, radio and television episodes, scripts, comic books, unpublished manuscripts, and fan-fiction. In addition, he reads mysteries by numerous other authors. He especially favors those that feature what he considers to be the classics, Nero Wolfe, Ellery Queen, Hercule Poirot, and Holmes's logical heir, Solar Pons.

When not immersed in the activities of his childhood heroes, David is employed as a licensed civil engineer, and lives in Tennessee with his wife and son. In 2013 he finally traveled to Baker Street in London, the location he most wanted to visit in the whole world, as well as other parts of England and Scotland on an incredible trip-of-a-lifetime Holmes Pilgrimage.

Questions and comments are welcomed and may be addressed to:

thepapersofsherlockholmes@gmail.com

Also from MX Publishing

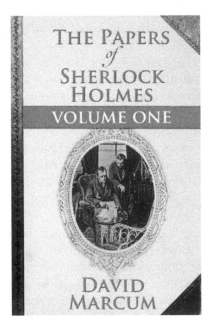

The Papers of Sherlock Holmes – Volume I

Traditional Sherlock Holmes stories from David Marcum

". . . here we have David Marcum showing us how it should be done. I hesitate to call any such collection flawless, but this, the first volume of The Papers of Sherlock Holmes *is as close to flawless as to not matter."*
– David Ruffle, *Sherlockian author*

MX Publishing is the world's leading Sherlock Holmes books publisher with over 150 titles.

www.mxpublishing.com

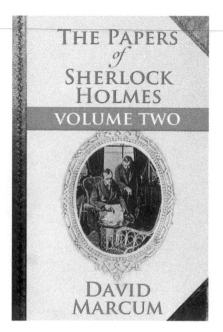
243

Also from MX Publishing

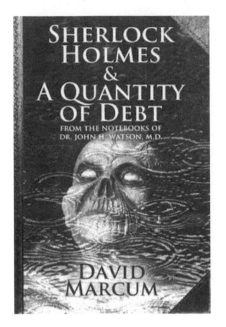

Sherlock Holmes and
A Quantity of Debt
Hardcover

Another traditional Sherlock Holmes story from David Marcum

"This is a welcome addendum to Sherlock lore that respectfully
fleshes out Doyle's legendary crime-solving couple in the context
of new escapades . . . ."
– Peter Roche, Examiner.com

MX Publishing is the world's leading Sherlock Holmes books
publisher with over 150 titles.

www.mxpublishing.com

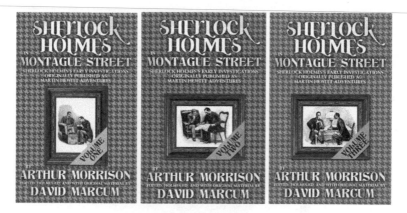
245

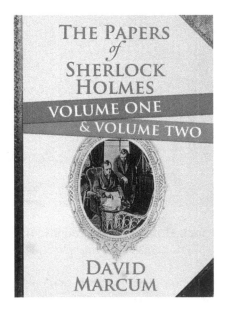